JASMINE IS HAUNTED

MORE BY MARK OSHIRO FROM TOR PUBLISHING GROUP

BOOKS FOR YOUNG ADULTS
Into the Light
Each of Us a Desert
Anger Is a Gift

JASMINE IS HAUNTED

MARK OSHIRO

TOR PUBLISHING GROUP

NEW YORK

This is a work of fiction. All of the characters, organizations, and events portrayed in this novel are either products of the author's imagination or are used fictitiously.

JASMINE IS HAUNTED

Copyright © 2024 by Mark Oshiro

All rights reserved.

A Starscape Book
Published by Tom Doherty Associates / Tor Publishing Group
120 Broadway
New York, NY 10271

www.torpublishinggroup.com

The Library of Congress Cataloging-in-Publication Data is available upon request.

ISBN 978-1-250-33729-0 (hardcover)
ISBN 978-1-250-33730-6 (ebook)

Our books may be purchased in bulk for promotional, educational, or business use. Please contact your local bookseller or the Macmillan Corporate and Premium Sales Department at 1-800-221-7945, extension 5442, or by email at MacmillanSpecialMarkets@macmillan.com.

First Edition: 2024

Printed in the United States of America

0 9 8 7 6 5 4 3 2 1

For all the spooky kids:
The grieving ones, the sad ones, the outcasts and black sheep.
I'm right there with you.

JASMINE IS HAUNTED

1

Jasmine Garza—freshly twelve, her black hair in two long braids down her back—rests her hand against the frame of her front door.

She can hear her new friend, Samantha Reyes, coming up the stairs behind her.

She's quick as she can be. She whispers to her house: "Please behave yourself."

Samantha is there, a little out of breath, and she smiles, and Jasmine's heart leaps.

She did it! *Finally*. She had invited a friend home, she actually said yes, and now, they've kicked off their shoes in the entryway, then they're in Jasmine's bedroom, pulling books out of their backpacks, and it feels . . . normal.

It's all Jasmine has wanted these last couple years: what everyone else already has.

And now, Jasmine's first friend in a long time—the first since she had to move twice in the last two years—is sitting on *her* bed. They're supposed to work on a group project for Mr. Theo's history class, and Samantha asked if they could do a report on the Philippine-American War. Jasmine let her lead; she wanted to make this whole process as easy as possible.

Which is why the loud knocking on the other side of the house sends dread tearing through her stomach.

She doesn't look up, hoping that she imagined it, that her mind is running wild because she's nervous.

Knock, knock!

"Is someone at the door?"

Jasmine looks up. "It's probably our landlord. He likes to bother us a lot. We just ignore him."

Her heart thumps faster.

She tries to read the book Samantha checked out of the library for them, her own fingers on the delicate charm on a chain around her neck, but she can sense it. She always can.

It's here.

The hairs on the back of her neck and arms rise up. She looks up again at her friend, but she's jotting something down in a notebook like nothing is happening. Does she not sense it?

Of course not. No one else ever does.

Please leave us alone, she wills. *Just this once.*

Her eyes drift over the words in the book again. She doesn't take in a single one.

The moment passes and Jasmine thinks, *You won't ruin this!*

The ghost doesn't respond. At least not in words.

Jasmine and Samantha both startle as the knocking begins again, this time from the wall behind Samantha.

Her almost-friend leaps off the bed. "Jasmine, what is *that*?"

Jasmine rises. "Uh . . . the landlord?"

Samantha gives her a look that says everything: *You're obviously lying.*

"I don't know!" Jasmine says. "Maybe it was an animal?"

But she knows what it is.

Jasmine has lived in three apartments these last three years, and this spirit—whomever or *whatever* it is—keeps showing up and making trouble. It never seems to bother Mami, either. Just *her*.

There's a slamming sound in the hallway, and Samantha stuffs the book she dropped on the bed back in her bag. "Is this a prank or something?" she asks, backing away from the bed. "It's not funny."

Jasmine doesn't know what to say. She inches over to her

bedroom door, and she peeks out into the hallway where the noise came from.

One of the doors to the linen closet swings open, then slams shut.

"I think maybe I left a window open or something," she says to Samantha, the lie sliding out easily. "Let me go check."

Check what? she asks herself in a panic. *You have to come up with a better cover story, Jasmine.*

She doesn't get to. As she edges closer to the misbehaving linen closet, the door flies open and a stack of towels plummets to the floor.

"No, no, no!" she says under her breath. She kneels down to pick them up when she hears Samantha's voice behind her.

"Jasmine, what's going on?"

She stands up, smacking her head on the handle of the linen closet door. Pain radiates over her scalp, and she falls back as the door slams shut.

"Are you okay?" Samantha runs up to her, but stops short. Her eyes dart up to the linen closet.

It is slowly opening again.

Jasmine presses a hand against it quickly, but something pushes *back*.

"It's . . . a raccoon!" She pushes harder. "It got in through the open window."

"A raccoon?" Samantha twists her face up. "In Santa Monica?"

The spirit pushes against the door again. Jasmine is about to explain how nature's trash pirates are all over California when another round of knocking echoes through the house.

Only this time, it's coming from the ceiling.

Jasmine watches the fear cross over Samantha's features as she looks up.

"I'm gonna go," she announces, then bolts back to Jasmine's room.

She groans internally, then scrambles to her feet, leaving the spirit to fling towels all over the hall. At her doorway, Jasmine nearly crashes into Samantha, who has her backpack slung over her shoulder.

"Stay!" she says, nearly breathless.

As if on cue, something heavy falls out of the closet, thumping on the floor, and Jasmine swears it sounds like someone whispers something to her.

Samantha doesn't even reply. She pushes past Jasmine and leaps over the pile of towels and clean sheets in the hallway, then yelps when the *other* closet door slams as she passes. Jasmine chases after her, and her project partner flings the front door open.

There's a man there, his jaw nearly on the ground.

León. The landlord.

"Ay, Dios mío," he mutters, turning to watch as Samantha leaves. "Jasmine, what's going on up here? I just got another noise complaint and you're at three warnings already."

There's a loud slam in the house, and Jasmine can't help her reaction. She laughs. Because of *course* her ghost chose this moment to act out!

León does not like her reaction. He scowls at her. "I'm going to have to talk to your mom about this."

Her heart drops. "Please—" she begins.

He doesn't let her finish. He turns and heads down the stairs, shaking his head.

The soft breeze from the ocean drifts over her face as she stands in the doorway alone. She likes living here in Santa Monica. It's the first time she and Mami have gotten to be near the ocean. On some mornings, if she's up early enough, she can even hear the waves crashing on the shore.

She wonders then if this is going to be the end of this place, just like it was for their apartment in Westlake and the one in Glendale.

"You *had* to do this today," she says with a sigh. "Why couldn't you just *not*?"

She spins back to the house and is met with silence.

"I don't know why you're doing this. Are you a child? Throwing a tantrum or something?"

Nothing.

"Answer me!" she yells.

Still . . . nothing.

She quietly closes the front door, then glances up at the photo of Papi. The pit in her chest grows as she stares at the man she hasn't seen in three years.

Because he's dead.

She breathes in deep and stares at the photo for a moment or two until her fingers find the charm on her necklace, the one Papi gave her before he left them all. She wears it every day, even though Mami swears it's going to break at any moment. But she can't take it off. Papi said it was his way of protecting her.

Yet when she walks back to the hallway to begin cleaning up the mess her ghost made, she isn't so sure that she feels protected.

"Four out of ten," she says to the linen closet. "You're not even an entertaining ghost. You're just *annoying*."

The closet says nothing back to her. It's just a closet.

o o o

Jasmine is back outside, sitting at the top of the steps with a tattered notebook in her lap. The cover is crisscrossed with Scotch tape to hold it together, so she opens it as delicately as possible. It is the other thing Papi left behind. He taught English at Los Angeles Community College, and during breaks, he would sit outside and observe the world around him. As the sea breeze flows over her, she turns the pages. There are poems. Doodles. Notes. She runs her finger along the sketch of a dog on a long leash far ahead of their owner, who yaps away on a phone. She reads a poem about the bright purple jacaranda flowers that bloomed along Vermont Avenue.

She's lost in the familiar words and images when she is pulled back into the present by the sound of boots on the steps. The sun is disappearing over the horizon, so there's a pink-and-orange glow around Mami's face.

"Hola, mija! What are you doing out here?"

"Nice day," she says, shrugging.

Her mami is clutching an envelope that's been torn open. "A very nice day," she says, turning to gaze at the setting sun. But then she gazes back at Jasmine, and she can tell that Mami doesn't exactly buy her answer.

Jasmine returns to the notebook. She isn't really reading it. She doesn't want to meet her mami's eyes.

Suddenly, the paint-speckled Doc Martens that Mami wears to work as a set dresser appear on the step below her, and Jasmine can't ignore her anymore. When she glances up, Mami's brown eyes are soft.

"Everything okay today?"

She nods.

"Well, let's head inside. I have some news to share with you while I start dinner."

"News?" Panic flares in her chest. *Oh no,* she thinks. *León did talk to her.*

"It's good news!" she says. "Come inside."

But Jasmine doesn't stand up. "Mami, I promise, I didn't do *anything*. It wasn't me!"

Mami laughs. "Jaz, it's okay." She reaches a hand down to help Jasmine up. "I mean, we have to do something annoying, but everything is going to be all right."

"Annoying?" Jasmine scoffs, then uses Mami for leverage to get up. "I'm a pro at handling annoying."

"Well, our lease is up at the end of next month, so I just told León that we'll be leaving then."

She stops dead in her tracks and lets go of Mami's hand. "What?"

"I know we've moved a lot already," she continues, unlocking the front door. "But I just found out from one of the gaffers on set—her name is Lara—that there's a great place opening up not terribly far from here. It's bigger. No stairs."

Jasmine frowns. "Mami, I swear I didn't do anything. It was the gho—"

Mami puts a hand on Jasmine's cheek. The gesture is both affectionate *and* stops Jasmine dead in her tracks. "I know you didn't. I just think . . . it's time. Time to move on, you know?"

There's something in Mami's expression that Jasmine can't place. She sees crinkles at the corners of her eyes, a tightness in the way she presses her lips together. But then she's turning away, heading into the house, and Jasmine follows, a new dread stitching itself to her bones.

They're moving. Again. It's because of the ghost, again. And Mami doesn't want to hear anything about it, *again*.

A thought surfaces that always comes to her in moments like this, when she can't ignore how much her life isn't like anyone else's.

Because Jasmine knows she is haunted.

She stops in the entryway. Looks up once again at the frameless photos tacked up on the wall. One is of Jasmine's first day of kindergarten; she wore a particularly intense frown that day because she didn't want to go. There's another where she's awkwardly clutching Tito, their orange tabby cat that ran away years ago.

And then there's the one of Jasmine cradled in her papi's arms as he smiles down at her.

He's been gone awhile now, and the whole time, all she's wanted is to hear from him again.

So why isn't the ghost Papi?

Why hasn't he ever tried to reach out to her?

Instead, she's stuck with a spirit who annoys her, who once tried to steal the charm around her neck, who just caused her only potential friend to run screaming from the apartment. Papi would *never* do anything like this to her.

She truly feels like the unluckiest girl in the world.

2

Jasmine stands at the end of the stoop, her backpack held at her side. She's had to do this so many times: another new apartment, another new neighborhood, another new school. They had only lasted a year in Crenshaw before this most recent move, and all Jasmine wants to do is go back to bed.

"Come on, Jaz," says Mami. She's on the sidewalk at the end of the short walkway in front of their house.

Jasmine doesn't move.

It's hot out. It's the second of October and they are in East Hollywood, so she's not surprised it's so hot out. This *is* Los Angeles, after all. But her head feels like it's full of bees. She doesn't want to go.

"Apúrate, mija," Mami commands.

She takes a step. "I'm going as fast as I can."

She does not go as fast as she can. She trudges toward her mami, who raises her eyebrows.

"Jaz, *please*. I have to get to set in an hour, and you know how traffic is here."

"We're only leaving early because you have to talk to everyone you see."

"There's nothing wrong with being friendly!" Mami slings her tote over her shoulder.

Jasmine groans. "Take me with you."

"You have to go to school today, amor."

Jasmine takes a few more sluggish steps. "But like . . . is that the *law*?"

Mami grins. "Actually, it is. Literally so."

"I'm tired of always going to a new school."

The smile on Mami's face disappears. "I don't like it, either," she says, her voice soft at first. Then, in a more musical tone: "But look at how beautiful this neighborhood is!"

Jasmine *did* love all the weird, colorful houses on La Mirada Avenue. But she'd just gotten used to living in Crenshaw, to all the good soul food nearby, to seeing Ronald, the landscaper at their apartment complex, every morning when she walked to school.

Unfortunately, it was the first day of school for Jasmine and *only* Jasmine. She's the odd one out, like always.

She feels like the unluckiest girl in the world.

It's hard for her to be present as her mami slips into her normal routine. Unlike Jasmine, Mami effortlessly meets new people. If you leave Aida Garza alone, she'll introduce herself to every human within a mile radius. So it isn't surprising that as soon as they make it beyond their house on La Mirada, Mami is already greeting their neighbor.

Her name is Ina Aguinaldo, and she has a blank canvas perched on a wooden easel set up in the alley between the Garza house and her own. Her shiny black hair is so long that it hangs past her waist. Her gray T-shirt is covered in speckles and smears of paint, and she studies the canvas.

Jasmine thinks she's the prettiest lady she's ever seen, so she doesn't say much after waving to her.

Moments later, Jasmine manages to pull Mami away from Ina to head down La Mirada to Lyman Place. They make a left at the next corner, where Mami meets Carl, a tall Black man with long locs, across from the big hospital. He'd been wailing away on his saxophone. Her mami puts a few dollars in the sax case open at his feet, and he nods at them both, then begins playing again. His music is loud and beautiful, but for some reason, the notes and the melodies make Jasmine feel a little sad, so much so that she has to look away.

She's relieved when they continue on, though Mami slows again as they approach The Intersection. One of Mami's co-workers had warned her about this neighborhood feature, and Jasmine had not understood why anyone would be worried about a street.

Jasmine gets it now. The Intersection seems like a crime against nature. Three major streets—Hoover, Sunset, and Fountain—all slam into one another in a chaotic explosion of lanes and crosswalks and signals. It takes them a couple moments to figure out the order of crosswalks they need to take to get to Jasmine's new school.

Who builds something like that?

Jasmine looks to her left, and a car zooms by, dangerously close to the curb. She reaches out to grab Mami's hand, but only grazes it. She pulls it back. Crosses her arms over her chest. She's not going to let a bunch of asphalt freak her out.

"You nervous?" Mami asks.

"Nah."

"It's okay if you are."

"Why does everyone in LA drive like they're playing *Mario Kart*?"

Mami shrugs. "Everyone has a place to be."

She hesitates. Then she puts a hand on Jasmine's shoulder. "Before, I meant if you were nervous about today. You know, starting at a new school."

"No," she says. "I've had a lot of first days, Mami. They're all kinda the same."

Mami squeezes her hand as the walk signal changes. "Very mature insight, Jaz."

They look both ways and cross over Fountain, where Mami unleashes another round of her patented cheeriness on another stranger: Diego, who stands behind a silver metal cart that gleams in the sun. He's got a round face and dark brown skin, and she spots some silver caps on his teeth as he falls into rapid Spanish with Mami.

She's gazing at the cups of sliced fruit on the edge of the cart when she feels the same sadness she did listening to Carl's music. Her fingers go straight to her papi's heart charm around her neck. It's been like this for years. The waves come and go, and she can't really control them. She simply has to ride them out.

The chirping of the bell on Diego's cart pulls her out of the thickness, and she follows Mami across the final crosswalk. "I'm so glad I found a fruit cart already!" she says, a cup overflowing with chopped fruit and Tajín from Diego in her left hand.

Kingsley Middle School is only a few blocks past The Intersection, but by the time it comes into view—other students streaming up the steps into the front entrance—Jasmine's sadness is replaced with the thumping heart of dread. She *has* had countless first days, but this one . . . this one *doesn't* feel the same.

Eighth grade. It's her last year before high school. So why does she feel like a little kid all over again?

Get it together, she tells herself. *You're practically an adult now.*

"Okay, mija," Mami says, kissing the top of Jasmine's head. "I hope today isn't too hard for you."

"I'll be fine," she says. "And you didn't have to walk me to school. I can get here on my own."

"I know. But I thought it would be nice before work gets too busy."

Mami tips her head to the side, and then her dark brown eyes get all glassy.

"What?" says Jasmine. "Oh, god, Mami, are you gonna *cry?*"

"No!" she says, then wipes at her eyes. "Maybe? I'm allowed to."

Jasmine laughs, and it washes her nerves away. "This is a No Crying zone. I promise I'll be okay, Mami."

This time, the two of them share a long gaze. Jasmine isn't sure what it means for Mami, but she knows what is swirling around in her head: They've been through a lot in the past four years.

She thinks that Mami looks . . . tired. Yes, that's it. Tired in a way that they don't really talk about, like they're trapped in bed under a blanket that's too heavy to toss off.

Jasmine smiles and throws her arms around her mami. "Te amo," she whispers.

"Te amo," Mami whispers back. "Try making a friend today?"

She smirks. "Only enemies."

Mami nods. "That's my daughter."

It happens again. Mami's eyes go shiny.

So Jasmine turns and darts into school without looking back. She's worried if she does, she might cry, too. Deep in her heart, her love for her papi stirs, and she wonders if he can see her. Is he worried, too? Does he know what they've been through since he left this world?

Beyond the doors, Jasmine sees Ms. Flores, the assistant principal who had helped Mami during registration. She nods at Jasmine, and she waves back before rounding the corner.

She finds the heart charm again. Imagines that Papi is watching her, and that he's proud of her.

It's enough to leave her feeling better as she heads to her first class.

3

As it turns out, Kingsley Middle School is pretty much like the rest.

Her classes . . . happen. Algebra I followed by World History, then English, then Life Sciences, and Jasmine does her best to keep up. She certainly feels like she's been dropped in the deep end of a pool, given that everyone else is a month into the lessons, while she is just starting. Her teachers are nice, though the only one who stands out is Mx. Chen, the English teacher who does a dramatic reading from a book called *The House on Mango Street*. Everyone is asked to discuss "sensory details" of their neighborhoods, and it is the only time Jasmine participates in anything all day. She's lived in a lot of places around the city, and it reminds her of her papi's journal, so she raises her hand. Tells the class about the swaying line of palm trees that rustle in the wind along West Martin Luther King Jr. Blvd. Mx. Chen smiles at her, then says, "What a wonderful contribution! Glad you're in my class."

Jasmine blushes. "Thanks."

When English class ends, Mx. Chen stops her before she leaves. They point at a small rainbow enamel pin on the strap of Jasmine's bag. "What does that mean?"

"Oh," she says. "Just that I'm queer."

Her English teacher smiles. "Well, since you're new, I feel obligated to invite you to this afternoon's GSA meeting. It's in the library. We're very small, but you're absolutely welcome there."

She thanks Mx. Chen and darts off. A school club? That's

not really Jasmine's style. Besides, she's never really lasted long enough at a school these past few years to get involved. Or to volunteer. Or to make friends.

At least not since Samantha.

Still, it's because of Mx. Chen that Jasmine finds herself in the library after school. It's not that Jasmine thinks things are going to be different this time. The request Mami made lingers in her mind: *Try making a friend today?*

Okay. Maybe she can make *one* friend.

The school's librarian is busy writing something while she stands in the doorway, unsure where exactly she is supposed to go. The library itself is a lot bigger than she expects, with high ceilings and huge windows that let in lots of light. There are plenty of towering shelves to the left.

"Do you need something?"

She looks up at the man, whose dark skin is shiny from sweat. "Mx. Chen? Do you know where they are?"

He smiles and points to the tables toward the windows. "Hang a left at the magazines," he says, "and you'll see the group there."

"Thanks."

"You new here?"

Jasmine nods. "Started today."

He waves from behind the circulation desk. "I'm Mr. Winters," he says. "You're always welcome in the library as long as I'm here, and I keep long hours, so I'm around a lot."

"Well, I like libraries," she says. "So I'll probably be here a lot, too."

He jots something down in a notebook on the desk. "Sorry, I was writing some poetry before you got here."

She senses the heaviness again, and her mind immediately goes to her papi's journal. She doesn't think what Mr. Winters is doing is the same, but as always, she can't control the connections she makes.

Jasmine shakes the weight off and turns away from Mr. Winters. She weaves around a couple tables and then, at the far end of the room, she sees Mx. Chen standing next to a circular table, where two other kids sit facing the opposite direction.

When she walks up to the table, Mx. Chen is already beaming.

"Members of the GSA," they say, extending their arms out, "I'd like you to meet Jasmine Garza! She's new to Kingsley Middle School."

The two kids turn around. The one on the right raises a hand in greeting and offers up a curt smile with lips painted black with lipstick. "I'm Bea Veracruz," she says. "Today, my pronouns are she/her, and I'm queer *and* genderqueer. I'm the club president."

She has on a black beanie, and dyed hair the color of a green highlighter pokes out from underneath it. Jasmine opens her mouth to comment on how much she likes it, but Bea turns back around quickly.

The other kid is smiling at her, and he raises a peace sign. "I'm Jorge Barrera," he says, and his thick curls shake when he moves. "He/him. And I'm the secretary."

She glances down at the small notepad in front of him, and there's a drawing there. Something . . . furry? When she leans over to look at it, Jorge closes it quickly. His light brown face immediately flushes red.

That was weird, she thinks.

"Well, I'm Jasmine," she says. "She/her pronouns. Just moved here from Crenshaw."

"Welcome," says Mx. Chen. "We officially meet once a week on Tuesdays, but we've all been known to bend the rules a bit."

Bea whispers something that Jasmine doesn't catch, then casts a quick scowl at her.

"Uh . . . okay," says Jasmine. "Can I join you today?"

"Absolutely!" Mx. Chen pulls out the chair to their right. "Sit, sit."

"Where are you from, Jasmine?" Jorge asks. "You totally look like you could be a cousin of mine."

"My parents are from two different parts of Mexico," she answers as she sits. "You?"

Jorge goes red again. "Well, we don't really know. I was adopted. But my papi is from Mexico, and my other dad is from Leimert Park."

"Cool!" Jasmine says.

Once again, Bea offers up another seemingly angry look, and this time, it's Jasmine's face that burns up. *What gives?* she thinks.

"Bea?" Mx. Chen says, prompting her to answer.

"Oh." Bea doesn't even glance up this time. "My parents are from Guatemala."

"Well, I'm from Taiwan," Mx. Chen says. "My parents moved us to San Jose initially, but I came down here to Los Angeles after college. And I've never left."

Jasmine nods but then she looks to Bea and Jorge. "So . . . what normally happens in these meetings?"

"Sometimes, we talk about books or movies and stuff," Jorge says. "But today, we were talking about—"

"—about our favorite cartoons," Bea cuts in.

"Be nice," Mx. Chen chides.

"Sorry," says Bea quickly. "It's just . . . we didn't expect anyone new to join us since no one else has this year."

"More members is good," Jorge says, practically whispering.

Jasmine decides that the energy at the table is way too weird, which she knows is a lot coming from someone who is haunted. Bea and Jorge do actually start talking about cartoons, but Jasmine only chimes in when Jorge says he loves *The Amazing World of Gumball*.

"Oh, me too," she says. "Definitely one of the best."

For a moment, Jorge looks thrilled. But then he shuffles through his notepad, and the moment is over.

By the time the meeting ends at 3 p.m., Jasmine can barely contain herself. She has to actively try not to sprint out of the library. She bids the three of them goodbye, then walks swiftly toward the library exit with her head down.

She is relieved once she's out of the school and walking home. *So much for trying to make friends,* she thinks.

Maybe being on her own is best. It's always worked in the past.

As she approaches The Intersection, her feet slow, like she's stuck in syrup. *Does* she really want to try to make friends? Why is she even making an attempt with these other kids? It won't matter anyway.

The world blurs around Jasmine as she comes upon Diego and his fruit cart. The heaviness settles in her chest again. There doesn't seem to be much of a point to anything. She nods at Diego, then looks away as quick as she can. Her eyes dart from one rushing car to another, all these people heading to some unknown destination. She wonders: Does anyone else feel like this?

Probably not.

○   ○   ○

That night, Mami comes home just as tired as Jasmine is. The production she's been working on has been more intense than usual. It's for some period piece, so Mami has been running around town to find antique furniture that fits the theme, then helping direct the construction of a set that has to be *exactly* to the director's specifications.

"I get why the director wants it this way," Mami says, riffling through the takeout menus she keeps stuffed in a drawer in the kitchen. "But Jaz, it's so *annoying.*"

They get their usual takeout order from Sanamluang Cafe: tom kha soup with tofu, and an order of pad see ew with chicken. The delivery driver arrives on a battery-powered bike and zips away so quickly that Jasmine is convinced it must be magic.

Mami asks her about her day, and Jasmine is honest: it was mostly uneventful, and she didn't make a friend yet. She even tells her about the GSA meeting.

"Well, you *tried*," says Mami, picking up some rice noodles with her chopsticks. "I hope you don't give up."

"I just don't get why they were so weird to me."

"You're new, Jaz," she says. "It's not always fair, but sometimes, it's gonna be hard to break into a group for that reason."

Jasmine narrows her eyes. "You sound like that project you worked on last summer."

Mami groans. "The one for LA Unified School District?"

"A *literal* after-school special."

She rolls her eyes. "I do not sound that cheesy."

"Some days, you do. You are a mom, after all."

Mami slurps up some of the tom kha soup. "And proud of it."

Just then, there's a short creaking sound above them. They both look up, and goose bumps rise on Jasmine's skin. In any of their past homes, they could have easily written it off as their upstairs neighbors. But this . . . this is the first time they've lived in a standalone *house*. Jasmine likes it so far. It's nice not to have neighbors on the other side of the wall, and it's so much bigger than the apartments they've been at.

Yet up until this moment, Jasmine wondered if this would finally be the place to break the pattern, that her ghost wouldn't follow her to.

Neither of them say anything at first, but then Mami resumes eating. "It's an old building," she says. "It's probably just talking back to us."

That was something she first heard from Tía Selena, Mami's older sister. She had a bizarre store out in Pasadena: the Mystic

Emporium. She claimed to sell "everything a wandering, inquisitive soul might need." Jasmine had only been there a couple times and never failed to get lost in the labyrinth of shelves overstuffed with crystals, incense, potions, spell books, and other objects she wasn't sure did what they claimed to.

Which is also why she wasn't sure that Tía's assertion that all buildings have a soul was true. Mami certainly didn't agree with her sister. To her, what Tía Selena believed was always a joke.

So Jasmine kept quiet, and she hoped the creaking *was* the old house being old.

4

It is early in the morning—before the sun rises, before the birds start chirping outside her window—that Jasmine senses something is in her room.

She opens her eyes quickly, and she is met with darkness at first. She turns her head to the left and finds the small beam of light casting on the far wall from the streetlamp outside the window. The more she stares at it, the more her eyes adjust to the shadows. Her gaze falls on her dresser, on the small reading chair in the opposite corner, then to the closed closet door.

Jasmine sits up and pulls her cobija close. She doesn't *see* anything in her room, but the sensation is still there. Like she's being *watched*.

It isn't the first time she's felt this, though. The details are usually different, but the feeling? Always the same.

In their apartment in Westlake where Papi died four years ago, it began as the whispering, as if someone was trying to talk to her just out of earshot. That's when she first sensed that she was being watched. When she told Mami about it, she'd dismissed her, had told her it was just grief.

By the time they got to Glendale, there were dishes breaking and falling all the time in addition to the whispering. Mami said she never heard anything, and they quietly left that apartment. Then there was the place in Santa Monica. Jasmine's ghost escalated toward the end, opening and closing doors whenever she was in the house alone. Except when Samantha was there, of course. She wished she knew what León had told Mami.

Then there was the Crenshaw apartment. They got more noise complaints, always when Mami wasn't home, but that time... Jasmine asked to move. She wanted to tell her mami that it wasn't just the noise—the slamming doors and cupboards and broken dishes—but the creepy presence that would run its fingers over the back of her neck. But ever since Mami had shushed Jasmine that day Samantha fled from their apartment, Jasmine hasn't had the courage to bring up ghosts again.

She likes this house. She really does. But as she sits there in the deep shadows, the sensation doesn't go away. She feels *watched*.

She wants so badly to be overreacting. She sits there, silent and waiting.

It starts off as a low groan.

The groan becomes a creak, as if someone is walking on the roof.

Maybe it's the house talking, she thinks. *It has to be.*

She wants to comfort herself with disbelief because she knows it will be easier. But she knows she's kidding herself. Ghosts are real, and she's had one tagging along in her life for four years now.

Then: "Ugh," she says aloud. "If this *is* the house talking, then keep it to yourself, okay? I'm trying to sleep."

She waits again.

She doesn't hear anything.

"Thank you," she whispers, knowing she isn't actually going to get a reply, yet she raises her hand and presses her fist against the wall.

She sighs.

"I think I just gave a house a fist bump," she says to herself.

And it isn't even the strangest thing that's happened in her life. Because she knows this isn't a house talking.

It's a ghost.

She briefly considers what existence is like for a ghost. What can they see? Hear? But then annoyance fills her brain. If *she* was a spirit, she certainly wouldn't be tormenting a family like hers over and over again. Didn't ghosts have better things to do? Weren't there actual evil people to haunt? She would absolutely spend her afterlife playing endless pranks on people who made the world worse.

Jasmine's face burns in the shadows. She hopes that she hasn't done anything to deserve this.

She tries her best to will the feeling away, but it continues to stick to her when sleep finally comes.

5

Jasmine goes to bed each night that week hoping for the best. Every time she and Mami have moved, it has taken a while for her ghost to announce its presence. In her mind, ghosts move slower than people, and somehow, hers eventually finds her.

She doesn't feel any ghostly touches. No loud banging. No broken kitchenware. Nothing. But every morning, she wakes up exhausted and on edge.

It still feels like someone is watching her.

On Friday morning, Jasmine is eager for a distraction, so she heads to the library first thing upon getting to school. She greets Mr. Winters, who is shelving books by the door, and then she heads to the fiction section. That *House on Mango Street* book sounded interesting. Maybe she just needs a good story to escape from the lingering fear in the back of her mind that it's all starting up again.

She's searching for Cisneros on the shelf to see if she has any other books when she hears the whispering.

At first, terror pulses through her, and she's brought right back to the Westlake apartment. But when she peers around the edge of the bookshelf, she sees two people she recognizes, fiercely whispering to one another: Bea and Jorge.

She hasn't seen either of them since the GSA meeting on Tuesday. Bea is wearing all black clothing again, though this time, her bright green hair is free of a beanie. Jasmine marvels at how long it actually is. Jorge, dressed a lot more plainly than

Bea, is pulling at the collar of his polo shirt, then pointing down at his notepad. She can't quite make out what they're saying, and she wonders if she should announce her presence and join them.

They're both staring at a spot between two reading chairs set up by the large bay windows. Bea holds up what resembles a power drill that Mami keeps in her big toolbox. It's black and orange, and there's a digital screen facing Bea.

Careful as she can be, Jasmine eases forward to hear better, hoping they won't see her.

"Are you getting anything?" Jorge says, no longer whispering.

"Not really," says Bea, and then she waves the device around. She spins toward Jasmine, who ducks back behind the shelf. "I know I'm not imagining this."

Imagining what?

"Wait," says Bea. "I think I got something!"

Jasmine hears their feet scuffling on the thin carpeting, moving away from her, so she quickly peeks again. Unfortunately, Jorge is looking directly at Jasmine this time, and he gasps loudly.

Bea lowers the device, which was pointed her way. "Jasmine?"

She steps out from behind the shelf. "Sorry, I was looking for a book and . . . what are you *doing*?"

The two exchange a silent look.

"Homework," Bea blurts out. Then she holds the device up again and waves it from side to side.

"Is that like . . . for Mz. Taylor's class?"

Jorge glances over at Bea, who ignores the question. She stops moving, and then her eyes go wide.

"Jorge," she says softly.

Jorge quickly looks at the screen. "Is that—?"

In an instant, it's as if Jasmine doesn't even exist. Bea's eyes go wide. "Definitely got something!"

Jorge looks as if he's going to explode. The two of them dart off toward the front of the library, the device held forward.

"We got it!" Bea cries out.

And then they're gone.

As Jasmine is left standing there alone, she isn't sure what's a worse thought: Bea and Jorge don't seem to want to make a new friend.

Or they don't seem to want to be friends with *her*.

○ ○ ○

Despite that she knows that there's a chance she'll run into Bea and Jorge again, Jasmine heads to the library after her last class. A part of her feels guilty; it's the end of her first week at Kingsley Middle School, and she spent the whole day reading a book. (She ended up checking out *Brown Girl Dreaming* by Jacqueline Woodson.) She isn't sure she remembers a single thing that her teachers said. But that still counts as learning, right? At least she was reading.

She drifts through the hallway as students rush past her to get out of the building as fast as possible, and she almost doesn't catch it.

It's Bea's green hair that gives them away.

Jasmine freezes. She watches as both Bea and Jorge peer around a corner about fifteen feet away, then duck back behind it. The crowd thins, and Jasmine realizes it won't be long before she is the only person standing in the hallway.

She could go home and do what she has been doing every day since she started at Kingsley: homework and writing in her notebook. But now, she simply *has* to know: *What are Bea and Jorge doing?*

Jasmine spots an open classroom and rushes inside of it. When she steals a glance down the hallway, Bea and Jorge are rapidly heading away from her. She nearly trips over her own feet as she exits the classroom, but thankfully, she doesn't alert them to her presence.

Jasmine also notices that Bea has that weird beeping device held up in the air.

She doesn't get too close, but follows the two of them down the hallway until they turn right. She suspects she knows where they are headed, so she picks up the pace. Sure enough, she manages to catch them entering the library.

Once at the door, she peers through the glass to see Jorge, his bag slung over his shoulder, talking to Mr. Winters at the circulation desk. Then, off to the left, Bea is . . .

Actually, Jasmine isn't certain. Bea isn't holding the device anymore. She's setting something up on one of the distant bookshelves.

And now Jasmine can tell it's a *camera*.

When Jorge suddenly walks away from the circulation desk, Jasmine takes a chance, her heart racing. She gently pulls open the door to the library and slinks inside, making sure she doesn't make a sound. Mr. Winters looks up and smiles, then returns to organizing his never-ending pile of books.

How are there always so many? Jasmine wonders. *Are they reproducing in here?*

Images of a library overflowing with multiplying books fills her head and she shudders. The paper cuts *alone* would be something of nightmares.

She sneaks forward, beyond Mr. Winters's desk and toward the big bay windows with all the reading nooks. Thankfully, she has a view straight down the aisle between shelves, and there, standing between them and whispering, are Jorge and Bea.

Jasmine moves to the next row of shelves and quickly creeps down it until she's just out of earshot of the other two. She peers over the tops of some books as Bea waves the beeping device about, and then she spots the camera Bea has set up on a lower shelf.

"I know the activity is localized here," Bea says.

Jorge sighs. "I feel like we're on a wild-rooster chase."

"Isn't it a 'wild-goose chase'?"

Jorge shakes his head. "Have you *seen* a rooster before? Try catching one."

"I just want to find it," Bea whines. "I know it's here. I can *smell* it."

"That's probably because it needs a shower."

Bea gapes open-mouthed at Jorge. "What a good theory, Jorge. What if the Sasquatch is using the showers in the gym after school?"

Sasquatch.

Sasquatch?!

Jasmine is so shocked by the word that she leans too hard on the books in front of her, which sends them spilling off the shelf. She backs away as they slam against the ground.

"There it is!" Bea yells, and to Jasmine's horror, both Bea and Jorge come running around the corner of the bookshelves, only to find Jasmine with a bunch of books at her feet.

"Hi, again," says Jasmine, her face burning. "Sorry I'm not a Sasquatch?"

Jorge's mouth is practically on the floor. "Jasmine?" he says. "What are you doing here?"

"I kind of had the same question for you guys," she answers.

Bea is *scowling,* her whole face scrunched up. "Were you *spying* on us?"

Jasmine pushes past the irritation burning in her and points at the camera. "Aren't you spying on Mr. Winters?"

Bea actually looks shocked. "Uh . . . *no!* Definitely not!"

"We were hoping to find—" Jorge says.

Bea gently backhands Jorge's arm. "Dude! Don't tell her!"

"I already heard you," Jasmine says. "It's not that big of a deal."

Jorge's mouth drops open. "So you believe in them?"

Jasmine hesitates for only a moment, and in that time, a hundred thoughts hit her like a tidal wave: *I mean . . . why not? I have a ghost following me. I'm haunted. I should tell them. Don't tell them. Don't say anything more! This is a terrible idea.*

Then: Is *a Sasquatch using the school gym?!*

"I don't see why not," she ends up saying. "There are lots of weird things in the world."

"Like *what*?" Bea says, the words more an accusation than a question.

It is like a compulsion. Her whole body is telling her not to say *anything* about her strange life, and yet the words fall right out of her mouth.

"Well, I'm haunted."

At first, neither Bea nor Jorge react. They simply stare at her with expressionless faces, and dread overwhelms Jasmine. Why on *earth* did she say that?

"Haunted," Bea says. Her tone feels cold, and her face is like stone.

"I guess," says Jasmine.

"You *guess*?" she says.

"It's just that . . . well, I've never told anyone before. I'm pretty sure that a ghost has been following me for years."

"*Years?*" Jorge shakes his head in disbelief. "What do you mean?"

Stop telling them anything, she thinks.

But her mouth says: "It's been around for like . . . four years now."

Jorge and Bea exchange a look.

"Four," says Bea, brushing green hair out of her face, and this time, she looks shocked. *"Four?"*

Jasmine nods.

For the first time since they've met, Bea smiles at Jasmine. "That's amazing."

"*Is* it?" says Jasmine.

"We might be able to help," offers Jorge.

"Well, hold on," says Bea. "We need to gather more information if we're going to take on the case."

"Case? What does that mean?"

"Well, you need to first become an official member of the GSA," says Bea.

Jasmine narrows her eyes. "O-okay," she says. "And how does that help?"

"Jasmine," Bea says in a serious tone. "Would you like to join the Gay Supernatural Alliance?"

Her first impulse is to laugh, but she sees the intense look of anticipation on the faces of Jorge and Bea. "Wait, *really?*" she says. "Is that what the GSA *actually* is?"

"We renamed it," says Jorge. "Mx. Chen knows about it, but they think it's just a joke."

"They said something about all young queer people having strange interests." Bea shrugs. "I mean, they're not *wrong*."

"So, do you want to be a member?" Jorge asks, eyes wide.

Jasmine gazes at both of them. "You're serious about this, aren't you?"

Bea nods. "My parents are actually professional supernatural investigators," she says. "They taught me everything I know, but I'm looking to start my own consulting company once I'm in high school. You know, people can hire me to take care of the supernatural problems in their lives."

"I'm sorry, they're *what?*"

"It's amazing," Jorge says. "Like, her parents have all this gear and stuff, and they track down all sorts of supernatural beings and help people."

"Gear?" Jasmine points to the weird device in Bea's right hand. "Like that thing?"

Bea holds it up. "An infrared thermal imager," she says. "It allows me to measure changes in temperature. It's why I thought you were the Sasquatch earlier."

When Jasmine continues staring at it, her eyebrows rise in confusion. "So . . . bigfoot."

"We don't think they like that name," Jorge says confidently. "I mean . . . what if a Sasquatch has tiny feet?"

"Okay, fair," she says. "But there's one on campus?"

"There's been sightings of something strange lurking around this place," Bea explains. "We're not all that far from Griffith Park, and who knows what sort of creatures come down from the hills?"

Jasmine glances at Jorge. "Looking for a . . . shower?"

He shrugs. "I don't know. Bea's much better at this stuff than I am," he says. "I'm here for support. And for . . ."

He clamps his mouth shut and presses his lips into a thin line.

"He'll tell you later," Bea says, running her hand up and down Jorge's arm to comfort him. "I'm sorry we've been so . . . so *secretive*. We didn't know who you were when Mx. Chen introduced you to us, and it's not like we could've told you about the *real* GSA then."

It hits Jasmine instantly: she is having an open conversation about ghosts and a Sasquatch. No one is laughing at her. Yelling at her. Calling her names or running screaming from her house. Her head spins, and she reaches out to carefully place a hand on a shelf to steady herself. "Sorry," she says. "This is just . . . it's a lot."

Jorge's face falls. "I know," he says. "But you can talk to us about it."

Bea extends a hand. "Jasmine Garza, would you like to join the Gay Supernatural Alliance?"

"Please," Jorge says, his dark brown eyes practically pleading. "We can help you."

The idea is so strange to her. For the past four years, she's done her best to survive the chaos at home. But had she ever done anything to try and *stop* the haunting?

No. Not really.

Could Bea and Jorge actually help her?

Maybe it is worth a shot.

Jasmine takes Bea's hand, which is warm and soft. "Okay," she says. "I'm in."

Bea shakes it, then lets go. "Well, you should tell us about what you're experiencing." She nods to Jorge, who takes out the small notepad she saw before from his backpack.

Her heart skips. She isn't sure she should be doing this.

Jorge flips to a blank page. Bea stares at Jasmine with those dark eyes of hers.

"Tell us about your ghost," Bea says.

So Jasmine tells them everything.

o o o

She tells them about Papi.

Westlake to Glendale to Santa Monica to Crenshaw to here.

Whispers to thrown glasses to opening cupboards to creepy caresses.

Running from one place to another.

Never feeling like she can settle anywhere.

o o o

The whole time, Bea and Jorge listen intently. He takes notes, and Bea occasionally interjects with a question, mostly when it comes to the details. What did the ghost sound like? Feel like? Smell like? That last one trips her up. She's not sure she's ever *smelled* the ghost. Jasmine provides what she can, even when she isn't sure why it's all so important.

When she is finished, they're still standing in the same spot between the shelves. Jasmine isn't sure how much time has passed, and for a moment, she's worried that the library has closed while they were all still in it.

Jorge shuts his notepad, and Bea's gaze lifts to the ceiling. She stays like that for a few moments, deep in thought.

"I've never heard of anything like that," says Jorge quietly, then he shivers. "Ghosts are so creepy."

Jasmine laughs, but then cuts it short when she realizes Jorge isn't joking. "Wait," she says, "you're in a school group *about* the supernatural."

He frowns. "Doesn't mean I have to like it all. I'm here to *study* it."

Jasmine wants to ask him more questions, but Bea cuts in. "You've given us a really strong case," she says. "I'll have to do some more research before I can suggest a plan of action."

Now it's Jasmine's turn to frown. "Meaning what?"

"Surveillance," she says, then gestures at the camera still sitting on a nearby shelf. "My parents also have a device. An EMF reader. It can detect changes in the local magnetic field whenever there is the presence of a spirit, so we'll probably need to use that."

Someone clears their throat nearby, and all three of them turn around to find Mr. Winters staring at them.

"Sorry, kids," he says. "Gotta shut down for the afternoon. Do you have anything to check out before I do?"

"No," says Bea quickly, then gestures with her head toward the exit. "We'll get out of your way."

As they head for the library doors, the hair on the back of Jasmine's neck rises.

A shiver runs down her spine. She looks over to Mr. Winters, who is waiting expectantly for her to leave. Her heart beats frantically, and she follows after her new friends. *What was that?*

Just beyond the library door, Bea stops and turns to Jasmine. "Jorge and I will get to your case soon," she says. "We're just really busy with other ones right now."

"Why don't you just ask your parents for help?" Jasmine asks. "You know, since they're paranormal investigators."

In an instant, all the warmth is gone from Bea. She folds her arms over her chest and draws her eyebrows together.

"No," she says. "I can do this without them."

Jorge steps closer to Bea. "We got this," he says, but his voice doesn't sound all that certain.

"Okay," says Jasmine. "So . . . what next?"

"Let's talk next week," says Bea, and then she and Jorge give Jasmine their phone numbers. At the exact moment she finishes, Bea salutes Jasmine. "We look forward to working with you, but right now, we need to go. We're hunting down La Llorona in a nearby park."

While they run toward the front doors, Jorge turns and waves. "So glad we could do this!" he cries out.

And then . . . they're gone. Jasmine is left standing in the hallway, one emotion crashing into another. There's shock, because she can't really believe what just happened in the last half hour. There's confusion, because Bea is one of the strangest people she has ever met.

But then there's . . . relief.

Relief because Jasmine told *two* people her secret.

And both of them believed her.

She sends each of them a text from her number so they have it. Jorge is quick to reply:

Sorry we ran off so quickly!!! On the hunt! 💀

She stares at the text message and thinks: *Is this really happening to me?*

6

Thoughts swirl around in Jasmine's head as she walks home, and she nearly enters into the crosswalk without looking up at The Intersection. A car honks sharply, and she's jolted back into the present.

Across the street, Diego waves at her, then rings the bell on his cart. She waves back, but her attention wanders. She waits for the walk signal while her mind drifts back to what she just experienced.

Jasmine traverses one of the crosswalks at The Intersection carefully when it's her turn and nods at Diego. There's a lull in traffic, so she quickly darts across Fountain before the walk sign lights up. At the other side of the street, she reaches into the neck of her shirt and runs her fingers along her chain. When she comes to the charm at the end of it, the weight in her chest returns.

Was I right to trust them, Papi? she asks, even though she's reached out like this a thousand times before and Papi has never answered.

Bumps suddenly rise all over her skin.

She knows this feeling.

Someone is watching her.

When she turns around, she expects to find Diego looking her way. But he's not even paying attention to her. There are a couple nurses in blue scrubs next to his cart, waiting for him to finish chopping some more fruit. An older Chinese woman walking a small white terrier passes by them. As far as she can tell, no one else is feeling what she's feeling.

Then she sees it.

His shadow.

Diego's shadow on the sidewalk to the right of him . . . it seems *bigger*.

It's a play on the light. It has to be. A person's shadow can't grow like that. She looks to Diego, and the two nurses are gone. He's staring off, and his gaze is . . . distant.

Jasmine looks back down at his shadow for a few more seconds, then shakes it off. Too much ghost talk on the brain. It's just a *shadow*.

The rest of her walk home is uneventful, even though her brain is full. Carl isn't out playing his saxophone that afternoon, which Jasmine is thankful for because she doesn't want to talk to anyone at the moment. When she heads down La Mirada, she picks up the pace, eager to get back to home.

But when she arrives at the alley between her home and Ina's, she slows. One of Ina's paintings—clearly unfinished—sits on an easel. Next to it, there's a small table with a palette, numerous tubes of oil paint, and a cup of dark, cloudy water. Her neighbor is nowhere in sight, so she slowly heads down the cement driveway toward it. There's no definable shape on the canvas, just a colorful brightness surrounding a very dark spot in the center.

Beyond the canvas, toward the end of the alley, there's a small garage separate from the house, and Jasmine glances over to see if Ina is coming. The garage door is open, and Ina's small green sedan sits inside of it.

Jasmine looks back at the painting. Somehow, the work-in-progress overwhelms Jasmine. She shouldn't be looking at this. It's like she's peering inside Ina's head without asking.

She instinctively reaches for her charm, and that's when she sees it out of the corner of her eye.

Something *moved*.

She whips her head to the side, expecting to see Ina, but there's no one there.

Bumps rise all over her skin.

"Oh, not *again*," she whispers.

Has her ghost finally found her? Did it follow her to school, then to Diego, *then* to Ina's?

The darkness under Ina's car . . . it looks like Diego's shadow.

Jasmine backs away from the canvas, her breath caught in her throat.

A door opens in the garage, and just like that, it all passes: Jasmine's instinct and the growing darkness under the car. Ina walks around her car, then looks up at Jasmine and waves.

"Hey, neighbor!" she says. One side of her head is shaved to the scalp, and she pushes the rest of her hair over it. Jasmine notices that her hands are covered with paint.

"You okay, Jasmine?" Ina says as she approaches.

"Oh, sorry," Jasmine says quickly. "I thought I saw an animal or something in your garage."

"We get raccoons in the backyard sometimes." Ina picks up her easel and repositions it, spinning it to face the garage so that the afternoon sun hits it. "They're little trash demons, so you have to be careful around them."

"Totally," says Jasmine. "We used to get them out in Glendale when we were close to the foothills."

She glances back at the garage, but there's nothing there.

Just regular shadows and a regular car.

"Glendale? Is that where you came from before this?"

"Ummm . . . that was a few apartments back," says Jasmine. "We moved here from Crenshaw."

Ina examines the canvas, then picks up the palette and pulls a brush out of her back pocket. "Sounds like you and your mom move around a lot."

"I guess."

"Can I ask you something?"

Jasmine's heart skips. "Uh . . . sure."

"It's kinda personal."

"That's okay."

"How long has it just been you and your mom?"

It's been four years, but the pain often feels just as sharp. Jasmine scrunches her face up.

"I'm sorry," says Ina. "I shouldn't have asked that."

"No, it's fine," says Jasmine. "It was a while ago."

Ina sets her palette back down on the small table. "It's all right if it isn't fine. I've had a bad habit of being very forward about this sort of thing since my partner died last year. I keep bursting my way into uncomfortable conversations like it's my job."

Jasmine holds back a gasp. "Oh, I'm sorry, too," she says.

"That's why I paint." Ina picks up the palette once more, then makes a dramatic line of red with her brush. She steps back from the canvas. "It wasn't something I did a whole lot before I lost Fatima, but it's really helping me channel my emotions."

Jasmine's skin bristles, and the sensation returns: someone is watching them.

She gazes back to the garage, but she doesn't see anything. She spins toward the street, but no one is walking by.

"I gotta go do some chores," she says. "Nice talking, Ina."

Ina gives her an odd look, then raises her brush in a goodbye. "See you around."

Jasmine wastes no time getting back home. She unlocks the front door and slams it behind her. In her mind, the faster she closes it, the less likely it is that the ghost will get inside.

Her heart is racing, and she is sure she's sweating from

everywhere. She slumps against the front door, convinced there's a puddle of sweat at her feet. *It's a ghost,* she reminds herself. *It can walk through walls if it wants to.*

Unless she's just overreacting and there is no ghost. She knows it's been a very strange day, between telling Bea and Jorge the truth, deciding to join the Gay Supernatural Alliance, and her unnerving experiences around Diego and Ina. She remains sitting against the door until her heart slows and her breath comes back.

When she's calmed down, she pushes herself up and walks into the kitchen. She makes some citrus tea with the kettle, then lets the silence of her new home swallow her up as she sips at the steaming mug. She has not adjusted to living in a house instead of an apartment. It feels so much *bigger,* even though there are still plenty of unpacked boxes strewn about. Mami has mentioned hanging more things on the walls, something they've barely done because . . . well, they always move at the end of their year-long lease.

What's different about this place? Why would Mami think this would be an exception to what has *always* happened?

But at least it's quiet. She pulls out some homework to work on, thankful that her usual torments don't seem to be around for now. When Mami comes home a couple hours later, she's still nose-deep in trying to catch up to where her science class already is. The two greet each other with smiles, and Mami comes over to kiss Jasmine's forehead. Then they settle into a familiar silence: Jasmine continues doing homework while Mami begins heating pans, dropping in garlic and onion to sizzle and fill the house with the best combination of scents. They eat pollo asado over rice and ask about each other's days. Jasmine says she might have made two friends, to which Mami responds by getting out of her seat and shaking her hips. She does this until Jasmine boos her, and then laughter rings out in their small dining room.

There's a moment where Jasmine thinks she hears the house groaning. But in this instance, she chooses to ignore it. Maybe that's why Mami wants to hang more things on the walls. She's *choosing* to make this place a home. Jasmine likes that idea, especially as Mami clears their plates and everything feels so *normal*. Not much in Jasmine's life fits that word at all.

7

There is lots of unpacking that weekend, and Jasmine helps Mami find places where everything should go. A lamp with a bright yellow shade fits best in the southern corner of the living room; the few coats they own go in a small closet near the entryway; Mami's books are alphabetized and put in a bookshelf in the dining room, since Mami likes to read while she eats.

Their two-bedroom house on La Mirada Avenue is beginning to take shape. Jasmine likes what she sees, but she's also a little afraid. They've never settled in a home like this before. *Should they be getting so comfortable?*

So when she heads out to school on Monday morning, she has one thought on her mind: Is it a good idea to let Bea and Jorge help her?

She's never really had anyone who wanted to help her find a solution before. Mami simply does not allow talk of ghosts, so Jasmine doesn't really try. A long time ago, in the Glendale apartment, Tía Selena came over and waved a burning clump of sage and placed weird crystals everywhere, but then Mami removed them and told Jasmine her tía had her heart in the right place. "But this stuff doesn't work. Papi is gone, mija. We have to move on."

At the end of Ina's long driveway, Jasmine's heart thumps. Sadly, Mami was right. Papi *was* gone, and this pesky spirit certainly wasn't him. That still didn't make her feel any better.

She glances over at Ina's garage. It's closed.

Jasmine sighs, then continues to Kingsley Middle School.

She waves at Carl, who belts a long melody at her. Diego is in his usual spot, and there's a crowd of kids surrounding his cart. She can tell he looks a little overwhelmed as he rapidly chops fruit and speaks Spanish even faster than his knife works.

She touches her heart-shaped charm. "Should I try, Papi?" she asks after she passes Diego.

She waits, leaving room for a reply she knows isn't going to come.

The Gay Supernatural Alliance can't make things *worse*, so she decides that it could be worth a shot.

Jasmine knows it's not going to be hard to find them. Even though she's only been here a week, it's clear that Jorge and Bea frequent one place more than any other: the library.

She pushes open one of the swinging doors and sees that Mr. Winters is finally *not* buried behind a towering stack of books. He is steeping a tea bag in a mug, his hand bouncing up and down. "Good morning, Jasmine," he greets, then nods in a predictable direction. "They're back there."

She's about to head off that way when he raises his free hand. "A moment," he says. "What exactly are y'all looking for in here?"

"Uh . . ." she says. "Books?"

He reaches behind the counter and produces Bea's digital camera.

Jasmine's heart drops. In all the chaos of the previous week, she forgot about it! Clearly, Bea did, too.

"I found it on the floor. Maybe she dropped it?"

She gingerly reaches out and takes it. "I'll give it back to them," she says. "Sorry."

One side of Mr. Winters's mouth curls up. "I know that they are convinced this entire school is crawling with monsters, but perhaps you could relay a message to your new friends that maybe their creature hunting should stay out of the library."

Even though this isn't really about Jasmine, she can't help

the heat that rises to her cheeks. "Okay," she says. "But . . . why didn't you give this back to Bea yourself?"

Now it's Mr. Winters's turn to look embarrassed. His gaze drops for a second. "I don't want to be too hard on her."

Jasmine is thoroughly confused. "Okay . . ." she says, drawing the word out. *Whatever that means,* she thinks.

Mr. Winters turns around, and Jasmine takes the opportunity to dart away from him. She heads straight for the back of the library, Bea's camera in hand. Seconds later, she finds Bea huddled up with Jorge in the far corner, waving the thermal imager up and down the wall. Bea is dressed very differently from the last time Jasmine saw her. She's wearing a pair of tight black denim jeans and a loose-fitting purple flannel shirt that she left unbuttoned. All her hair—which Jasmine assumes is still highlighter green—is tucked under a beanie.

"I swear there was something here," Bea says before turning around, then her eyes go wide. "Jasmine! You're back!"

But Jasmine doesn't say anything. With a frown on her face, she holds out Bea's camera.

Instantly, both Bea and Jorge gasp in horror. "Where did you find that?" Jorge says, his hands on both sides of his face.

"I didn't find it anywhere," Jasmine says softly. "Mr. Winters did."

Bea gives herself a face-palm. "Oh, *no,*" she says. "I must have left it on the shelf last week."

"Mr. Winters told me that he didn't want to say anything because it would give you a hard time. What did he mean?"

Jorge actually *winces.* Bea looks away.

"It's nothing," she says. "I think he just isn't convinced that our school is a hotbed of activity yet."

Jasmine can't explain why, but she senses that Bea just lied to her. She pushes past it, though, because both Bea *and* Jorge look so uncomfortable.

"Well," she says, "he told me that maybe we shouldn't be monster hunting in the library?"

Bea scoffs at that. "He's trying to hide the truth," she says.

"We just got a reading a couple minutes ago," Jorge says, nodding. "I really think there's something here."

"Sasquatch?" Jasmine asks, then gives the camera to Bea.

"No," she says. "We have gotten conclusive evidence that a Sasquatch is *not* using the locker room showers in the morning."

"Turns out it was the PE teacher, Mr. Yancey," says Jorge, then he twists up his face in disgust. "I will never get the image out of my head of him walking out of the showers with just a towel around his waist."

"So no Sasquatch," adds Bea, "*but* I think there might be a werewolf around. There's a full moon soon."

"A werewolf?" Jasmine laughs, but the others don't. "Wait, seriously?"

Jorge nods his head. "We've captured some howling before."

"Could be a dog," Jasmine says.

"Or it could be a werewolf," Bea says matter-of-factly. She tries to turn the digital camera on, but nothing happens. "Battery's probably dead," she says, but then hands the camera back to Jasmine. She swings her backpack around. "Good thing I always carry a spare one."

After Bea digs around in her backpack, she pulls out a small black rectangle, then gestures for the camera back. She swaps out the battery, and then Jasmine finds herself huddling up next to Bea, her heart beating, her eyes locked on the now illuminated screen on the back of the digital camera.

Is it possible that Bea's camera caught something in the library?

The idea seems silly to Jasmine as Bea searches through the files, flipping past chaotic, blurry images of what look like hallways, bookshelves, and even a selfie of Jorge, who is sticking his tongue out.

"What?" Jorge says, his face reddening. "I was just testing it out."

Bea ignores him as she lands on a video, then hits the play button. "This is it," she says. "I hope we got something. I don't know how long it recorded before the battery went out."

Jasmine squeezes closer, and her heart thumps again as she watches. She sees Bea setting up the camera on the shelf, then stepping back and holding up a peace sign. When she steps away, there's a clear shot of the wide-open reading area and the computer desks.

"Okay, we were all inside the library at this time," says Bea. "We don't need to watch this."

Using the touch screen, she fast-forwards through the three of them talking. It's weird to see them from a distance, but Jasmine keeps her eyes locked on the screen. "So, if there isn't a Sasquatch, then won't there not be anything on the footage?" she asks.

"You never know," says Bea. "Maybe we caught your ghost."

"Do ghosts even come out during the daytime?" Jorge asks. "Maybe that's why we haven't able to catch one before."

Bea frowns. "Maybe," she says. "But it's not like ghosts have to *sleep* or anything. My parents say they don't exist by our rules."

Jasmine's stomach twists at that. How can Bea talk so casually about all this? *And* with her parents?

She doesn't understand it.

On the screen, Bea gestures at the camera, so she stops fast-forwarding. Jasmine hears Mr. Winters tell them they need to leave. As she remembered, Bea and Jorge dash away and—

She gasps.

Something moved.

A *lot* of things moved!

"What was that?" Jorge whispers.

Bea nearly drops the camera. "Wait, lemme rewind it."

They all huddle closer as Bea drags her fingers over the touch screen to back the video up a few seconds. Sure enough, as soon as Bea and Jorge are out of sight, the camera appears to move *toward* Jasmine.

"Is that Mr. Winters doing that?" Bea wonders aloud.

But then the camera pans, and the librarian is clearly in view.

Jorge reaches over and pauses the video. "I don't like this," he mutters.

"Don't be so scared," Bea says, her tone a little harsh. "It's just a video, okay? We don't know exactly what we're looking at."

"All right," Jorge says, moving back to Bea's other side. He shakes his arms about wildly, as if he's trying to fling his fear away. "I'll try."

Bea resumes the video.

And Jasmine cannot believe what she is seeing.

The view tilts to the side, back and forth, and then the camera moves even closer to Jasmine. Mr. Winters walks past it, obscuring Jasmine for a moment, and then Jasmine is walking, too, following right behind him, and *the camera pans to follow her.*

"Did someone pick up the camera?" Jorge asks.

Took the words right out of my mouth, she thinks.

"I think you might be right," says Bea softly, pausing the video again. "But who got in the library that late? We would have seen them come in through the doors. How did we not hear them, either?"

A thought comes to Jasmine and she blurts it out. "Why is it filming *me*?"

Bea looks at her and frowns. "What?"

"It's following me, isn't it?"

"Jasmine," Bea says, her eyes wide with wonder. "Could this be your ghost?"

Her heart is fully in her throat. "I don't know," she says. "I mean . . . it's never done anything like *this*. Why would it change all of a sudden?"

Bea narrows her eyes, then nods. "I like the way your mind works," she says. "You're asking the right questions. Which makes me believe that we have to find the *motivation* for this spirit."

Jorge grins awkwardly. "Maybe they want to ask Jasmine for a book recommendation?"

"Who wants to read in the afterlife?" Bea says.

He raises his hand. "I would."

Jasmine points at the screen. "Keep playing it. I wanna see what happens before the recording ends."

Bea obliges, and they watch as the camera drifts toward the front desk. It pauses, then veers sharply to the left, toward the big bay windows. Jasmine's heart races again, and then bumps rise all over her skin.

It's happening. She feels it *everywhere*.

Something is watching her.

She doesn't peel her eyes away from the screen, however. She can't. She needs to know. The camera seemingly floats toward the windows, then turns to the right. There is a big screen on the wall there—one of the TVs that Mr. Winters has mounted that usually display announcements or book recommendations. There's enough light from outside coming in that she can *definitely* see the camera reflected on the blank screen.

And she can definitely see that *nothing is holding it up.*

Her heart drops as the video comes to an end. The final image is of the carpet as the camera falls to the ground.

She turns around, unable to resist the urge to look, to acknowledge that something really is watching them. But all she sees are bookshelves, posters on the wall, and the windows against the far wall.

Jorge gulps loudly. "Did we do it, Bea?" he says. "Did we just capture evidence of something supernatural?"

Her mouth is still open wide in shock. She nods her head and says, "I think we did."

She gives Jasmine a deadly serious look. "We captured a ghost on camera."

Jasmine can't hold it in any longer. "Help me," she says, her voice much louder than she intends. "Help me find out why I am haunted."

This time, Bea doesn't hesitate, doesn't gaze at Jasmine strangely, doesn't do that weird thing where she makes Jasmine feel like a stranger. Her expression is serious as she nods. "Of course," she says, then turns to Jorge. "This makes it an official case. You know what that means."

He nods with importance. "Case name."

"Case name?" repeats Jasmine.

"Oh, we name all our cases," says Jorge. "Sasquatch was 'Hairy Bathroom.'"

Jasmine groans. "That's gross."

"Well," says Bea, "if you'd seen the hair Mr. Yancey was leaving behind in the drain, you'd name it that, too."

"I hate that," she says.

"Still a good name," says Jorge. "Then there was 'Bark at the Moon,' which was our werewolf case. And 'Everything Sucks,' which was our chupacabra case."

Jasmine nearly chokes. "El chupacabra is real?!"

"The case is still open," Bea says. "So, Jorge, what do we call this one?"

"'Spirit in the Shelves'?" he suggests.

"Snappy. I like that. But Jasmine's ghost isn't just haunting a bookshelf, remember?"

He thinks for a moment. "How about 'Spirited Away'?"

"Perfect." Bea turns to Jasmine. "Operation Spirited Away begins today. Are you ready to participate?"

Her smile is awkward. "I . . . guess? I don't know what that actually means."

Bea reaches out and clasps Jasmine's shoulder. "I know this must be a lot, but we are experts."

"Or sort of like experts," Jorge adds, wincing. "We're definitely getting there."

Bea lets go. "You're in good hands. I promise. We'll figure this out."

And Jasmine so desperately wants to believe that.

8

Jasmine does not anticipate that when the Gay Supernatural Alliance said they would take on her case, Bea and Jorge meant *that day*.

She's standing outside her apartment on La Mirada, Bea and Jorge at her side. She texted Mami and said she was bringing some friends over, fully expecting that she'd still be on set for a few hours. Unfortunately, Mami texted immediately back. She was sending messages in all caps. That's how excited she was that Jasmine had "made some actual friends" and that maybe now, "you'll be a real girl!"

Her words exactly.

But that wasn't the worst part. Mami had texted her *from the apartment*. She had gotten the day off due to two of the stars coming down with food poisoning, and now she was planning all these little treats she was going to make for Jasmine and her new friends: her epic rolled tacos con papas y queso. Her jugo de piña that was so creamy and refreshing. Maybe even some cookies. All things Jasmine loved, but this was a problem. A huge problem.

Bea pulls out a new device that's all black with a thick handle and a digital meter that faces her. She waves it in the direction of Jasmine's home.

"What are you doing?" Jasmine says harshly. "Mami will see you!"

"EMF reader," Bea says, frowning at it.

When Jasmine casts a panicked look at Jorge, he nods. "It

measures electromagnetic frequencies, which is supposed to be the easiest way to detect spirit energy."

"It's not 'supposed' to do that," Bea snaps. "It *does* do that. But I'm not getting anything yet."

Jasmine doesn't know what she could possibly catch from this distance, but that doesn't matter. Someone is waving a ghost hunting device at the very place Mami is currently inside.

Bea spins around. Waves the reader about.

"Do you see anything yet?" Jorge asks, then jams his hands in his pockets. He's shrinking again, like Jasmine has seen him do before when he gets nervous. "Maybe there's like . . . a haunted tree or something around here."

"Can *trees* be haunted?" Jasmine asks.

He shrugs. "I don't know."

"Wouldn't that make all books haunted, then?" she says.

His eyes go wide. "Oh. That's a good point."

Bea lowers the device. "I'm definitely not getting anything out here. We'll have to go inside."

Jasmine sucks in a deep breath. "Okay. I should warn you again, though. Mami *really* doesn't like talk of ghosts and spirits and stuff anymore."

Bea doesn't hesitate. "Oh, that's fine. Jorge's dads are skeptics, too."

"Huh?" Jasmine raises an eyebrow at him. "Really?"

"Yeah," he says, and looks down and rubs the edge of his shoe against the sidewalk. "Well, it's mostly Papi. He doesn't really like me talking about this stuff, either."

"I'm sorry," she says. "But it's not that Mami is a skeptic. I think it's more that she doesn't want to acknowledge it anymore. We used to be able to talk about it, but we haven't for a while."

Jasmine hesitates. "Actually . . . you two are the first people I've talked to about my ghost in years."

One side of Bea's lips curls down. "That sounds hard."

Jasmine waves it off. "We just have to be careful, that's all."

She leads her friends up the stoop, digs her keys out of her pocket, and then, just before Jasmine puts her key in the lock, she turns to Bea. "Wait, how would you like me to introduce you to Mami? What pronouns?"

Bea smiles warmly. "Actually, if you could use they/them, I'd really like that. Not feeling very girly today."

"And I'm still fine with he/him," says Jorge.

She nods. Looks forward. Accepts that she's got to take a step forward if she's actually going to do this. Reaches up and touches her papi's charm. *Help me if you can,* she thinks.

Finally, Jasmine unlocks her front door. Mere seconds later, Mami is greeting them all, her eyes alight with excitement. She makes quick introductions of Bea and Jorge and both their pronouns. The house is full of savory scents, and Jasmine's mouth is watering as her heart bounces along in terror. But Bea mentions nothing of ghosts, and Jorge isn't as frightened as he was outside the house, so Jasmine allows herself to let some of her guard down.

Jorge quickly hops up on a stool at the island in the kitchen, and Mami places a plate of her rolled tacos in front of him. Bea slides onto the stool next to him, asks what kind of oil Mami fries her tacos in, and soon, it's like both Bea and Jorge have known Mami for years.

"So are you kids doing homework today or what?" Mami asks after finishing off one of her tacos. She glances over at Jasmine. "Not that I'm saying you have to immediately start doing schoolwork, mija."

And just like that, Jasmine's blood races through her. "Uh, yeah," she says. "We've got some stuff to do together."

Bea isn't nearly as hesitant. "We have a school science project we're working on as a team," they say. "Is it okay if we work on it in Jasmine's room?"

Her mami looks like she's going to explode with joy, and it takes everything in Jasmine not to laugh. It at least relieves her frayed nerves.

"Please, don't let me bother you," Mami says. "If any of you need anything, feel free to ask."

Jasmine is still at the end of the island, so she starts to back up, hoping that Bea and Jorge will follow. Bea is quick to get the hint, and they get up and stand next to Jasmine.

"These are so good, Ms. Garza," says Jorge, then stuffs another taco in his mouth. As he's chewing, he grabs one more.

"Jorge," Bea whispers harshly.

"Yes, science!" he says with a mouth full of taco. "We've got *so* much science to do."

Mami frowns. "Okay," she says, and that's when Jasmine thinks this whole thing is going to derail right then, but then Mami winks at her. "I'm just glad you're all here."

This is her sign. Jasmine darts away toward the back of the house, and thankfully, Jorge and Bea are right behind her. By the time she gets to her room, she thinks her heart is going to explode in her chest.

Bea drops their backpack on the floor. "Cool room," they say, glancing around, and then they're digging in their bag. They pull out an even larger device than the one they were waving about outside. The entire thing is black and has a large screen on one side and numerous switches and buttons.

"What's *that*?" Jasmine asks, trying to keep her jaw off the floor. "Please tell me it's not louder than the EMF meter."

Jorge sits gingerly on the edge of Jasmine's bed. "It's pretty cool," he says. "Bea's parents showed me that one once. It measures both electromagnetic energy *and* temperature."

"It's definitely a good tool for a ghost hunter's arsenal," Bea says, nodding. "Think of it like both a thermal imager *and* an EMF reader."

They turn the device on. "You told me before that you can usually sense a spirit in the room with you, so the second you feel something, let me know. I'll scan the room to see if your ghost is here and manipulating heat."

"Manipulating heat?" Jasmine says, then sits next to Jorge. She notices that one of his hands is trembling. She reaches over and grabs it to hopefully comfort him, and he scoots a little closer to her.

"Spirits are always coming from their realm," Bea explains while they flip a few switches. "And we don't know a whole lot, but it's clear that they're able to affect temperature."

"How do you know so much about ghosts?" Jasmine asks. "Just from your parents?"

Jorge flinches as Bea sighs. "Sure, from them," they say. "But I do a lot of studying on my own. There's a lot of great information out there, and I'm always trying to learn."

"You're definitely helping us," says Jorge.

Again, Jasmine is aware that both of them are talking around the truth about something in Bea's life. But Jasmine also knows this isn't the right time to bring it up.

Bea isn't saying anything. They slowly turn around the room, and the device they're holding makes a very soft buzzing sound, almost like a phone vibrating. "I'm not getting anything," they say, then lower the device. "What's the trigger for your spirit?"

Jasmine frowns. "The what?"

"What's the common thread for all the appearances of your ghost for the last week or two?"

"I don't know," Jasmine says. "Just in this house, you mean?"

Bea nods.

"There doesn't seem to be a pattern."

"Does it always happen in the same part of the house?"

She shakes her head. "I mean . . . I haven't lived here long.

But I don't think the ghost ever stuck to one part of any of the apartments I used to live in."

"Hmm." Bea paces the room. "Same time of the day?"

"Nope."

Jorge squeezes her hand. "Is there something you're doing each time that might be similar?"

"Good question!" Bea says.

"I really don't know," Jasmine answers, glancing over at Jorge. With her free hand, she touches her charm.

"Okay, you might want to keep track of those things," Bea suggests, then brings the device up again. "Write it down in a journal or something."

Jasmine thinks of the notebook, which is sitting so close to her in the dresser, and her sadness returns, settling in her chest.

"I can do that," she said. "I'll start today."

"Perfect," says Bea. "The more information we have, the better."

Jasmine is about to ask what sort of information Bea would like when two things happen at the same time: Bea's device begins to buzz rapidly, and the wall behind Jorge and Jasmine creaks.

This time, Jorge squeezes Jasmine's hand *hard,* so much so that one of her knuckles cracks. "Sorry," he says in a whisper.

But Jasmine isn't thinking of that. Her heart is in her throat. Something is in the room with them.

The tiny fine hairs on her arm rise, and she watches in horror as Jorge raises his arm, too.

"You feel that?" she asks.

He nods.

Bea's eyes are wide, and they hold up their own arm, gazing at it in wonder. "Is this what you meant?" they ask. "The feeling of being *watched*?"

"Yes," says Jasmine. "So I assume it's happening to you, too!"

Bea gulps, and the device buzzes away. "This isn't like the library."

Jorge is shivering even worse than before.

"Are you okay?" Jasmine asks.

"I *r-really* don't like g-g-ghosts," he stutters.

"But . . . you're a ghost hunter," Jasmine says. "Like . . . willingly."

"I have to face my fears somehow," says Jorge.

Bea raises a finger to their lips. "Shh. Something is happening."

Sure enough, the creaking rings out again. This time, it comes from the ceiling, and all three of them gaze up.

"Could be raccoons up there," says Jorge softly. "Or possums. We had those once in our house."

As if the house is responding to him, a long groan stretches out.

Bea holds the device up higher. "I don't think that's an animal. Because the temperature just dropped."

They wave Jasmine over, and she sidles up to Bea. On the colorful screen, there is a batch of colors: greens, yellows, reds. Jorge is still on the bed, so she sees his body on it, almost entirely in red and orange. Bea tilts the reader upward, and there, floating over the ceiling, is a blob of dark blue.

"What is *that*?" Jasmine whispers.

"I think that's your spirit, Jasmine," Bea announces. "Say hello."

Her voice cracks. "Hello?" she says.

Nothing happens.

"Jorge, start recording," Bea demands softly.

He pulls out his phone and aims the camera at the spot.

And his phone flies out of his hand *toward* the ceiling.

A yelp escapes from Jasmine, and then she clamps a hand over her mouth.

All three of them can't stop staring at what is happening.

Somehow, Jorge's phone appears to be stuck to the ceiling.

"Well, this is new," says Bea, practically breathless. "I've never seen anything like this. Not even my parents have!"

They reach out for Jorge. "This could be my big break."

"Okay," says Jorge, who slides off the bed and joins the two of them on the other side of the room. He then sucks in a deep breath. "But also . . . how do we get my phone?"

"In a second," says Bea, crouching down. They rummage around in their backpack with their free hand, and Jasmine watches as they pull out the digital camera. "I need to capture this."

But before Bea can even turn the camera on, it tears out of their hand and smashes against the dresser.

Which is of course the *exact* moment that Mami opens the door to Jasmine's bedroom.

"Everything okay?" she asks as she raises an eyebrow. She has a plate of cookies in her hand, and the scent hits Jasmine next. "What was that sound?"

"I dropped my camera," Bea says quickly, then squats to pick it up.

Jasmine heads to Mami and takes the plate of cookies. "Gracias por las galletas, Mami," she says. "We're just working on our project."

Mami glances at the device in Bea's hand. "With that thing?"

Once again, Bea doesn't hesitate, despite Jasmine looking like she's about to panic. "Oh, we're learning about temperature!" They turn the device around so Mami can see the screen. "It's pretty cool. We are supposed to document different spaces."

"Wow," says Mami, squinting at the device. "We never did anything like this in school."

"You also didn't have cell phones," says Jasmine, which immediately feels like a terrible mistake because then she can't help but look up at the ceiling as quickly as possible. Sure enough, Jorge's phone is still there

"Okay, okay," says Mami, putting her hands up. "I'm old, I get it."

Jasmine feels a drop of sweat on the side of her head. "I still love you, though," she jokes.

"Glad to hear it," Mami says, sticking her tongue out.

Jorge gasps beside Jasmine, then she feels his hand in hers. Bumps rise all over her skin.

Jorge's phone is no longer on the ceiling. That would be a good thing, except now it's floating *above Mami's head.*

Jasmine can't move. Can't speak. Can't seem to breathe.

Mami steps away from Bea, who hasn't noticed what's happening. "I should probably let you all get back to work, then."

"Thanks, Ms. Garza," Bea says, then finally glances up. A sound leaves their mouth, and Jasmine isn't quite sure what it is. It's kind of like a cross between a bark and a screech.

Mami tilts her head to the side. "You okay, Bea?"

"I'm perfect," they say, smiling. "I just . . . make sounds sometimes. When I'm excited. About science!"

Then Bea meows.

This is a disaster! Jasmine thinks.

"Then make as many weird sounds as you like," Mami says. "I'll check in later. Enjoy the cookies and the science!"

About seven hundred years pass as she leaves the room and shuts the door. At the moment it closes, Jorge's phone drops from where it had been floating and Bea majestically dives out and catches it.

Jorge, meanwhile, is gasping for breath. "What *was* that?" he says. "How is that possible?"

Bea's eyes are wide with delight. "I can't believe it," they say. "Jasmine, you really *are* haunted!"

Jasmine isn't exactly thrilled with that pronouncement, but she smiles anyway. "Yeah. I know."

"You have a spirit who can manipulate temperature *and* physical space," they continue, spinning around, waving the device about. "I've never seen a ghost with this level of energy!"

Also not exactly what Jasmine wants to hear. "So what am I supposed to do now?"

Bea is silent for a moment as they walk around the room, and then they shut the device off. "Well, I'm not getting any more abnormal readings, so I think your ghost has left us for the moment."

Jasmine senses Jorge's relief at her side as he leans against her. "That's good."

"I think we'll have to set up some cameras one night," they continue. "Maybe I can grab some of my parents' infrared monitors. And then we should think about making contact."

"Why would we make contact?" Jasmine says, slightly panicked. "What would that do?"

Bea frowns. "Well, what if we can't determine the ghost's motivation? We might have to ask it what it wants, you know?"

"I guess," she says.

"If you keep a log starting today, I think that would be very helpful. Remember, we're trying to figure out this ghost's motivation. That's how we'll know why it's doing all of this, and maybe we can stop it from bothering you."

"And I won't have my phone stolen again," Jorge adds, shaking his head. "I didn't know ghosts could do *that*."

Jasmine scratches her head. "So . . . just keep track of the haunting and let you know?"

"Exactly!" Bea says. "We'll get to the bottom of this. I promise."

But it doesn't make sense to Jasmine. What could a spirit ever want from *her*? The very idea seems so unfair to Jasmine. She's barely a teenager. What could she possibly do to help someone who is *dead*?

She touches her charm. *Where are you, Papi? Why aren't you here?*

A terrible thought occurs to her: Maybe Papi hasn't shown up because he doesn't need her anymore.

She doesn't share this thought with the rest of the GSA. She hears them talking about plans and devices, but the words are in one ear and out the other. Jasmine is somewhere else for the moment: MacArthur Park. Four years ago. The breeze on her face. The sun on her arms. Papi and Mami are holding her hands and she skips toward the dulcería on the corner.

It's one of her favorite memories, so she visits it like a miniature vacation. She's only brought back to the present when Jorge starts coughing, having choked a bit on one of her mami's galletas.

Bea is slapping him on the back. "Breathe, Jorge, breathe!"

He glares at them. "Dude, I'm *trying*. That's why I was choking."

"Oh. Right!"

Jasmine offers to get some water, but when she opens the door, Mami is already a few feet away, a glass of water in hand.

"Do you have a hidden camera in my room?" Jasmine asks. "Maybe hidden in a stuffed animal or something?"

"No, mija," she says, handing the water over. "I simply have *ears*."

It marks the end of this part of the investigation, though. Jorge and Bea both say they need to get home, so they gather their things quickly. Jasmine follows them toward the front door and watches as shoes are put on and goodbyes are offered to Mami.

"Remember," Bea says, "make sure to write your entries down!"

A flash of terror flows through Jasmine. "Uh . . . yeah, of course."

After they're gone, Mami rubs her hand along Jasmine's back. "You still have some homework to do?"

"A little," she says.

"Well, there's still some food left, so I don't think I'll make dinner. Let me know if you get hungry again."

"Do you have any blank notebooks?"

Mami raises an eyebrow. "Probably. Do you need one?"

Jasmine nods.

She sets off toward the living room and Jasmine is close on her heels. She begins rummaging through boxes until she triumphantly raises a notebook with a red cover high above her head.

"Perfect," says Jasmine as she takes it. "Te quiero, Mami."

"Te quiero back," she says.

In her room, Jasmine keeps it simple:

#1

GSA investigated my ghost today. It made the walls creak, grabbed Jorge's phone and stuck it to the ceiling, and then made it float over Mami's head. It also threw Bea's camera aside. We were in my bedroom.

She still isn't sure what else she should write, so she leaves it at that.

It doesn't make Jasmine feel better. If anything, documenting what happened feels *worse*. When she reads back her words, it's like she's a scientist describing something in the field. They're nothing like the poetry or witty observations her papi used to make. Maybe they're not supposed to be, but she closes the notebook with a profound sense of disappointment hanging over her.

9

Mami is making breakfast the next morning when Jasmine, all showered and dressed, walks out into the kitchen, leaving her book bag by the front door.

"Sorry for the rush," she says, sliding some scrambled eggs over a couple of small corn tortillas on a plate. "We're back on set today, so I have to be there in an hour. Hot sauce is in the fridge."

Jasmine goes and grabs the Cholula to drench her eggs in. "You didn't have to cook anything up. I could have grabbed a Pop-Tart or something."

"I am trying to ensure my daughter eats more than processed frosted rectangles."

"Aren't *you* always the one finishing off the box?"

Mami smirks. "I am an adult, and I get to make the mistakes around here."

Jasmine hops on a stool. "Sí, señora," she says.

Her mami gasps. "How *dare* you. I am a señorita to you, mija."

"And I'm just being respectful! You *are* the adult, after all. My senior citizen."

Mami rolls her eyes. "It was nice meeting your friends yesterday," she says. "They're much more polite than you are."

"You know I'm a troublemaker."

"I'm replacing you with both of them. Two new kids for the price of one."

"A steal, Mami."

Jasmine picks up a tortilla and folds it in half. Some of the eggs fall out, but she stuffs a big bite in her mouth as her mami watches her. "What?" she says after swallowing.

Mami's eyes go all shiny. "Just thinking about yesterday," she says. "It's been a while since you've had anyone over. Not since Samantha, if I remember correctly."

Jasmine gulps her food down. "Uh, yeah. Not since then."

Mami turns away and serves herself some eggs. "I think it's a good thing that you're trying. And Bea and Jorge seem like fun kids."

"They are." She takes another bite, but keeps her eyes on Mami.

"And I loved that you didn't bring up any of that spooky stuff you're always talking about."

She stops chewing. Still keeps staring at Mami.

"'Spooky stuff'?" Jasmine says.

Mami dismisses her with a wave. "You know what I mean," she says. She looks down at her wrist at the slim silver watch she wears. "Sorry, I'm in a rush!"

She floats off with her plate of eggs and tortillas toward the back of the house, oblivious to what she's just done. A few moments later, Jasmine can hear muffled salsa music coming from Mami's bedroom, meaning that she's resumed her morning routine.

Suddenly, Jasmine's appetite is completely gone. *Spooky stuff.* The way Mami said it—so casually, so matter-of-factly—grates on her nerves. Is that how she thinks of it? That Jasmine was just in a phase or something?

She dumps her remaining food in the trash. Mami's music is still there in the background, so she quickly washes off the plate and sets it aside to dry.

She doesn't understand. Does Mami think she made up ghosts? How can someone change their mind so *completely*? She remembers telling Mami about seeing a glass fall out of the cupboard in the kitchen back in Glendale, and how Mami took her fear seriously. She walked Jasmine through the entire apartment, opening every cupboard and door, showing her that nothing was hiding there. She didn't call it "spooky stuff."

What changed?

She knows that her ghost doesn't seem to bother anyone else, but Mami can't believe that she's making *everything* up, can she?

Jasmine grabs her backpack and lingers near the entryway. She hasn't brushed her teeth, nor has she said goodbye to Mami, but her skin prickles with anger. She thinks she will say something mean if she talks to Mami right now.

So she ducks toward the front door, opens it, and heads out without a word to Mami. A pang of guilt hits her, swells in her gut and spreads up into her chest, almost like molten lava is traveling up into her throat. She's never left without saying something to Mami, but right then, Jasmine can't face her.

She decides that she has to rely on the GSA to help her.

Because she can't rely on Mami.

o o o

Jasmine is standing just beyond the doors of the library, frozen. As soon as she crossed the threshold, the sensation smacked into her: she's being watched.

She creeps toward the front desk, pulling both straps on her backpack tight so her bag is flat against her back.

"Hello?" she calls out. "Anyone here yet?"

She silently scolds herself. *What if it* is *a ghost? Do you expect it to answer you back?*

Still, it's odd that no one seems to be in the library. Why was it unlocked?

She peers over the circulation desk, but notices that Mr. Winters's office light isn't on.

There's a thump behind her, and she spins around. There

aren't many shadows in the library because of all the morning sunlight pouring in through the bay windows. Which is why she notices the darkness in the far corner to her right.

Her instinct flares again. It looks a *lot* like the shadows she saw near Diego and in Ina's garage.

Thunk!

In front of her, at the foot of a tall shelf, a large bound book hit the floor. She narrows her eyes at it. She walks briskly over to the book and picks it up. It's a dictionary.

"Ha, ha," she says. "Okay, ghost, *are* you trying to talk to me? This has literally *every* word in it, so it doesn't help."

Silence.

She places the dictionary back on the shelf.

And she's met with a long, hideous creak.

At first, her mind is right back in her new home, the walls groaning and moaning. But it's not quite the same sound here. It's higher pitched. It rings out again, and then she catches movement out of the corner of her eye.

The bookshelf.

It's leaning.

Instinctively, her hand juts out and she pushes back, which immediately feels ridiculous because even if she wanted to, she couldn't hold up one of these enormous bookshelves all by herself. But the bookshelf leans farther over, and books begin to spill from the shelves.

"Oh, no, no, no," she says, and she's got both hands on it, trying to shove it back, but—

It's not falling over. Gravity should have gripped it by now, sent the entire thing tumbling over, but it's more like . . .

Like something else is already holding it back.

She lets go. The shelf stays in the same precarious position, and a few more books tumble forth.

"What is going on?" she whispers. She darts around the edge

of the shelf to the next aisle, and she's not shocked to discover that no one is there.

"I don't get it," she says. "What kind of spirit are you?"

"Jasmine?"

Startled, she lets out a small yelp, and another book flops onto the ground next to her.

Mx. Chen is standing at the entrance to the library, their face twisted up in confusion. "What are you doing in here, dear?"

Panic ripples through Jasmine. She casts a glance down at the haphazard pile of books on the floor.

"Where's Mr. Winters?" they ask, stepping forward. "Do you need help?"

"Sorry, Mx. Chen," she says. "I think one of the shelves broke and a bunch of these fell off."

It's a lie, yes, but only sort of one. Something about this bookshelf is broken if it can lean over on its own and shake some books loose.

"Oh, well, let me help," Mx. Chen says, brushing their straight black hair out of their eyes. They crouch down beside her and begin picking up books, tucking some under an arm.

There's a bang as Mr. Winters bursts through the double doors, out of breath and his forehead shiny with sweat.

Which is when the bookshelf creaks again, and the books cascade down on Mx. Chen.

Jasmine yelps as she helplessly grabs for the shelf, but it's pointless. Mr. Winters rushes over as a book bounces off the top of her head and flies off somewhere while Mx. Chen cries out.

Mr. Winters presses his back against the bookshelf and gives it a shove. "Watch it, Jasmine!" he calls, and she dives out of the way of a veritable book tsunami, slamming against the floor and scraping her knee on the carpet.

She glances back, and the librarian heaves the bookshelf upright, just as Mx. Chen is able to push themself up.

"Are you okay, Jianming?" Mr. Winters says, grabbing them under the arm.

"I think I just drowned in some books," Mx. Chen says, then grins. "I'm all right, I promise."

Jasmine's knee is stinging, and any second now, her heart is going to beat so fast that she'll overheat and burst into flames, but neither of those things are her main concern at the moment. She scrambles to her feet, eyes wide, and she stares at the two books floating above Mr. Winters's head.

This isn't happening. This isn't happening.

Except it *is*.

She remembers Samantha's screams tearing away from her apartment, and she wonders if it's only a matter of time before both Mr. Winters and Mx. Chen peel away, shouting and shrieking. Jasmine wishes more than ever that she could stop this, but her ghost *never* listens to her.

She grabs a few books while still on the ground, then stands quickly. "I don't know what happened," she says, then stacks the books in an empty spot on the shelf next to her. "But we should check to see if the others are okay."

The lie slips out easily, and Mx. Chen and Mr. Winters exchange a look. "What others?" Mx. Chen asks, raising an eyebrow.

"I heard someone else in here earlier," she continues, and her eyes keep darting between the teachers and the books, *still* floating above their heads. *Stop it!* she tells herself. *They'll notice!*

Mr. Winters sighs. "Was it Jorge and Bea?"

"No!" Jasmine blurts out. "I was alone, I promise!"

"I had to run out," Mr. Winters said. "Realized I forgot to lock my car door after I opened up here."

Just then, there's a knock on the main entry doors to the library, and one of them swings in slowly.

And to Jasmine's great relief, Jorge pokes his head inside.

"Is e-everything okay?" he says, and his poor face looks panicked. "We heard some loud noises."

Bea's head appears above Jorge's, then . . . an EMF device, waved about in front of the two of them.

Both Bea and Jorge look from Jasmine to the books floating above the two adults, and their eyes bulge.

"Mr. Winters, I think this might be my fault," Mx. Chen says and then they're drifting toward Bea and Jorge. Mr. Winters follows, and Jasmine watches as the floating books drop to join the others.

Mx. Chen glances back at the pile, then puts their hands on their hips.

"This whole monster-hunting thing has gotten out of control," they say. "I indulged it because I was so happy that any student was interested in the GSA this year, but this?" They gesture back toward the mess of books where Jasmine is. "This is too much."

"But—" Jasmine begins.

"Were you looking for Sasquatch again? Convinced there was a vampire in the shelves?" They shake their head. "Never mind. It's not important."

"But we weren't in here," says Bea while approaching. Jasmine spots a SHE/HER pin on the strap of her backpack. "We sensed some sort of activity in here and—"

Mx. Chen raises a hand. "Not now, Bea. The three of you will help Mr. Winters clean up the library this morning, and then that's the end of any supernatural talk in GSA, okay?"

Jasmine hears Jorge's gulp in that terrible silence. "Yes, Mx. Chen," he says, then nudges Bea.

"Yes, Mx. Chen," Bea adds. "Promise."

They both come inside and make their way over to Jasmine. *What happened?* Bea mouths at Jasmine, but she just shakes her head. How could she possibly explain everything that just transpired? She doesn't even understand it herself.

The three of them begin to gather the books strewn about the floor, but Jasmine keeps an eye on the two adults. Their English teacher is saying something in a low, harsh whisper to Mr. Winters, but she can't make it out. Soon, Mx. Chen storms out of the library, leaving one of the double doors swinging back and forth. Mr. Winters just stands there for a few seconds before he turns toward Jasmine and her friends.

"I'm sorry about that," he says, shaking his head. "What happened in here, Jasmine?"

"I don't know," she says, even though she *does* know. She can't tell her friends all the details just yet. "When I got here, I thought someone else was here. Maybe the bookshelf is just old and broke."

He takes the books from Jasmine. "I suppose," he says, but she notices that there's a sheen of sweat over his face.

"No," says Bea. "We sensed—I mean, *heard* something and came running over."

Mr. Winters catches Jasmine's gaze, and he must see how worried she looks. "I'll be okay," he says. "It's just a shelf. The books are fine. Doesn't seem like anyone got hurt."

He goes silent.

"You said you sensed some activity in here," he says to Bea. "Is that true?"

Bea nods. "Yeah, my EMF reader detected a huge burst of activity as we approached."

"And we heard this low groaning sound," Jorge adds. He shudders. "It was *awful*."

"So . . . ghosts," says Mr. Winters.

Jorge grimaces and nods. "Ghosts."

He looks back to Jasmine. "Is that what *you* think happened here?"

Mr. Winters's face does not do what she expects it to: he looks like he wants the truth.

She isn't sure what to say to him. This isn't what she's used to, either.

She shrugs. "I don't really know," she answers.

He nods at her, then wipes the sweat off his brow while smiling sadly. "You kids head to morning classes, okay? I'll get this fixed up."

"You sure, Mr. Winters?" Jorge asks, setting down some books. "We can help."

"I know," he says. "I'd like to do it, though."

The three of them don't hesitate to get out of Mr. Winters's way. However, upon reaching the door, Jasmine still can't shake the interaction. She looks back to the librarian.

He hasn't moved from the spot where they left him. He reaches out and touches one of the shelves, and then he sighs. Deeply.

Jasmine suddenly realizes this isn't a moment she should be watching. Heat rises in her face, and she finally ducks out of the library.

She wants a moment alone with Bea and Jorge, but Jasmine is immediately met with the shocked, confused faces of more students than she can count. She doesn't know any of their names because she's never made time to get to know anyone outside of the GSA.

"What happened in there?" asks a tall girl with pigtails in her jet-black hair. "We heard someone yelling."

Yelling? Jasmine thinks. *Does she mean Mx. Chen?*

"You mean screaming," says another. "What was all that screaming?"

"Uh . . ." is all that escapes Jasmine's mouth. Why do all these other students suddenly want to talk to her? What exactly did they hear out in the hallway?

"Sorry," says Bea, and they grab Jasmine's arm. "Important meeting happening soon, gotta go!"

And with that, Bea drags her off toward the science wing, Jorge trailing behind. Jasmine glances back once and sees some of the gathered kids pointing at her, then saying something.

"What's going on?" she whispers. "I don't understand!"

They round the corner and Bea finally stops. They tear off their beanie, and green hair spills out. "There's some serious supernatural activity happening here at Kingsley Middle School."

"Jasmine, it was weird," says Jorge between deep breaths. "I've never heard anything like that. I thought that maybe the library was caving in or falling apart."

"What?" She shakes her head at him. "No, that's not possible. I didn't hear any of that, and I was *inside* the library."

Bea insists on every detail, and Jasmine tells her what she can in a hushed voice. More and more students are passing behind them, and a few cast strange glances at Jasmine.

"Like my phone in your room?" Jorge asks, eyes wide.

"Yeah," says Jasmine. "Exactly like that."

"Okay, so, can you write all that down?"

"Yeah. I'll add it to my other entry from when you guys were at my house."

Bea clasps her hands together. "Perfect! Keep it up. I don't know if we have enough information to figure out the pattern, but this is a good start."

"*Is* it?" Jasmine says, frowning. "Mx. Chen and I almost drowned in books."

"All information is good information. And it sounds like this was *definitely* your ghost, since it acted the same."

Jasmine isn't sure about that. Her ghost hasn't ever dumped a shelf full of books on her. Maybe it's trying something new?

"I think it's time," Bea announces, ignoring what Jasmine

says. "The Gay Supernatural Alliance needs to escalate their investigation. Clearly, this ghost is trying to get our attention!"

"Escalate?" Jasmine raises an eyebrow at Bea. "Didn't Mx. Chen just tell us to knock it off with all the ghost talk?"

Bea waves a hand. "Oh, they'll come around. Especially once we pull off what I'm planning."

Jorge lets loose a whine. "Which is?"

Bea smiles with utter glee. "I think it's time for us to capture a ghost."

10

It isn't easy for Jasmine to concentrate for the rest of the day.

There's an odd, uneven energy in Mx. Chen's class. She never felt like it was directed at her specifically, but Jasmine knows that the book waterfall from earlier certainly threw Mx. Chen off their game. There are lots of starts and stops, some hesitating, and at one point, they seemed to forget what they were teaching.

Jasmine can't help but feel bad. It's not like Mx. Chen deserved to experience . . . whatever happened in the library. Up until this point, Samantha had been the only real collateral damage outside the Garza family.

She hopes this isn't going to become a thing at school, too.

At lunch, Bea details as many possible theories on how to "catch" a ghost. Jasmine pushes her food around the tray, and Jorge just sweats. A lot. He really, *really* seems to dislike any talk of ghosts, yet never excuses himself or asks to change the subject. She wonders why he is so intent on facing his fear, but there's no good point in Bea's deluge of theorizing for Jasmine to ask.

She hears of salt circles. EMF traps. Jars with candles inside them. Rituals and chants and spells. Clearly, Bea *has* done her homework, but it still seems so impossible to Jasmine. You can't *catch* a ghost, can you?

After school, Jasmine takes her sweet time walking home. She gets some fruit from Diego to quell the hunger pangs in her stomach, who tells her about a car crash he'd seen an hour earlier. One of the drivers got out of their busted car with a slingshot and starting flinging marbles at the person who rear-ended them. It sounded very Los Angeles to her. When Diego bids her goodbye, she catches him looking away as something slides over his face.

Oh. Sadness.

Her own returns, and then all the hairs rise on her arms. She doesn't stick around to find out what triggered them; she scurries away as soon as the crosswalk light at The Intersection changes.

Carl is packing up his instrument when she comes upon him. She ends up giving him her unopened bag of fruit from Diego because her appetite simply isn't there anymore. Carl thanks her and says he'll write a song for her. "A trade," he explains.

"You don't have to do that," she says.

He shakes his head, his locs swaying. "I return all kindnesses given to me, Jasmine."

"Thank you," she says, her face flushing with heat.

When Carl walks away, his shadow stretches longer than it should.

Jasmine is practically jogging by the time she gets to Ina's long driveway, where she lingers at the end of it. Ina is sitting in a wooden chair in front of a canvas on an easel, and beyond her, the garage door is open.

She doesn't see any weird shadows, so her shoulders droop in relief.

Ina only offers a quick glance, then returns to the canvas on the easel. Jasmine watches as Ina flicks paint here and there.

Ina stands and gestures to the chair with her paintbrush. "You can sit," she says. "If you want, that is."

Her stomach groans, but she walks over to Ina anyway. When she sits, her eyes leap from color to color on the canvas. This is a new piece, and like the last one, it's so bright and chaotic all over, except for a dark blotch in the center.

"How do you know?" Jasmine asks.

"Know what?"

"Know what to paint."

Ina hesitates, then points to the chair with her brush again.

Jasmine slides her book bag off her back and sets it next to the chair as she sits down. Ina doesn't say anything at first; she stares at the canvas, then begins to add streaks of orange along the edges.

"I almost never know," she says, so quiet at first that Jasmine isn't sure Ina is talking to her. "I might have a notion some days. Like, I might wake up and think, 'Hey, I want to paint the ocean today.'"

Jasmine squints. "Is that supposed to be the ocean?"

Ina's laugh is hearty. "No, not at all. It's abstract. Meaning that the idea I have isn't represented literally on the canvas."

Jasmine hesitates. "It's the feeling of it."

"Yes! Very much that."

"So you get a feeling and then . . . try to figure out how to express it, right?"

"More or less."

"So why does this one kinda look like the one you were painting before?"

Ina sighs. "I'm working on a series," she says. "And I'm still thinking about the language of it, so to speak. Kinda like if you're writing, you don't always know what words you're going to use to say what you want until it happens."

She points to the dark center. "This is the common language across all these pieces. Just something I've been thinking a lot about lately."

Jasmine doesn't say anything else. After a while, something appears to take shape on Ina's canvas. She thinks it's a tree, buried within the chaotic lines and strokes, but she doesn't tell Ina that. Like the feeling she had earlier that day in the library with

Mr. Winters, she thinks that maybe she is witnessing something that she shouldn't.

Her nerves flare. Her ghost is *back*.

After a quick glance at the very normal garage, she gathers her bag and leaves her neighbor to her work. Somehow, she knows that Ina won't be bothered by a silent goodbye. Once home, Jasmine flops onto the couch and stares up at the ceiling, waiting for evidence that her ghost has followed her here.

The couch squeaks as she turns to the side. It's an old thing, light green and a little dingy. Mami and Papi bought it when Jasmine was super young, and Mami doesn't want to get rid of it. Secretly, Jasmine doesn't want her to, either. It's comfortable. It reminds her of Papi and how often she'd find him curled up on it napping. Well, whenever Mami wasn't napping on it, that is.

Her thoughts race, jumping from the memory of Papi on the couch, then to the events in the library, then to Bea's insistence that they catch a ghost.

You can't catch a ghost. It's just not possible.

Is it? She doesn't actually *know*, she supposes. She's never tried it. No, she and Mami have always run from one apartment to the next. How would you even go about catching something that doesn't have a physical form? Bea seemed to know about those sorts of things, and maybe one of their devices would aid them in the task.

Still, it seemed absurd. She didn't want to catch a ghost. She wanted them to leave her and Mami alone.

Jasmine doesn't move for hours. A part of her wants to write in her notebook, but the words in her mind . . . it's like they have an edge to them, each one too sharp. They'll hurt her on the way out. So she turns to the side and clutches one of the pillows on the couch to her heart, holding it tight.

She sighs.

She knows what she wants.

She knows it is impossible.

"Are you out there, Papi?" she whispers. "I just want to know."

For a moment, she thinks she hears something in the back of the house: a low groan. But it's probably just the foundation shifting once again.

She is still on the couch when Mami bursts through the front door a few hours later. Jasmine can smell some sort of takeout seconds after—Thai, probably.

"Mija? You home?"

"Yeah," she calls out. She hears Mami set her keys down on the counter in the kitchen, followed by the rustling of plastic bags.

"Where are you?"

Jasmine clutches the pillow tighter and sighs. She should probably get up and go say hello, but she doesn't feel like moving.

It doesn't matter, because Mami is standing over her moments later.

"¿Estás bien, mija? ¿Te sientes enferma?" She reaches down and presses her hand on Jasmine's forehead.

"No," she says. "Just tired."

Mami scoots in next to her. "Long day?"

"Maybe."

"Bad day?"

"No, not at all."

"So . . . ?"

"Lo extraño," she says.

Mami sighs this time. She knows exactly what Jasmine means. "I miss him, too, Jaz. Every day."

"Do you think it'll ever . . . stop?"

"Stop what?"

"Stop feeling like this."

Mami looks away. "Oh, Jaz, I don't know. I've been doing this just as long as you."

She turns back, and her eyes are red. That same pang of guilt she felt in the morning returns, and she buries her face under the pillow. "I'm sorry, Mami."

Mami rubs her hand over Jasmine's back. "No, mija, you have nothing to be sorry for. We have to feel this out. Hiding it away is not going to solve anything."

For a brief flash, it looks like Mami is going to say more about it, but then she purses her lips and stands up. "Anyway, I had an annoying day at work, so I didn't want to cook. I got our favorite from the Thai spot on the way home!"

"Thanks, Mami," she says.

"We'll get through these feelings together, okay?"

Jasmine nods, but as Mami leaves the living room, something burns in Jasmine. There's a thought—half-formed, uncertain—building in her. *Hiding it away is not going to solve anything.*

A moment ago, Mami felt like she *wasn't* hiding it all away. It was brief, but it was *there*.

She remembers that Bea told her to write down each time she sensed she is being haunted, so she pushes herself up from the couch. She can't hide away from this feeling. In her room, she pulls open the top drawer of her dresser and retrieves her notebook. Before closing the drawer, she presses her hand lightly on Papi's notebook.

Then she finds the words she needs to describe what happened:

#2
———

In the library this morning, I found it empty. I sensed someone was watching me, and then a book fell from a shelf. A dictionary, to be exact. Is my ghost trying to talk to me? (Too many words in a dictionary for there to be

> a specific message.) Then one of the big shelves started to tip over even though there wasn't anyone around. Mx. Chen and I were nearly buried in books. Mr. Winters acted weird about it all. Does he believe in ghosts?
>
> Felt three more instances of something watching me. I think my ghost is following me to school and back. Don't know why it's not always making itself known at home, though.

Then, after reading back what she wrote, Jasmine adds one more sentence on a new line:

> I miss Papi.

She closes her notebook and returns it, wishing that this didn't have to leave her feeling so empty.

11

Jasmine doesn't want to talk about ghosts or hauntings that week. She also doesn't want books falling on her head or cell phones floating in the air or houses to groan and creak at her. What she wants is to be a mountain. Just chilling in the air with a bunch of trees all over her and nothing to worry about. Yes. A mountain. Most definitely.

So she keeps to herself, avoiding the library and grabbing her lunch to go so she can eat it in the central courtyard instead. Kingsley is her fourth school in four years, and *this* is what she's used to: avoiding other students and eating lunch by herself. The familiarity of it all gives her comfort as she drifts through the week. She passes by the library a few times, but ignores the urge to dart inside to see if Bea and Jorge are there. At home, a routine starts to develop as Mami and Jasmine see each other over breakfast and are reunited each night over dinner. Jasmine listens to stories from set and asks lots of questions about the brewing drama between the two leads. "I'm pretty sure they're in love with one another," Mami says, rolling her eyes. "I wish they'd just talk to one another and stop torturing the rest of us."

Jasmine bites back a quip. She wants to say, "Kinda like my ghost," but she chooses to keep the peace.

No ghosts. No spirits. None of that.

On Wednesday, Jorge texts their group chat: Sorry we haven't seen you all week! Bea thinks we found a fairy (other than me, of course) on campus!!!

Bea quickly follows up: Keep writing down your observations, Jasmine! Can't wait to hear from you.

She hearts both texts, but doesn't say anything.

For the most part, her week goes fine. She doesn't see anything new. No strange shadows or floating objects, so maybe everything is finally going to be . . . normal.

Jasmine is a mountain. Rising high, doing *nothing*.

Her week floats by just like she does, each day blurring into the next. She isn't sure she's remembering anything she's told by her teachers, in any of the assignments she completes in class, or while doing homework, but at least she's not actively failing anything.

On Friday morning, the first thing she notices upon arriving at Kingsley is Jorge Barrera.

He's standing at the top of the short set of stairs, and he's got his hands hooked into the straps on his backpack, pulling them every few seconds. He doesn't see Jasmine at first because he's also pacing back and forth, but he looks down at her when she's at the bottom step.

"Jasmine," he says, and he's clearly out of breath. His face is shiny with sweat, kinda like . . .

Like Papi used to get.

She buries the thought away. "Hey, Jorge," she says.

"Everything okay? I haven't seen you since the library."

Guilt burns in her chest. Maybe it was easier for her to be in her own world, but she can see on Jorge's face that he's a little bit hurt. She's not used to anyone at school caring where she's been.

"Yeah," she says, then walks up the steps to him. "I just . . ."

She is going to tell a little white lie, but she shakes her head. "Sorry, this is new for me."

"What is?" he asks.

"Having a friend."

He nods. "No, I get that. You've moved a *lot*."

Her smile is wide and genuine. "Yes. Exactly. So it's like . . . I haven't had much practice checking in with my friends."

"Well, it's partially our fault," Jorge says. "It's been a busy week for the Gay Supernatural Alliance."

"More fairies?"

"Turns out I truly was the only one," he says.

Jasmine laughs at that. "So, what was it?"

"Well, we haven't had any more ghost activity, but we got a report from a kid in my science class that there might be a monster living in the basement."

"There's a *basement* here? I didn't know we had basements in California."

"We can't find the entrance!" Jorge says, exasperated. "But there are some really weird doors that are locked all over campus."

He then turns and pushes through the doors into campus. Jasmine follows for a few seconds, and then he points to a blue door next to the administration office. "That one, for example. There's no sign on it. And we watched it for three hours yesterday. No one ever comes in or out of it."

"Weird," she says.

Jorge doesn't respond to her as he stares at the door. She notices that he is *still* sweating.

"Are *you* okay?" Jasmine asks. "You seem nervous."

"What?" he says, then wipes at his brow. "Oh. I always am."

"Like, more nervous than usual."

He grimaces. "That bad?"

"Sorry," she says. "I didn't mean for it to come out like that."

A grin spreads across his face. "No, it's okay. I *am* like this all the time. It's like my default setting."

That makes her laugh. "So . . . what's going on?"

For a moment, it seems as though answering will cause Jorge pain. His face twists up, and he quickly looks away from her.

"You don't have to tell me," she says gently.

"No, it's fine. It's just . . . well, remember what Bea suggested on Monday for your case?"

"I do remember," she says. "I've been thinking about it a lot."

"Me, too." Jorge hesitates. "I know we're always talking about how I'm trying to face my fears, and I'm realizing I'll have to soon. Especially if we're able to capture a spirit."

Jorge looks off again. "I have a lot to tell you, but maybe it'll be easier if I start at the end."

He gazes back to Jasmine, then takes a deep breath.

"I *want* my house to be haunted."

12

"I'm sorry, *what*?"

Jasmine's jaw is practically on the ground as Jorge's face flushes red.

"I didn't say anything before because I didn't want to overwhelm you," he explains. "I feel like this all affects you differently, especially when you told us what it's been like for the past few years."

Gratitude spreads in Jasmine, warming her face. "Yeah," she says. "Thank you for saying that."

"So it has to be weird to hear me say that I *want* something like that."

She turns one side of her mouth down. "I'm not sure you actually want that, Jorge. It's not fun being haunted."

"Someone passed away in our home a couple years ago," he blurts out.

Her heart leaps into her throat. "I'm sorry," she says.

"It's okay." Jorge's face reddens. "I didn't know how to tell you that."

"What happened?"

Just then, the bell to head to first period rings out.

Jorge frowns. "Can you come to my house tomorrow?" he asks. "I'll explain it all."

Jasmine's heart thumps loudly. "Do you live close by?"

He gives her his address, and when Jasmine checks it on her phone, she discovers they only live a few blocks apart. "I'll have to ask Mami about it," she says.

"Tell her she can come, too. My dads would definitely love to meet her." His face flushes red again. "I've told them about you."

It is Jasmine's turn to feel the heat in her cheeks. "Really?"

"Yeah, I haven't had many friends aside from Bea, so they're excited."

Jasmine cannot remember a time since Samantha when someone expressed interest in being her friend. "I'll be there," she says.

"Perfect. I'll send you our number so your mom can call."

Then Jorge runs off, still clutching the straps on his backpack. Jasmine stands there, trying to adjust to what she just learned, when the warning bell echoes in the hallway. She shakes herself free of her shock and sprints to class.

o o o

After a day that crawls by, Jasmine is practically leaping out of her skin waiting for Mami to come home from work. She barely has time to kick off her Doc Martens before Jasmine unleashes a thousand questions on her about Jorge and his dads.

"Slow down," she says, caressing Jasmine's face. "One thing at a time, mija!"

Jasmine explains it all in a breakneck pace, and by the end, even Mami can't stop smiling. "Okay, I love this idea. Gimme his dads' number. I'll call them now."

It is the first time since they moved to this house that Jasmine is overflowing with excitement. She sits in the kitchen, just out of earshot of Mami's conversation, but she can tell it sounds like it's going well. When Mami sticks her head in the room and holds a thumbs-up, it's Jasmine's turn to do a little dance.

She made a friend, one who wants her to come to *his* house.

And she definitely wants to celebrate it.

○ ○ ○

Mami is hilariously insufferable on Saturday morning.

She is standing at the end of the island in the kitchen, pointing to an enamel Pride heart pinned to her blouse. "Do you think this is too much?" she asks.

"Too much what?" Jasmine says, sipping on the hot chocolate her mami makes from the small yellow box. "Too much gay? Wow, Mami."

She purses her lips. "Jaz, you know that's not what I meant."

"Who knew my mami would turn into a homophobe once she met my friend's dads?"

"Not a homophobe, mija! Remember I'm bi?"

"So you're just self-hating, then."

Mami narrows her eyes. "I greatly dislike how knowledgeable the youth are these days. Can't you go back to being ignorant like I was at thirteen?"

"So you want me to live in the Dark Ages, then?"

Her mami groans. "Please, Jaz."

"Mami, the heart is cute. You should wear it."

"Gracias, mija." Mami walks over and plants a kiss on the top of Jasmine's head. "¿Estás emocionada?"

"A little," she says, finishing off the chocolate. "And a little nervous."

"Trust me, estoy más nerviosa que tú."

"Por qué? You're an adult. Adults don't get nervous."

Mami laughs so hard that tears roll down her cheeks. "Oh, mija, I can't wait until you find out how wrong you are."

Jasmine's heart flops about as they walk to 1261 N. Westmoreland. It ends up being a much easier walk than the one she takes to school. They cross no major, terrifying intersections, yet Jasmine feels worse than she usually does.

Ghosts. She's thinking of ghosts. She *wants* to know more

about Jorge, but what if she doesn't like his explanation for desiring a haunted house?

The Barrera house is tucked in between a set of duplexes and resembles the small home that Mami and Jasmine live in. There is a gnarled oak in the front yard—which is hardly a yard because of the massive roots jutting out of the ground. A small stoop leads to a gray metal door, and the whole house is the color of mint chocolate-chip ice cream.

Jorge's dads are standing at the doorway as Mami and Jasmine approach. Both of them are tall, much taller than Jasmine expected. Xavier Barrera looks a lot like Jorge, though. His skin is golden brown and thick brown curls fall around his head. He's also got a very bushy mustache. Virgil is a Black man with a bald head and is a lot burlier than his husband, like he used to play football.

Virgil waves at the two of them. "Welcome!" he says, and Jasmine likes how soft his voice sounds.

Jorge rushes out between them and hugs Jasmine. "Glad you could make it," he says. "Bea will be here any second!"

Jasmine's nerves flare again. "Okay," she says. "Are you fine with that?"

"Yeah," he says. "I talked to her last night. She knows you know some of it and promises to mostly sit and listen."

She smiles, then turns to Jorge's dads. "It's nice to meet you, Mr. Barrera," says Jasmine, then frowns. "Misters Barrera?"

Jorge's dad laughs. "Jorge calls us Papi and Dad. But you can call me Bald Barrera if you like." Then he gestures to his husband. "That's Mustache Barrera over there."

Mustache Barrera runs a hand over his namesake. "And proud of it."

Bea arrives as Mami is introducing herself to the Barreras. Like the first day she met her, Bea is wearing black lipstick and dark eyeshadow, and she's got a pin on her beanie that reads FEELING KINDA FEMME.

"Wow," says Jasmine. "You always have the best looks."

Bea blushes. "Thanks!"

They're all quickly invited into the Barrera home, and Jasmine marvels at how neat everything is. There's a couple of crosses on the wall—she recalls that Jorge said that he was raised Catholic—and some absolutely adorable family photos, including one where Jorge's dads are holding him not long after he was born.

"Always cute, that one," says Bald Barrera, pointing at the photo. "Right from the start."

"Daaaad," whines Jorge. "You promised not to do that."

His laugh is hearty. "No, that was Papi who promised. I said *nothin'*."

"Well, this is a perfect time to leave the adults alone to talk about me," says Jorge. "Can we go to my room now, Papi? Dad?"

"Sí, mijo," says Mustache Barrera. "It was nice meeting you, Jasmine."

Mami and the Barrera dads immediately fall into conversation as Jorge gestures for Jasmine and Bea to follow him. He leads them down a short hallway—also lined with more deliciously adorable portraits of Jorge that Jasmine vows to take photos of with her phone—to his room in the back of the house.

Jasmine gasps when she steps inside. His walls are *covered* with posters, flyers, drawings . . . she isn't sure that there's a bare spot anywhere. She steps toward the wall to her left as Jorge flops onto his bed. There is a hand-drawn flyer for some type of concert taped up next to a poster of Finn and Rey from *The Force Awakens*, which is partially covering a map of Los Angeles with shiny star stickers on it.

"Wow," says Jasmine, turning around as Bea shuts his door. "There's so much to look at!"

"Jorge's room is pretty cool," says Bea, who is kneeling on the floor, rummaging through her backpack. "I feel like there's something new on the walls every time I come over."

"It's just all the stuff I like," he says, then points at a spot behind Jasmine. "That poster is signed by most of the voice cast."

She spins and gazes at the large poster for *The Owl House,* and there are signatures all over it, each one signed over the character that the person voiced.

"That's *amazing*!" she says. "Oh, I love that show so much. I wish we'd gotten more of it."

"Same!" says Jorge. "R.I.P. *The Owl House.*"

She points to the map with all the stars. "What's this for?"

"Places I've visited in the city," he says. "Like museums and parks and stuff! I want to go *everywhere.*"

She examines the map more closely. Even though she's lived all over Los Angeles, it's such an enormous city, and somehow, Jorge has been to way more places than she has.

She glances down at Bea, who made a little pile of objects on the floor. She notices the thermal imager next to a bag of salt and a crucifix.

"Hi," she says. "What's actually happening?"

"Nothing," Bea says. "I'm keeping my promise to Jorge, but I wanted to bring some devices just in *case* something happens."

"Nothing has happened here," Jorge says quickly to Jasmine, his eyes wide. "Like, *ever.*"

"It can't hurt to be prepared," Bea says. She places a small glass vial full of a purple liquid, then sits back. "Okay, that's it. Every contingency is in place."

Jorge takes a deep breath. "So," he says. "About my house."

Bea reaches over and grabs Jorge's hand. "You're with friends," she says.

It makes Jasmine feel warm, and she relaxes, too. "Exactly," she adds. "You told me someone died in your house."

He takes another deep breath. "Mi abuelo."

When he says it, his eyes go glassy, but they don't break contact with Jasmine.

So, Jorge lost someone, too, just like she lost Papi.

The questions bubble up to the surface:

Does it ever get better?

Do you talk to him in your head?

Do you wonder if he can hear you?

"I'm sorry," she says. "I know how hard it is."

"It was a couple years ago," Jorge says, letting go of Bea's hand. He lies on his back and stares up at the ceiling. "Papi took it really hard, especially since Abuelo lived here with us. After he passed, Papi started going to church more. But . . . I don't know that that helped."

Bea pulls off her beanie and fiddles with it. "He never seems to want to talk about it, either," she says softly. "It's like . . . I can always tell he is sad, but he doesn't say anything about it to anyone."

"We're all sad," says Jorge. "I miss him a lot. Like, *every* day."

Jasmine sighs. "I know the feeling."

"I figured," he says. "It's just that . . . I need to talk to him again. And if I'm afraid of ghosts, then I won't be able to."

Her heart sinks. "Oh, Jorge, I . . . I don't know that that's *possible*. I haven't been able to speak to my ghost for four *years*."

"Maybe there's a way to reach him," he insists. "But I can't try if I'm always terrified."

"Can I ask *why* you need to talk to him again?"

Bea looks away, a sadness lingering on her face, and *that* makes Jasmine nervous. Jorge can't seem to look at her, either.

"Guys, what is it?" she asks. "Is it bad?"

Jorge's eyes are now red, and he starts to cry. "I said something awful to him the day before he died," he says, and then he chokes back a sob. "I have to talk to him again so that he knows I didn't mean it."

The effect is instant. Jasmine's grief crawls up from her stomach and grips her chest. She feels an immense sadness for Jorge, too, because she gets it. She gets wanting to have just one more conversation with someone you lost. What would she say to Papi if she could? What would she tell him?

That she loved him and missed him.

And that she wanted him back.

There's a stone in her throat, and now, *she* is the one who can't look at her friends.

"I'm sorry," Jorge says. "I'm upsetting you, aren't I?"

She reaches up for her charm as she turns. "Oh, god, Jorge, no! Please don't feel bad. I get sad sometimes when I think about Papi."

Even Bea isn't her usual cheerful self. "Yeah," she says. "It's . . . hard."

Jorge looks at her and nods, but she shakes her head. "Not now."

"What?" says Jasmine.

It's happening again, she thinks. What isn't Bea telling her?

Her friend pushes past the moment with a big smile. "Uh . . . well, I want to try a summoning of Jorge's abuelo at some point."

Jorge arches his eyebrows. "Bea . . ." he says.

"Look, we should at least *try,* right?"

Jasmine is still lightly clutching her heart charm when she shivers, and then it rushes over her skin. Bumps rise everywhere.

Something is already here.

She holds her breath in and stills, waiting for a strange sound or some unexplainable event. But this time, she experiences something she's never felt from a spirit: the air around her goes *freezing.*

She can't stop her teeth from chattering, and that's what grabs the attention of Bea. Her eyes are open wide. "Jasmine, is something happening?"

"It's s-s-so cold," she says, rubbing her hands up and down her arms. "Don't you feel that?"

Bea doesn't hesitate. She holds up the device she spoke about earlier, pressing a button on the side. The screen comes to life, right as the lights in Jorge's room flicker.

Jorge bolts upright. "That's new," he says.

But Jasmine isn't looking at the lights, or at Bea or Jorge, or trying to find a ghost.

Because she is absolutely sure she can see it.

Her eyes are locked on the corner of the room behind Jorge, right where his headboard meets the wall. It seems like a trick of the mind at first: the corner itself seems *darker* than the rest of the room. She wonders if it's because of the lights, but they're not flickering or dimming.

Bea is waving the temperature reader about, and she steps in front of Jasmine. "There's definitely a massive drop in here!" she says, and she's not hiding her excitement. "Wow, I thought we'd only get a reading in your abuelo's old room."

Jorge shudders. "Wait, I can feel it now, too!"

Jasmine glances over his shoulder.

There's something there.

She can't help that she jumps upright.

"What is it?" says Bea, turning around. "What do you see?"

The shadow grows slowly along the edges, and her mind shoves forward a memory: the darkness in Ina's garage. Diego's shadow seeming bigger than it should be, or Carl's growing longer the other day.

Is this happening *again*?

"Do you *not* see that?" Jasmine asks, pointing.

Both Jorge and Bea stare into the corner, and then, completely in sync, they turn to Jasmine, confusion on their faces.

"No," says Jorge. "What are you talking about?"

The shadow twists in the corner in a way that makes it seem

like it is a living creature, but it has no real shape. The hairs on Jasmine's arm rise up as the darkness grows, and then—

She can feel it. It's staring at *her*.

"There's something here," she says, trying to keep her voice from breaking. "It looks like—like a shadow, I guess."

Jasmine backs up again, and this time, her shoulders bump against Jorge's door. Her breath catches in her throat.

"Point to it," says Bea. She kneels on the ground and grabs something she took out of her bag.

Jasmine points a shaking finger toward the corner.

And something very much like an appendage reaches *back*.

She covers her mouth to prevent the scream building up inside, and Jorge scrambles off the bed toward her. He keeps looking at the corner, but to Jasmine's frustration, he can't seem to see what she sees. The shadow shrinks back and remains where it is.

Bea moves quickly. She tears open a bag, and then upends it slowly, pouring a white substance on the carpet in Jorge's room.

"Bea!" Jorge says sharply. "What are you doing?"

"A circle of salt," she replies. "It's the most basic way to capture a spirit."

She draws a circle with the salt, but stops when she's closest to the corner with the writhing shadow.

"Okay, Jasmine, I need you to call the ghost forward."

"*What?*" Jasmine and Jorge say in unison.

"They can't cross a line of salt!" she says. "So you need to get it to move here and then I'll complete the circle."

"How do you call a ghost?!" she says, trying to keep her voice low so the adults don't hear her. "What does that even mean?"

"I don't know!" Bea shoots back in a harsh whisper. "I've never spoken to one!"

"Maybe it's like a dog?" Jorge suggests, sidling up to Jasmine.

Jasmine's mouth drops open. "A dog?"

Then she glances at the shadow.

"Here, ghosty ghosty?" she says, then frowns. "Come here, spirit?"

"Don't sound so unsure!" says Bea, standing outside of the incomplete circle, the salt raised above the empty space. "Command it!"

"You can't command ghosts!"

"How do you know?"

"Because I've been begging mine to leave me alone for years!" she says.

It's as if all the air is sucked out of the room. Bea shakes her head. "Why?" she asks. "Why would you want that?"

"Never mind!" Jasmine says, then points to the corner. "It's *shrinking*! What do I do?"

"Anything!" Bea says sharply. "We need to get it in the circle."

"What if 'it' is actually mi abuelo?" Jorge's face is twisted in panic. "Shouldn't I do something?"

"I don't care who does what," Bea says. "Just get it over here."

Jorge grabs onto Jasmine's arm. She glances at him; his eyes are red.

"Hola, abuelo," he says, his words shaking as much as he is. "Would you come toward me for a second?"

The shadow twists and turns a few times, but continues to grow smaller. Jasmine is certain her heart is going to burst out of her throat, and she touches her charm again.

I wish you could help me, Papi, she thinks, but that hasn't worked before, so she clears her throat.

"Spirit, I need something from you," she says, her voice barely above a whisper. "Would you leave the corner for me?"

It doesn't make sense, but Jasmine feels like the shadow *hears* her. For a moment, it lingers there, its shape mostly the same.

She lets go of the charm and extends a hand. "Come," she says. "I promise it will be okay."

The moment breaks. The shadow appears to erupt, spreading all over Jorge's room, and Jasmine ducks to avoid it. And then—

Nothing.

It's gone.

Jasmine rises and looks around the room. The posters and photos are all still there, and nothing seems to be damaged. The shadow is no longer in the corner, and Jorge cowers alongside her.

"What's happening?" says Bea, the package of salt raised above the ground.

"Nothing," she says. "It's . . . it's gone."

"Hmph." Bea lowers her arm. "So you don't see it at all?"

She shakes her head. "It like . . . exploded. Or something."

Jorge lets go. "So it's gone?"

"Yeah, I think so."

"Do . . . do you think it was *him*?"

Bea kneels down and tries her best to scrape the salt into a pile, which is proving very difficult because it's all on carpet. "I don't know," she says. "It's sometimes not easy to tell what a spirit actually is. It could be anyone. Or *no* one."

Jorge sags. "Oh."

"No one?" says Jasmine. "What does that mean?"

Bea begins scooping up what salt she can back into the bag. "Well, some theories about ghosts are that they're like . . . remnants of energy. Like maybe they're moments of strong emotional currents that we're experiencing now, even though they happened a long time ago."

"So, like, they're just history?" Jorge says. "Like a recording?"

"Could be," Bea says.

Jasmine wipes away a line of sweat running down her temple. Her heart is still pumping furiously, but it also hurts, like a big bag of cement is sitting on top of her chest. She doesn't know if anything Bea is saying is correct. But it must be possible. What if the ghost in Jasmine's life *is* random? What if it isn't a departed soul at all? What if she and Mami have simply been tormented by *bad feelings* all these years?

"I think we need your vacuum," Bea tells Jorge.

"I'll go get it," he says.

Once Jorge leaves, Bea stands. "That was pretty wild," she says. "I don't think I've ever experienced that much supernatural activity at once!"

"Yeah," says Jasmine.

"I mean, I didn't *actually* experience it, since I couldn't see anything. I wonder why that is."

She goes back to collecting the salt, and Jasmine is left with her emotions swirling around in her head. *This is a hobby to her, isn't it?* she thinks. The realization grows: just like Jorge, Bea *wants* to be haunted. Maybe for a different reason, but the desire is there all the same. She wants to see the things Jasmine can see and feel the things she does, too.

She can't possibly understand why Jasmine wants it all to go away.

Jasmine helps Jorge when he returns. He tells them that he'd given his dads a story about another science project and spilled salt. Bea and Jorge laugh about it, but Jasmine finds she doesn't have any words at the moment. Her mind is a terrible storm, and she just wishes it was quiet.

Her friends talk about what they might do next—Bea is convinced they'll have better luck at school—and soon, Mami comes to fetch Jasmine so they can get some errands done. The two of them take a few minutes saying their goodbyes, and then, unsurprisingly, Mami falls into another conversation with Jorge's dads. Jasmine is used to this, so she leaves her mami inside. Bea and Jorge follow Jasmine out of his house.

"We'll talk on Monday," Bea says.

"Definitely," says Jasmine.

"Thanks for coming over," Jorge says. "I'm . . . I'm really glad you were here."

"Of course," she says. "I'm glad I was, too."

She has questions for Jorge, but this doesn't seem like the right time. What time *would* be good? When could she ask him if his heart still aches like hers does? Does he talk to Abuelo throughout the day? Does he resent that he hasn't visited him?

And does he think the spirit in his house was his abuelo, or did Jasmine's ghost follow her *again*?

Those aren't the kind of questions that you ask someone you've only known a couple weeks. Jasmine waves to Jorge and Bea, and, as always, she keeps it all to herself.

13

Time seems to keep escaping from Jasmine.

She goes on errands with Mami, and the rest of the afternoon passes in a blur as they move from one store to another. The farmer's market at the Grove is usually one of Jasmine's favorite places to visit, but she doesn't get any honey sticks to snack on. She doesn't ask for samples at the ice cream shop where they serve wacky flavors like Hot Honey Waffle or Lavender Chai. When Mami wanders over to her favorite produce stand, Jasmine stays back, sitting at the end of a bench. She aimlessly watches Mami chat with the man handing her vegetables.

It's hard for Jasmine to get her mind off what she saw in Jorge's bedroom, and it doesn't help that she still seems to be the only one who witnessed it all. It replays again: the dark, twisting figure, hiding off in the corner. The thing that looked like . . . an arm.

It *was* an arm, wasn't it?

She watches the people around her go about their day, all of them unaware of what she's going through. Do any of them have unwanted ghosts in their lives? Are they bothered by creepy noises or floating cell phones? Probably not. Sitting there in a crowded farmer's market, Jasmine feels utterly alone. It is a strange sensation; she always thought feeling lonely meant you were by yourself, but that isn't what she knows anymore.

When Mami approaches, she runs her fingers through Jasmine's hair. "Everything all right, mija?"

Jasmine looks up and offers a tiny smile. "I don't think I slept well last night," she says.

"Nap time, then!" says Mami, who is *always* game for some sleep.

After taking the bus home—Jasmine dozes off on Mami's shoulder for most of the ride—they put away the perishable food and leave the rest of the stuff on the counter. Mami gives her a kiss and heads for the couch, the native nap habitat of Aida Garza.

But Jasmine herself . . . she can't sleep. She lies on her bed for a while and stares at the ceiling. She tries closing her eyes, hoping she'll doze off. The house, however, is *too* quiet, and it feels like all her thoughts are echoing off the walls of her room.

Why is this all happening to her?

And *only* her?

She isn't sure how much time has passed when she hears the couch characteristically squeaking, meaning Mami must be up. The light in her room is different, dimmer than usual, like it gets late in the afternoon. Maybe she *did* fall asleep and just can't remember it.

She gets up and goes to her dresser, then fishes out her notebook. She writes a quick entry for this round of haunting:

#3

Went to Jorge's house. While we talked about his abuelo, a weird shadow came out of the corner of the wall. I think it reached out to me at one point, but then it exploded.

She puts it back in the dresser and heads out to the kitchen, certain she heard Mami rummaging around in there. She finds Mami standing next to the stove, zoning out and staring toward the dining room table.

"How was your nap?" Jasmine asks.

"Fine," she replies without looking.

Sometimes, Mami gets like this when she's deep in thought,

so Jasmine starts to put away some of the non-refrigerated items they got at the farmer's market. She gathers jars of local-made adobo and jam and sticks them in the pantry, then puts the apples and avocados in the fruit basket on the counter. Mami finally snaps back to attention and helps Jasmine finish the rest.

"I really enjoyed the Barreras," she says, pulling a piece of dried apricot out of the trail mix she bought. "I'm glad we went over there this morning."

"Me, too," says Jasmine, though her heart rate quickens when she thinks of Jorge's room.

"Virgil gave me some ideas of how I could decorate this place. I really want to put some effort into that."

She gulps down her fear and sits at the island. "So . . . we're actually going to try to stay here?"

Mami raises an eyebrow at her. "Yes, mija. I never *plan* on moving. It just sort of . . . happens, you know?" She waves her hands in the air.

"I mean, not *really*," she says.

"What's that supposed to mean?"

Jasmine knows she should drop it, but she presses her hand to her throat and feels her papi's charm. "That isn't the real reason we move all the time."

Mami raises a finger. "Oh, Jaz, please don't start with that again."

"Why not? We *never* talk about it anymore."

"Because there's no point!"

Mami's voice echoes loudly in the room, and she turns away from Jasmine for a moment. "Sorry," she says, then spins back, a smile on her face. "I didn't mean to take my frustration out on you."

"But *why*, Mami? I don't ever talk about ghosts or anything anymore. You know, all that 'spooky stuff' you don't like. So why can't we talk about it now?"

"You don't understand, Jaz. It's a hard subject for me."

"Because of Papi?!"

"No," she says, and once again, Jasmine can hear the irritation creeping back into her voice.

But it only emboldens her. "Do you think I made it up before? Is that why you won't let me talk about it?"

"No."

"Then *what*?"

"Do we *have* to do this now?" Mami rubs at her temple. "I just woke up from my nap."

"But if we don't talk about this now, we *never* will!" she says sharply, and then her voice pitches higher. "Just like every other time!"

She immediately regrets yelling at Mami, who stares at her with her mouth agape. Fear pierces her heart.

And then the hair rises on the back of her neck.

"Jaz, we don't talk to each other like that," Mami says. "Apologize."

She's trying to get the words out, but the telltale bumps spread over her arms and legs, so she sputters a whole bunch of nonsense.

"Jasmine?" Mami puts her hands on her hips. "Ahora mismo."

Not now! Jasmine thinks. *Not. Now!*

She sucks in a breath, but it gets stuck.

Because there's a shadow growing behind Mami.

Jasmine slides her stool back so fast that it falls backward, slamming against the tile floor. She reaches out and grips the edge of the island for stability.

"¿Qué está pasando contigo?" Mami says.

Jasmine knows she has to control herself because Mami's rapid Spanish is what she slips into when she's angry or afraid. "Nothing!" she says. "I'm sorry for yelling at—"

She doesn't finish her sentence because the shadow—much

like the swirling thing in Jorge's bedroom—pulsates and oozes, then reaches a shapeless appendage toward Mami.

"Stop!" she screams, then clamps her hand over her mouth. The shadow stills.

"Jasmine Garza," Mami says, her voice even and furious, "*you* stop. I don't know what's gotten into you!"

She extends the hand that was over her mouth. "Mami, would you come here?"

"What?" Mami twists her face up. "Why?"

The shadow begins moving again, inching closer to her mami.

"*Please,*" she begs. "Just come over here, okay?"

She throws her hands up in frustration, then walks around the island. The whole time, Jasmine keeps her gaze locked on the shadow. The edges of it are like wisps of smoke, and it spreads down the cupboards like a puddle of syrup.

Mami reaches for Jasmine's hand, but is startled upon touching it. "Jaz, you're *freezing!*" she says.

She still doesn't look to Mami. The shadow pours forward slowly until one part of it touches the island's counter.

"Can you hear me?" Jasmine asks.

"Of course I—" Mami begins.

"Not you," she says, and she finally breaks from the shadow, to grab Mami and turn her around. "Can you see it?"

"See *what?*" Mami says, panic filling her voice. "What am I looking for?"

She pushes past the disappointment that clings to her and addresses the shadow. "If you can hear me, will you leave us alone? *Please.* I don't know what else to do."

Mami's breath catches in her throat.

"Please. Just leave us alone."

The shadow shrinks, slowly at first, and then it's like a vacuum sucks it up and out of sight.

Jasmine doesn't even realize how tightly she is holding herself until the shadow disappears. Her whole body sags with relief, and she leans against Mami for support.

"Jasmine, what is it?" she asks. "Who were you talking to?"

Even in her exhaustion, she still manages to muster up some anger. "You won't believe me."

Mami kneels down in front of Jasmine. Holds her face in both hands. Examines it.

"I think I made a mistake," she says, her voice tiny and distant, like she is only talking to herself.

She stands, then steps back, wiping at her eyes.

Is she crying? Jasmine thinks.

"Mami, what are you talking about?"

"I hope you'll try to understand that I've been trying my best."

Jasmine's heart is beating in her throat. "You're scaring me, Mami."

"I need you to answer this question truthfully."

"Okay."

"Even if you feel like you *shouldn't* tell me the truth, you have to."

She grabs both of Jasmine's hands.

"Jaz, were you just talking to a ghost?"

Her mouth falls open. Mami was right; her first instinct is to lie, to make up some story about practicing lines for a play she wants to audition for. She's glad she doesn't have to lie, because it wouldn't even be a good one. Jasmine has no interest in acting and has told Mami that a thousand times.

Still, the words don't come out easily. Her mami's gaze implores her, though, and she frowns.

"I'm not sure," she says. "But I think I was."

"Ay, Dios mío," Mami says, but then she pulls Jasmine in for a tight embrace and kisses the top of her head.

"I'm sorry," she continues. "I thought I was doing the right thing. That if I ignored it all, it would just go away."

Jasmine pulls back. "That *what* would go away?"

Tears spill out of Mami's eyes. "Ghosts. Spirits. All of it."

"But you thought that was a phase," Jasmine says, and she can't keep the despair out of her voice.

"For a while, I did. I thought maybe you heard some conversation between me and your tía, and you acted them out or were playing pretend. I never saw a ghost, never heard what you did, never experienced any of it."

"And us moving?"

Mami reaches down and picks up the stool that Jasmine knocked over. "I know this probably isn't satisfying to hear, but denial is addicting. The more I tried to ignore what you were telling me, the more I believed it. The *easier* it was to believe what I told myself."

She tucks the stool flush with the island.

"I have an idea," she says. "To figure this out, and to start to make this up to you, Jasmine."

Jasmine raises an eyebrow. "Okay."

"You are probably going to like it."

"All right."

"A *lot*."

"Mami, what are you talking about?"

She pulls her cell phone out of her front pocket. "I'm going to call Tía Selena."

At first, Jasmine isn't sure she heard that correctly. She tilts her head. "What did you say?"

"I think it's time to ask for some help," she says. "But I need you to not feed into her worst—"

Jasmine can't contain herself. "Tía Selena is coming *here*?"

"Mija, please—"

"Like, coming to our house?"

Mami groans. "I haven't even called her yet. Please don't make me regret it."

Jasmine *squeals*. "Mami, you won't regret it at all!"

She presses on her phone screen. "I feel like I already am. But I have to do this."

Before she dials her sister's number, Mami gives Jasmine a sad look. "I want you to know that this isn't the end of *our* conversation, though. We have a lot more to talk about when Tía Selena gets here. But I'm really, truly sorry, and I hope I can earn your forgiveness."

As Mami puts her phone up to her ear, Jasmine resists the urge to spin around the kitchen, even though she wants to. All her fear and anger—it's gone. Evaporated just like that weird shadow thing. *Maybe they'll all be gone forever,* she hopes silently.

Tía Selena is coming over. She doesn't know when, but right then, it didn't matter. She hasn't seen her tía since Christmas in the last apartment. Even then, it hadn't been a long visit; as soon as Tía started talking about "color vibes" and "spirit messages," Mami had picked an argument with her, and soon, they were both snapping at one another. Mami was a "boring disbeliever" and Tía "lived with her head in the clouds."

It's possible that they might start bickering again, but Jasmine doesn't care. Tía Selena is who Jasmine wants to be when she grows up. Maybe she doesn't believe in all the weird stuff she does, but her *energy* is what matters. Jasmine has never met someone so wholly themself, and *that* is what she wants to be.

She glances over at Mami, who is holding her phone away from her ear and frowning. Even from halfway across the room, Jasmine can hear Tía Selena shouting, her joy so infectious that she smiles.

"Is she coming over?" Jasmine whispers.

Mami holds up a finger. "Selena, take a deep breath," she says. "Just let me know when you're free to—"

Her eyes go wide. "Oh. Well . . ." She looks at her phone again. "Yeah, that works for us. Okay, nos vemos pronto."

When she hangs up, Jasmine has already figured it out. "She's coming over today, isn't she?"

Mami rolls her eyes. "Not you, too," she says. "I can't deal with both of you flipping out on me."

"So that's a yes?"

Mami nods and Jasmine lets out a whoop of excitement. *Then she starts salsa dancing around the kitchen.*

"I'm going to regret this," Mami mutters.

But then she reaches out and grabs one of Jasmine's hands. The two of them spin and twirl about, and then Mami pulls her into a hug.

"I am really sorry," she says. "I meant what I said earlier."

"I know," says Jasmine. "You already said that. More than once. Can we talk about it later?"

"Of course, mija." Mami squeezes her tighter. "But for now, Tía is on her way, so it's time to prepare for all the chaos."

"Guacamole, then," she says.

"You handle that, and I'll start with the chile pasilla."

The two of them fall into silence after that as they focus on chopping, slicing, frying, and mixing, though Jasmine has a lot on her mind. But she knows that there will be time to talk later, so she lets the sounds of the kitchen take over.

14

When Tía Selena arrives, it is *always* a production.

Jasmine hears her first. Somehow, Tía Selena must have found a spot out front, because the sound of Maná reaches Jasmine in the kitchen. She perks up, then glances at Mami.

"Ay, qué molesta," she mutters, then wipes her hand on the dish towel. "Mija, you wanna go let her in?"

"Gladly," says Jasmine. She puts the bowl of guacamole she completed in the fridge and skips to the front door.

She flings it open as Tía Selena's music cuts out, and Tía is standing outside her car, her arms raised.

"Jasmine!" she cries, and she shakes her arms back and forth. They're both covered in bracelets and bangles, so she basically jingles as she moves. She always wears brightly colored dresses, and today is no exception: she's got on an outfit that makes her look like she's exploded from a bouquet of flowers.

"Tía!" Jasmine rushes forward and embraces her. She smells earthy and sweet at the same time, a mix of cinnamon and pine. She stays there as Tía rubs her back.

"Te extrañé, Jasmine," Tía says into hair. "I'm glad to be here."

"Yo también," she says, then pulls away. "Please tell me you brought some."

Tía Selena winks. "Who do you think I am?"

She reaches into a pocket—because of *course* Tía only has dresses with pockets—and hands Jasmine a small mango Pulparindo, a chewy, savory candy that Jasmine is obsessed with.

"You're a goddess," Jasmine says, taking it.

They walk hand in hand to the house, and Mami is at the door, a smile on her face.

"Selena," she says. "It really is good to see you."

When the two of them hug, they hold each other much longer than Jasmine held Tía. She can even see Mami's face over Tía's shoulder, and Mami's eyes are red.

"Your aura," says Tía, "it seems muted today."

Mami yanks back. "Okay, could you come into the house *before* you start doing all that?"

"I'm just saying." Tía turns around and winks at Jasmine again. "Your mami is *very* muted."

Jasmine winks back at her.

Once Tía Selena bursts into the house—it really is the best word to describe it, and Jasmine stores it away to write down later—she begins sniffing the air. "Interesante, interesante," she repeats, then moves deeper into the kitchen, running her fingers over the countertops.

"Selena, you know this isn't going to work." Mami stands with her hands crossed at the edge of the hallway. Jasmine comes to join her after closing the front door, and Mami loops an arm around her shoulder. "Why don't you just listen to what Jasmine has to say?"

"Me?" Jasmine points to herself. "En serio, Mami?"

Mami squeezes her again. "I was telling the truth earlier," she says. "I haven't really listened to you in a while. It's not fair, so . . . yeah. I'm being serious, mija."

Tía Selena plops down in a chair at their small dining table. "Dime, sobrina. What's been happening here?"

She glances up at Mami and can see the fear that crosses her face. But she nods. "Tell her. Everything."

Jasmine joins her tía at the table while Mami heats up some water for tea. While she does, Jasmine starts talking. She isn't quite sure where to start. Years ago, Tía Selena had known about the spooky events in their Glendale apartment, so it wasn't like she needed a full update. So she begins with Samantha; it seems fitting for that to be the first thing Tía Selena hears about.

She tells her tía *everything* about this ghost that's been haunting her. The whole time, she listens intently, only occasionally glancing over at Mami, very much as if they're sharing a wordless secret. When Jasmine is done, Tía Selena leans back in her chair and stares up at the ceiling.

"You know what I'm going to say, Aida," she says softly.

"I was afraid of that," Mami mutters. She places a hot mug of chamomile tea in front of Jasmine, as well as a plate of cookies she bought at the farmer's market earlier that day.

"Afraid of what?" Jasmine asks, reaching for one of the cookies.

"The energy in this house," says Tía Selena, staring directly at her. "It's absolutely *twisted*. You can't feel it?"

She shakes her head. "I don't really *feel* it. Except the times when I sense there's something in the room."

"And you don't hear anything besides the groaning or creaking now and then?"

"Nope." Which isn't a lie. She knows she is leaving out the events in the library and at Jorge's house, but she only wants to focus on her own home for now.

"So maybe it isn't what you think it is," Mami says, standing near the island. "Maybe it's just an old house."

"With a dark shadow spilling out of the walls?" Tía Selena says, her words sharp. "Come on, Aida. Don't deny it. Didn't you tell me on the phone you wanted to stop doing that?"

Her mami's face flushes red. "I just don't want the same thing happening."

"Hi, I'm right here," says Jasmine. "What on earth are you two talking about?"

The two sisters trade yet another look, and Jasmine groans.

"That! That thing you keep doing! I see it! I know you're keeping a secret from me!"

"You know the Zamora family is special, right?" Tía Selena says, then rolls her eyes at Mami. "Still don't think you should have kept his last name."

Mami raises a hand. "Not the time, Selena. You know it was too complicated to pull off after he passed. I didn't want to deal with it."

Tía turns back to Jasmine. "Anyway, that's not important. You should know about your heritage. What you came from. What you're *made* of."

Jasmine twists her face up. "I mean, I know where Mami came from. And Papi, too. Is that what you mean?"

Tía Selena doesn't get to answer. At that precise moment, a large creaking rips out above them, followed by a terrible silence.

"Is that what you've been hearing?" Tía Selena says, her voice low.

"Yeah," says Jasmine.

No one says anything for maybe a full minute, and then sure enough, the ceiling groans from a different spot, this time closer to Jasmine's side of the room.

"Is there any way to get into the attic?" Tía asks.

"The landlord knows," says Mami. "I've never found it."

"I'm not sure that matters, hermana."

"Maybe it's a raccoon or something. I've heard they can get pretty big, Selena."

The wall next to the table practically moans, as if someone is pushing on it very hard.

Tía Selena actually jumps out of her chair. "Dios mío," she says. "That's not a raccoon."

"I always think it's raccoons," Jasmine explains, "but it never is."

"This can't be happening again," says Mami, and she heads

back to the other side of the island, then stands with her hands on it, leaning forward. "Selena, we have to stop this now."

"Stop what?" Jasmine asks.

"You think I can stop this myself?" Tía says, throwing her hands up. "I'm just like you, remember?"

Jasmine's mouth falls open. "Like what?"

"Well, we know how this ends!" Mami shoots back.

"You don't know that!"

"Do you want to go through it *again*?"

"Stop it!" Jasmine yells, and her heart drops when she realizes just how loud she was.

"Jaz." Mami puts her hands on her hips. "I know it's been a trying day, but let's all keep our voices at an even level."

"Lo siento, Mami, I promise. But . . . what are you two talking about?"

Mami presses her lips together hard, and Jasmine is certain she's about to get another coy answer when Tía sighs.

"Tu abuela . . . she could talk to the dead."

Jasmine whips her head in Tía's direction. "¿Qué?"

"The recently deceased, I should say," adds Tía, and she sits back down. "Only for a little while before they moved on, but . . . we both saw it."

Mami moves back to the table and sits in the only other empty chair.

"Mami, is that true?" Jasmine asks.

"It is," she says.

"Can *you* talk to the dead?"

Mami's laugh is sharp and bitter. "No, mija. Not at all."

"And neither can I," says Tía Selena, though she sounds far sadder than Mami did.

Jasmine isn't really sure what she feels. Shock? Confusion? She shakes her head like a soaked dog. "I . . . don't know what to say to that."

"Do you want me to tell her the story?" Tía asks Mami.

She nods. "You're better at it anyway."

"A story?" Jasmine sips her tea. "About . . . what? Abuela? Is that why you don't really talk about her?"

"Tu abuela Griselda," Tía says, smiling, "era habladora."

"Habladora?" She frowns. "A . . . talker? Speaker?"

"It's the word our village had for what she was," says Mami. "Someone who could talk to the dead."

"And this was *normal*?"

"Oh, baby," says Tía, "habladores go back generations in Tunapa, and most were in our family."

"I think we both have been keeping too many secrets," Mami says, reaching out for Jasmine's hand.

She takes it. "But what does that *mean*? Did ghosts visit her? Did she visit them?"

"Well, it's complicated—" Mami begins.

"And you said *recently* deceased," Jasmine adds, taking her hand back and pointing at Tía Selena. "Meaning . . . that if they'd been gone for a while, she couldn't say anything to them? How exactly did this work?"

Tía gives a wry smile. "Well, you would know the answer if you let me tell the story."

Mami suppresses a giggle with her hand.

"Sorry," says Jasmine.

"Estás emocionada," says Tía. "I understand. And we both know that this is a lot to tell you all at once. I urged your mami to share this with you earlier, but . . ." She sighs. "I do get why she didn't."

Mami actually looks embarrassed when Jasmine glances at her.

Tía Selena sits up straight and places her hands on the table. "Okay, pues . . . where to start?"

"Our village," says Mami. She gazes at Jasmine affectionately. "I think you would have loved where we grew up."

Tía nods. "Tunapa. It's very small. Less than a thousand people. And it is a magical place. Our ancestors are from there, and our people believe it is where our magic came from. Your mami and I grew up hearing all kinds of different stories about the origin of the habladores."

Mami laughs. "Remember mami's tía had a story about hadas and some war in another realm?"

Tía Selena rolls her eyes. "As if fairies are real."

"I'm sorry, *are* they real?" asks Jasmine.

"Who knows?" says Tía. "The point is that we don't know where the magic came from. There are myths and stories, but in the end, what mattered to *us* was that our mami was magical. There were times long before us when multiple habladores were in Tunapa. But when we were kids? There was only one: Abuela Griselda."

"We both grew up watching our mother talk to people who had recently passed," says Mami. "It was . . . strange. We never could see who she was talking to, but she would sometimes wake in the middle of the night and she'd be having an entire conversation with someone who wasn't there."

"Well, wasn't there to *us*," adds Tía. "But she knew information that was impossible to get. She sometimes even found out that someone in Tunapa had died before anyone else knew. She could only speak to souls that had departed under sudden or tragic circumstances, though. It was never someone who'd been dead for a long time."

Jasmine can't help the disappointment that blooms in her. If there was even a chance that she was magic, this already disqualified her from talking to Papi.

Mami gazes at her sister. "I think it allowed those people to say goodbye," she says, and her voice drops. "It was sad a lot of the time. The messages she passed on, I mean. Just hearing the last words of someone . . ." She looks back to Jasmine. "It was heavy, mija."

"Why didn't you tell me any of this?" Jasmine asks. "Did Papi know?"

"I told him long before you even existed," says Mami. "He knew everything."

"And he believed you?"

"Yeah," she says. "He was great about it. Was always bugging me to tell you, too. Said that he grew up with all kinds of wild stories from his own family that he wanted to tell us someday."

Jasmine sighs at that. If only she'd had more time with him. "You know," she says, "I would have believed you."

Once more, the sisters exchange a panicked look. "Baby, it's not about you believing us," says Tía. "I don't think we ever thought that."

"Then *why?*" she says, heat rising in her face. "I could have known something that might have helped us, Mami!"

"No, you couldn't have," says Mami, a hint of anger in her tone. "Because the power died with your abuela."

Her breath catches in her throat. Jasmine hadn't met Abuela Griselda because she'd died long, long ago, before Aida had ever met Edgar Garza and married him. She never thought much about *how* she had died because it hadn't seemed important. To Jasmine, Abuela was a distant collection of funny stories and an unmoving face in a few photographs.

She shakes her head. "Mami, I don't understand."

In an instant, tears spring to her mami's eyes. "We knew something was going wrong for a while."

Tía Selena reaches out and grabs her sister's hand, and Tía's bracelets jangle. "Our mami . . . they started visiting her more and more," she explains. "She couldn't sleep. She couldn't eat. Couldn't do anything without a spirit visiting her. At first, it was a few times a day, then maybe once an hour, until it was happening over and over again."

Mami wipes tears away. "Those last couple weeks, spirits from all over Sonora y Chihuahua . . . estaban visitándola."

"Visiting her?" Jasmine twists her face up. "Because people had *died*?"

"We'll never know," says Tía, whose own face is wet. "Because one night, they just took her."

"Took her?!"

"It's the only way we both know how to describe it," says Mami. "One night, the souls came for her. We could actually see them for the first time. She was surrounded by this terrible darkness, and then she was just . . . gone."

At the word "darkness," Jasmine chokes. She coughs so hard that Mami stands up to pat her on the back.

"¿Estás bien, mija?" she asks.

"Cookie down the wrong pipe," she says, then takes a drink of her now lukewarm tea.

Darkness.

Like the shadows she has seen all over the neighborhood *and* in her house.

She gulps down more tea. "And this power she had . . . it's gone?"

Tía Selena nods. "Tunapa hasn't had a single hablador since. It's like the magic evaporated overnight."

"It's still hard to talk about," says Mami. "It's why I snapped at you a few minutes ago. On the same day, I lost my mami, and our community lost this power. It makes me angry. I don't understand it."

Jasmine nods. In a way, she gets why Mami decided to keep this to herself. Telling the truth and facing it . . . it's terrifying. She realizes that maybe she should tell them about what's happening at school. And what happened that morning.

The words form on Jasmine's tongue. She is so close to the truth.

"Spirits are real," Tía says, "and we don't always know why they stick around instead of moving on. That's got to be what is happening here, but . . . there are no more habladores. So we can't ask the spirits why they're sticking around."

And just like that, Jasmine deflates. She has just learned of a legacy of magic in her family, but it has disappeared alongside a person Jasmine never got to meet.

What if there's nothing I can do? she thinks.

"So, you don't have any theories?" Jasmine asks.

Tía Selena shakes her head. "Not right now, but I also haven't been in this house except for the last hour or so. I would need to spend more time here."

She stands then, and Jasmine's heart sinks. "Well, thanks for coming over and listening."

Tía raises her eyebrow. "Oh, baby, I'm not leaving."

Mami reaches out for Jasmine's hand again. "I invited your tía to spend some time here. I think it will be good for the both of us to have her around."

"Really?" Jasmine puts a hand on her chest and feels her papi's charm through her shirt. "This isn't a joke?"

"No," says Tía Selena. "I was getting up to go get my suitcase from the car. Wanna help?"

She half expects her ghost to react, but there's no response as Jasmine rushes up from her chair. The house is quiet.

She lets herself fall into the joy of Tía Selena because it helps drown out her ringing disappointment. The Zamora family is magic.

And Jasmine didn't get the kind that would have helped her solve this whole problem to begin with.

15

When Monday rolls around, Jasmine finds Jorge and Bea standing outside of Kingsley Middle School. Bea's beanie is not only gone, but she's dyed her hair a bright pink and is wearing a pair of matching pink overalls.

"Whoa," says Jasmine. "I love that color on you."

Bea grins wide. "Yeah, I'm still feeling kinda femme this week, so I wanted to lean into that."

Jorge actually scoots in and hugs Jasmine, and she squeezes him back. "Thanks again for this weekend," he says. "I know it was a lot."

"No prob—" Jasmine begins.

"Which is why we need to strike *now,*" says Bea. "We've had a confirmed supernatural event happen twice in the last week, so I came ready for the next step in Spirited Away."

Her heart beats rapidly in her chest. "Uh, what would that step be?" Jasmine asks.

Bea swings her backpack around in one smooth movement and opens it. Inside, Jasmine sees multiple electronic devices and the same bag of salt from Jorge's room.

"Oh, no," she says. "I think I've had my fill of ghosts lately."

"Nonsense," says Bea. "We have twenty minutes before first period starts, and we only need five of those to set things up in the library."

"I thought we weren't supposed to do any ghost hunting stuff in the library."

"Well, maybe just this once is okay," says Jorge, though he doesn't sound all that sure. "Especially if we're successful."

"That's the spirit," says Bea, then she grins again. "Well, not *the* spirit. Let's go capture yours!"

Jasmine does not get a single moment to put a word in. *This is happening too fast,* she thinks. Plus, why is Bea so certain that Jasmine can summon her ghost to cooperate? Jasmine has no idea how to do something like that. She jogs to catch up to Bea and Jorge, who have already made it through the front doors and are about to round the corner to head to the library.

"Hold up!" she calls out. "How are we doing this?"

Jorge slows down so Jasmine can catch up. "Bea has a plan," he says. "We're going to use one of the private study rooms."

"The what?"

"They're on the opposite side of the library from where we meet," he explains. "Hang a right at Mr. Winters's desk instead, and there's four private rooms students can book."

"So Bea thinks we can use those?"

"Yeah. I guess the idea is that spirits aren't ruled by physical boundaries like walls, so we can entice it to come to us."

Jasmine still isn't so sure about this. She wasn't able to get the ghost in Jorge's bedroom to do much of anything she wanted. How are they possibly going to pull this off?

When Jorge and Jasmine head inside the library, Mr. Winters is at the circulation desk. "Bea's already in your room," he says. "Make sure you're not late for class, either. I can't write passes for you."

"We'll be quick," says Jorge.

Will we? Jasmine wonders. She waves at Mr. Winters as they pass by, but he buries his attention in a book.

They head to the right after the circulation desk, and as Jorge described, there is a short hallway with four doors in it, two on each side. The farthest one on the left is open, and Bea pops her head out of it. "In here!" she whispers.

The room itself isn't very big; it feels like it's about half the size of Jorge's bedroom. There are two small desks on either side of the wall and a large lamp in the corner, and the space is otherwise very plain, which doesn't fit with how Mr. Winters has decorated the rest of the library.

"This is a very boring room," Jasmine remarks while looking down at Bea, who is crouching on the ground and removing things from her bag.

"Apparently, they're 'distraction-free' rooms," says Jorge. "So you don't even have anything to do but study in them."

"Well, it works for us," says Bea, and she sets the bag of salt in the middle of the floor. "Less stuff to move out of the way."

"Bea, what exactly are we doing?" Jasmine puts her backpack down and picks up one of the devices. It whirs to life in her hand. She nearly drops it before Jorge gently takes it. He presses a button on the side that she accidentally tripped, and it turns off.

"I think our technique on Saturday was flawed," Bea says. She grabs the bag of salt and replaces it with the device that Jorge took from Bea. "It doesn't make sense that we tried to use you to get a spirit to do our bidding. I'm sure you noticed that your ghost doesn't do what you want."

You have no idea, she thinks bitterly, then touches her papi's charm. *I'm useless.*

"So I took something from my mom's files, and I think it will help."

She reaches into the front pocket of her overalls and produces a small tape, then pops it into a device.

"Is that a tape recorder?" Jasmine asks. "Mami said she used them all the time growing up."

"It is," Bea says excitedly. "And I realized my mom had a

recording of a ghost speaking, so maybe that will bring the spirit in this library to us."

Jasmine shakes her head at Bea. "You did not just say the words 'recording of a ghost speaking' out loud, did you?"

"Wait," says Jorge, his voice wavering. "You didn't tell me about this."

"Relax, you two," says Bea. "It's not what you think it is. It'll be much quicker than this weekend."

"How loud is it?" says Jasmine. "Because Mr. Winters isn't that far from us. What if he hears it?"

"Guys, *please.*" Bea stands up and frowns at them. "I know what I'm doing. This is going to work."

"But it didn't work last time," Jorge says softly.

"Are you on my side or not?" Bea snaps. Her face flushes red, though, and she looks away.

Like the feeling she had over the weekend, Jasmine knows that there's something *big* Bea is keeping from her. "Let's be quick, then," she says, choosing to keep the peace.

"Stand over here," Bea says, pointing to the side of the room to her right. "I'll be over here with the salt."

She tosses a small tripod to Jorge. "Set one of these up next to you, and I'll attach the EMF recorders so we can capture whatever it is we find here."

Bea makes quick work of it all while Jasmine stands and watches. She has to admit that it does look like Bea knows what she's doing. So why is Jasmine so quick to judge?

Something about this still doesn't feel right.

Moments later, Bea takes position opposite Jorge and Jasmine. "I'm going to press play on the tape, and no matter what happens, we can't talk. We have to let the spirit come to us without interruption."

Jorge reaches down and grabs Jasmine's hand with his own,

which is unfortunately quite sweaty. But she doesn't let go because Jorge is shaking.

Truthfully, she's scared, too.

Bea draws most of a circle with salt, but leaves an opening on one side of it. She puts the nearly empty bag on the desk, then turns on all the EMF recording devices.

"Ready?" she says, her eyes wide in anticipation.

Once again, the thought pops into Jasmine's mind: *This is fun for her.*

"Sure," she says, once again stuffing all her emotions deeper within herself, even though it's testing her patience. Will Bea ever understand why Jasmine doesn't want to be haunted anymore?

"Do it now," adds Jorge, "or I'll chicken out."

Bea nods, then steps into the circle. She picks up the tape recorder, and hits play. The tape begins to move through it, and there's a soft, crackling sound that comes from the speaker on it.

Jasmine tries to breathe as quietly as she can, and she waits for some horrible noise to fill the room. After another thirty seconds, the tension is unbearable, and she squeezes Jorge's hand too hard.

"Ouch!" he says.

"Shh!" Bea puts a finger up to her lips.

"Where's the ghost talking?" Jasmine whispers.

"Yeah, I don't hear anything," says Jorge.

"It's because you're not ghosts," Bea says. "We can't hear it."

"Can't hear what?" Jasmine asks.

"The ghost talking," Bea says, as if it's the most obvious thing in the world. "Only they can."

Jasmine's mouth drops open. "So . . . is it like those whistles for dogs? But . . . for ghosts?"

"Please be quiet," Bea begs. "Just give it a couple more minutes. We don't have much time left."

She closes her mouth, despite that she has about a hundred different things she wants to say. She is met with utter silence. If she focuses, she can hear the small tape spinning in the recorder.

Is this a joke? Jasmine wonders. *Maybe there's a hidden camera in here.*

She gazes up at the ceiling, but it's just as plain as the rest of the room.

That's how she notices it, though. At first, she thinks it's a cobweb up in the corner above her head, but as she stares at it—

Yeah. That thing is definitely growing.

It's a small blemish, but then it starts to spread, like a damp spot on a cloth, and Jasmine is so preoccupied in her horror that she doesn't even realize that the room isn't silent anymore.

The sound is delicate, and it reminds of her of Mami wrapping presents, or maybe rustling a plastic bag in another room.

But it transforms as the shadow grows. The noise is like . . . like someone whispering, but far away, like they're in another room.

"Jasmine?" says Jorge. "Are you okay?"

The darkness in the corner continues to grow, still as shapeless as it was in Jorge's room. She can't tear her eyes from it.

"Do you see something?" Bea asks.

"It's here," she says, right as all the hairs on her arm rise. She lifts her arm up and shows it to Jorge.

"Oh, I don't like this," he says and lets go of her. "Bea, maybe we should stop this."

He looks *terrified*. She wonders if he's right, but Bea whoops loudly.

"It's working," she says. "The EMF reader is picking something up. Some localized change in energy!"

Jasmine has no idea what that actually means, but she has a guess.

The shadow is now *enormous*, covering the entire ceiling. The sound that accompanies it definitely resembles whispering, but she can't make out a single word. It's exactly like the sound she and Mami would hear in their first apartment, the one in Westlake. She clutches her papi's charm, then glances down at Jorge. He's got the EMF reader in his hand, and sure enough, the gauge is swinging heavily toward the red end of the spectrum.

"Does it look like it did at Jorge's?" Bea asks.

She nods as she stares up at it. "Yep."

"Is there anything different this time?"

"I can hear something."

All at once, it hits her: *Is it trying to speak to her?*

She blurts out the words that form on her tongue. "I might be an habladora. They run in my family."

"A what?" Bea says. "A talker?"

"A spirit talker," Jorge says, almost breathless.

She whips her gaze back down to Jorge. "You know what that is?"

"Your mom and my papi . . . they're both from Tunapa!" he says. "Did she not tell you? They found out this weekend when you came over."

"We had . . . a busy weekend," she says, her mind whirling.

"Could someone explain to me what you're talking about?" Bea demands. "Also, is that spirit getting closer? Should I close the circle?"

"I don't know!" Jasmine says, much louder than she wants to, but she's completely lost. "It's hanging from the ceiling. How do the boundaries of a salt circle even *work*? Does the air count?"

"I—don't know," says Bea, uncertainty creeping into her voice. Then she pulls out a tiny notebook from a pocket in her overalls—*How much stuff is she carrying in there?* Jasmine wonders—and jots something down. "I'll do some research."

The whispering intensifies, but it's all gibberish. Jasmine doesn't make out a single word from it all, but it's so loud it feels like it's in her head. She backs up into the desk behind her, then clamps her hands over her ears.

She looks up and bites back a scream.

The shadow has loomed toward her. It is no longer a shapeless mass; a large portion of it is stretching out, but not like an appendage this time.

It looks like a head.

She knows it deep in her heart, even if she can't prove it: this spirit is a person. She can feel something in it that's human, that's real, but all it can do is loom closer and closer. She doesn't even know if it's the one whispering at her. Is that something else?

"Close it," she tells Bea, and her voice trembles like Jorge's. "I don't know if it will work, but it's like a foot from me. *Please.*"

Bea doesn't hesitate. Jasmine looks away from the shadow long enough to see her finish closing off the circle of salt. The second she finishes, the whispering stops abruptly.

A bone-chilling silence fills the room. Jorge stands up. "The EMF reader," he says. "It's just green now."

But Jasmine has her attention devoted upward.

Because the spirit most definitely is not gone.

She doesn't know how to explain it, but it is examining her. She thinks then that "it" isn't fair. So she adjusts her mind.

They are looking at her.

"Did we catch the ghost?" Bea asks.

"No," she says. "But they're still here."

"How do you know?" says Jorge.

"Because I'm looking at the spirit right now."

Bea gasps. She takes something out, and then there's a click and a flash. Jasmine isn't sure that's going to do anything, but she's too preoccupied to tell Bea that.

She stares into the darkness.

The darkness stares back.

Is this what ghosts are? Has the whole world gotten them wrong? She's always seen them in movies and TV shows as white, wispy things, like clouds of smoke and vapor. But this . . . this is more like motor oil, especially in the way that it moves. The spirit dances from side to side, staring deeply at Jasmine. Do they want to speak to her? Is she *broken* because she doesn't have the abilities of the habladores?

"What do you want?" she asks, so softly it's barely a whisper. "Why are you here?"

She knows Jorge and Bea are watching, but for the moment, it's just her and the spirit in that room. She lifts her arm up to touch it, and part of her mind screams at her: *This is what white girls do in horror movies before they get killed!*

But this isn't a horror movie.

"Jasmine, don't," says Bea. "We don't know what's happening here!"

It is the first time Bea has sounded so frightened, and it causes Jasmine to break her attention. She looks over at her friend, and Bea's eyes are wide and her eyebrows are pitched high.

"This stuff is serious," she says. "Please don't."

Jasmine chooses to believe her. She lowers her hand, and as she does, the shadow slowly shrinks away from her. She watches as the spirit on the ceiling shrinks to the size of a puddle, then a cobweb, then a spot.

And then they're gone.

"They left," she says.

Bea lets out a whoosh of air. "I'm sorry," she says. "I know I pushed us hard to capture the spirit, but . . . I don't know what I'm doing."

She plops down in the chair next to her, and Jasmine can see the despair on her face. Jorge moves to Bea's side and gives her a short hug. "It's okay," he says. "I feel like I was about five seconds away from peeing myself, if that makes you feel better."

She smiles. "I don't know that you wetting yourself makes me happy, but . . . thanks."

"Well, for what it's worth," says Jasmine, "I also don't know what I'm doing."

"What was it like?" says Jorge. "Did the spirit look like the one in my room?"

She nods. "Very similar. Acted like that one, too. But this one . . . they seemed to be staring at me."

When they both give Jasmine an odd look, she sighs. "I don't know, you guys. I'm guessing as much as you are, but . . . I think I'm right about that. That feeling of being watched was overpowering."

"All important details," Bea says. "Can you make sure to write a detailed entry in your journal? For science."

Jasmine realizes she didn't write about what happened on Saturday afternoon before Tía Selena came over. Her memories crash together, and she reaches out and grabs the edge of the desk as a wave of dizziness hits her. It passes just as quickly as it arrives, but it's not short enough that Bea and Jorge don't notice.

"Are you okay, Jasmine?" asks Jorge.

She knows Bea means well, that she's trying to get to the bottom of this. But Jasmine doesn't want to answer any questions. She wants to *ask* them.

Is she a broken habladora? Is she letting her ancestors down?

And why won't these spirits leave her alone?

"I have to go," she says.

She picks up her backpack and rushes out of the study room as fast as she can. She nearly crashes into Mr. Winters as she does so and mutters a quick apology to him.

Before she makes it to the double doors and into the halls of Kingsley Middle School, she does hear what Mr. Winters says to Bea: "Why is there salt all over my study room?"

16

Even though Jasmine is an absolute expert at ignoring people she goes to school with—she *has* been doing it for years—she does feel bad for not talking to Jorge and Bea for the rest of the day. She isn't quite sure what she'd say to her friends yet. That she's overwhelmed? That she's worried she's a disappointment? That she wants to treat her haunting as something more than a science experiment?

Actually, that's exactly what she wants to say.

She spends lunch in Mx. Chen's class reading, and she is thankful when they reveal that they have a secret cupboard full of snacks. Jasmine takes a granola bar and some cheese crackers to quell her rumbling stomach. She somehow survives after-lunch classes and then bolts out of school faster than she ever has before.

Jasmine rushes past Diego, Carl, and Ina with barely a wave at any of them, not just because she wants to be back at home. There's also a fear in the back of her mind: she might see more of those shadows again, and she doesn't want to give them a chance to reveal themselves.

At home, though, she's delivered a shock she should have expected: she's not alone.

After the events of that morning, she completely forgot that Tía Selena was staying with them. She busts through the front door, only to encounter a very surprised Tía waving a burning hunk of white sage in the entryway.

"Jasmine," she says, her other hand on her heart. "You gave me a fright."

"Lo siento, Tía!" she says, then gives her a hug. "I'm just not used to there being people here when I get home."

"What's got you in such a rush anyway?"

"Just wanted to be home," she says. "What are *you* doing?"

Tía smirks. "Just giving this place a cleanse, for a start. I keep telling your mami that she needs to take this stuff seriously, but you know her. Stubborn to the core."

Jasmine sets her backpack down next to the shoe rack and slips off her bright red Chucks. "You told Mami to cleanse this place?"

"I tell her to cleanse every time you two move," she says, and she waves the gently smoking sage around some more.

"So why doesn't she do it?"

Tía stops. "She just believes differently, that's all."

"But *how*?" Jasmine heads toward the kitchen as her stomach lets her know that it's still pretty empty. "Both of you saw the same stuff when you were kids. Right?"

"Yes," her tía says. "I suppose so."

"So then how can she believe something different about the same thing?"

Tía follows behind her and places the sage on a tiny porcelain plate on the counter. "It's not that simple, Jasmine," she says. She opens the fridge and pulls out a bowl filled with colorful sliced fruit and sets it on the island. "Yes, we experienced the same thing, but we feel differently about it."

She thanks Tía for the fruit and scoots up to the island in a chair. Before she can say anything, a bottle of Tajín is placed alongside the bowl. "You read my mind," she says.

"It's the only way to truly enjoy it."

Jasmine picks up a piece of mango after dousing the fruit in the spicy seasoning. "Can I ask you more about back then?"

"Sure." Tía spears some cubed watermelon with a fork. "What do you want to know?"

"What was it like living with magic?"

A grin fills up Tía's face. "Exactly the same as this," she says, gesturing around her. "It didn't really feel any different, especially since your mami and I never had magic ourselves. Only Abuela Griselda did at the time. The magic was always passed on to a new generation."

"Until it wasn't."

Tía sighs sadly. "It was never gone long. Maybe a few months. But now, it's been like . . . forty or fifty years. Your relatives back home . . . they believe it left with Griselda."

"So Mami just doesn't believe in magic anymore, then."

"I wouldn't say that," says Tía Selena, and she picks up some mango. "I think you should have your own conversation with her. I don't want to speak for her."

Jasmine slumps in her chair. "I guess," she says. "But I didn't like it when she started ignoring everything that was happening."

Tía is silent in thought for a moment. "Here's what I'll say, Jasmine. To your mami, what happened to Abuela Griselda was so terrible that she sees magic and ghosts and spirits . . . all of it, as a *curse*. She wants our mami back more than anything."

Her heart sinks. How long has she wished the ghost tormenting her was Papi? Wouldn't she give up magic to have him back as well?

"You went quiet on me, baby," says Tía.

Jasmine offers a weak smile. "Just thinking, that's all."

Tía drops the subject after that. The earthy scent of sage still fills the house as Jasmine finishes off the fruit and then heads back to her room. She pulls out her notebook from the drawer and starts writing.

#4

The weird shadow spirit thing appeared in the kitchen and almost touched Mami, but then went away.

#5

My ghost made the walls creak while Tía Selena was here.

#6

I think we summoned my ghost at the library, and I think they were staring at me. Bea's salt circle might have worked, too. The shadow ghost is definitely a person. I feel it's true. And I have to come up with a better name than "shadow ghost" or "weird shadow spirit thing."

Then she sketches out what the spirit looked like, even though drawing isn't really her strong suit. In the end, they kind of look as if a maple syrup monster is hanging from the ceiling. She can't seem to get them quite right.

She can't talk to ghosts because she doesn't have the power to; that died with her abuela.

She can't get the spirits to leave her alone.

She can't speak to Papi.

She can't, she can't, she can't.

A tear falls on the page, and Jasmine shuts the notebook quickly, then tucks it away in her drawer. She hasn't cried about Papi in a year, and an uncomfortable shame spreads in her heart, burning her face and her ears. Shouldn't she be over this by now? It's been *years*. Why does this *still* hurt so much?

Her bed is an easy comfort, so she lies on it, staring at nothing.

As the sun slowly moves toward the west, the shadows grow in her room.

"I'm going to find a way to get rid of you," she says. "I promise."

If her ghost is around, they don't respond to her.

17

Jasmine doesn't see the other members of the Gay Supernatural Alliance until lunch the next day. She's so lost in her head that she forgets that she was avoiding them for the time being. As she makes it to the line of kids collecting their lunch for the day, she hears her name.

"Jasmine! Jasmine!"

To her right, Jorge comes barreling through a group of eighth graders in line who glare at him. "Sorry," he says. "It's important."

"Hi, Jorge," she says.

"Is everything okay?" he asks. "You kinda left quick yesterday."

"Yeah, I'm all right. It was . . . a lot."

"Excuse me," says one of the students that Jorge pushed past. "You're not cutting, are you?"

He looks back at her. She's a tall Asian girl with short black hair, and her face is twisted up in annoyance.

"No," he says. "I already got my lunch. I'm just talking with my friend."

"Okay," she says, though she still doesn't look too happy. "Just don't cut."

He nods. "Anyway, I feel the same way," he says to Jasmine. "But having you around helps me feel less scared."

"Thank you," she says, and she means it. "Is Bea doing okay?"

"You know her. She's doing research and trying to figure out why this is happening. But she definitely wants to talk to you."

Jasmine frowns and moves up farther in the line.

Jorge's face falls. "Oh."

"Sorry," she says. "I don't know that I want to be part of any more research, Jorge. It feels weird."

"Why don't you just tell her, then? I know she can be kinda forceful, but every time I tell Bea that things are too scary or intense, she does listen."

"But how many times have you gotten to that point? It seems like Bea does what she wants until you tell her to stop."

He sighs. "I guess I hadn't thought of it that way."

She glances behind Jorge. At a table not too far from them, Bea is watching them.

"I don't want to keep ignoring this, though," she says as the lunch line moves up again. "Like, it was so relieving to tell you two about my ghost, and it felt even better to tell my mami and tía. So . . . do you think she'll *actually* listen, Jorge?"

He nods. "I do."

She takes a deep breath. "Okay, then."

Jorge waves Bea in their direction, and she comes bounding over. Her beanie is back, and she's also got on a pair of thick-framed black glasses. Once she's closer, Jasmine notices that Bea has a THEY/THEM pin made out of the genderqueer flag colors, and she makes a mental note to use the right pronouns.

"Hi," says Bea. "I think I should apologize."

Jasmine shakes her head. "No, it's okay, I—"

"You're not cutting, either, are you?" asks the same girl from before.

"No one is cutting," says Jasmine. "Chill."

Bea smiles awkwardly at Jasmine. "Anyway, I really think I got caught up in the moment. Jorge has had to remind me to be more aware, and I definitely let the excitement yesterday take hold of me."

"I mean . . . I get that," says Jasmine. "But there's so much happening so fast, Bea. I don't feel like I've gotten a chance to breathe in the last couple weeks."

"You're right. Like, a hundred percent right."

She raises an eyebrow. "You agree with me?"

"Oh, absolutely," says Bea, and then they lower their voice. "Jorge can vouch, but we've jumped from one paranormal thing to another, and we've only recently focused on ghosts."

Jorge nods as the line inches closer to the counter. "Yeah, we only *talked* about hunting ghosts before."

"But what does that have to do with anything?" Jasmine asks.

Bea's eyes go wide. "Jasmine, we haven't seen this much paranormal activity happening at one time *ever,* and certainly not in this school. Everything else at Kingsley was monsters. Creatures. Rumors of other terrible things."

"Well, I don't know that we could ever prove that there were gnomes in Mr. Yglesia's closet," Jorge says. "I'm pretty sure they were rats."

"Not important!" says Bea. "Because I want to do things differently, especially so that the three of us don't get overwhelmed."

"Okay," she says. "I like that idea. But how?"

It's one of the few times that bashfulness passes over Bea. They suck in a deep breath.

"I think we need to involve my parents."

"Your parents?" says Jasmine. "You mean the professional supernatural hunters? Or whatever you called them?"

"Yes, them," says Bea. "We might actually be in over our heads, and I really believe we're close to something huge."

Jasmine is about to tell Bea that she's not sure they have the same goals in mind when someone touches the back of her neck.

She whirls around, ready to yell at someone for being creepy and weird, but she's left staring at . . .

Nothing.

Well, there's the rest of the cafeteria, going about their lunch.

The girls who were worried that Bea and Jorge had cut in front of them aren't there. She spins back, and she realizes that they've moved far in front of her. The line has left them behind.

"Jasmine?" says Bea, their face full of concern. "What's going on?"

She can't answer because someone touches her again, and this time, it's followed by a terrible chill in the air around her. A tiny yelp escapes her mouth. There's a table not too far from her, and everyone at the end closest to her stares in her direction.

"Did you just feel that?" says Jorge. "It feels *really* cold in here."

Bea doesn't hesitate. They quickly swing their backpack around to the front of their body—*How do they do that so smoothly?* Jasmine wonders—and dig inside of it. They produce one of the EMF meters that was in the study room, and Bea switches it on.

"I know this is probably scary," says Bea. "And I know the other day, I wasn't great about that. If you want to leave, we will go right now. But *look*."

They spin the EMF meter around, and the indicator wavers rapidly from green to red. "There's definitely something here, Jasmine."

"What do we do?" says Jorge. "And why is it happening here?"

"I don't want this happening here!" Jasmine whispers harshly. "Not in front of the whole cafeteria!"

She looks around again, and unfortunately, even more of the students are gazing her way.

This. This is worse, Jasmine realizes. Up until this point, she hated that no one could see or hear her spirit.

But she had never considered this possibility: that people could witness Jasmine being haunted.

"Everyone is looking at me," she says. "Pretend like we're going to get lunch, okay?"

Bea and Jorge don't argue with her, but it doesn't really

matter. After Jasmine takes a few steps, she hears a terrible scraping sound, then the horrified gasps of some of the students in the cafeteria. She's only able to look to her right quick enough to see a trash can sliding over the tile toward her.

She screams even though she was determined not to draw attention to herself, because it's a can of garbage traveling at a high rate of speed, and anyone would scream. Unfortunately, that means the entire eighth grade is looking at Jasmine as the garbage can tips over in front of her shoes.

She manages to dodge out of the way of greasy paper plates, soiled napkins, and some weird orange sludge that doesn't look like something that should be served to a human being. But the damage is already done. The cafeteria is dead silent, and people *definitely* saw a trash can try to throw itself at Jasmine Garza.

Bea still has the EMF meter up, and they gulp loudly. "Jasmine."

She glances at the reader. The little orange arm isn't moving anymore. It is stuck to the right side at the very edge of the red.

"I can't do this anymore," she says, and she does what she should have done the second she felt someone touch her on the back of her neck. She makes a beeline for the cafeteria doors as multiple pockets of whispers surround her. But it's not the sound of a shadow spirit; it is the gossip of her fellow eighth graders. Some of them are even pointing at her.

This is my worst nightmare, she thinks.

She races toward the open double doors.

And they slam shut in her face before she makes it to them.

Some of the students cry out. Jasmine ignores them and tries to shove the doors open. "No, no, no," she mutters, pushing as hard as she can on the crossbar, but the door doesn't respond.

"Jasmine!"

She turns around, and Bea and Jorge are right in front of her. She desperately hopes that she's about to be shown that she's being very silly and you have to pull the door open, but Bea's face tells her everything.

Her friend looks panicked.

"Jasmine, take a deep breath," they say. "It's going to be okay."

"I just want to leave," she says.

As if on cue, the door behind Jasmine swings open, and one of the school administrators is standing there.

"What's going on?" she demands.

She seems familiar, and it takes a second for Jasmine's memory to jog: Ms. Flores, the assistant principal.

"Nothing," Bea blurts out. "The door got stuck, that's all."

You could hear a pin drop in the cafeteria as Ms. Flores looks around the room. Jorge grips Jasmine's upper arm so hard that she has to resist the urge to squirm out of it.

"Well, get back to lunch," says Ms. Flores. "You still have twenty-five minutes."

Jasmine makes for the door, but the assistant principal is still blocking it. "You don't need to be wandering the halls during lunch, Ms. Garza."

It feels as though every cell in Jasmine's body wants to run, but instead, Jasmine turns around, her friends on either side of her, and slinks toward the serving area in the cafeteria. She isn't hungry in the slightest, but with Ms. Flores watching, she has to pretend she is.

She hears it from a kid she's never met, never seen, never talked to. She knows that's like . . . 99.9999 percent of the students at Kingsley Middle School. That doesn't make it sting any less when she passes this boy with a high fade and light brown skin who scoffs and says, "Is that girl being haunted by trash?"

She wants to whip around and say something smart to him as his friends snicker at their table, but the mounting epiphany keeps her moving straight ahead.

She knows she is haunted.

No one else is supposed to.

The whispers of gossip echo in the cafeteria until they clash together, filling her ears. She wavers before she reaches the servers behind the metal counter, and she thinks she hears Bea and Jorge ask her if she's okay, if she needs anything, but her vision blurs. The world turns upside down as she sways from side to side.

Then Jasmine collapses on the spot.

18

Jasmine has few eternal, iron-clad truths that she completely believes in. But one is that she and hospitals will always be mortal enemies. As she sits on the uncomfortable examination chair in Kingsley Middle School's nurse's office, she mentally adds "school nurses' offices" to be included in her anger.

The small room smells weird, first of all, as if someone left out a bunch of candy and it was slowly rotting, and then they tried to clean it with bleach, and *then* they sprayed perfume to mask the smell, which only made everything worse. There were layers to the stench. The walls were adorned with those cheesy motivational posters that adults always seem to think are helpful. They always have animals or really vague scenes in nature, and then there's a bright line of text with something that's supposed to inspire people. She reads one that says, "Tomorrow is always a chance to change today," beneath the image of a dog shaking off water. Next to it, a sloth hangs from a tree, and below it, the text reads: "The effort is always worth it."

She wonders if these animals consented to their images being used to spread fake positivity. She hopes they get justice someday.

Nurse Simpson, a tall and thin white woman, has a nice smile, though, and she offers one when she returns with a mug of water and a tiny paper cup that has an ibuprofen in it. "Your tía is on her way," she says. "You can definitely take the day off to rest, okay? And make sure to hydrate as well."

Jasmine nods and then takes the pill with a large swig of

water. Her head spins for a moment, and she takes in a few deep breaths as Nurse Simpson told her to, hoping the pain will go down soon. She is thankful she didn't hit her head when she passed out, but her headache is killer. She reaches for Papi's charm and touches it through her shirt briefly, then closes her eyes.

Today sucked, she thinks. *Wish I could talk to you about it.*

She lies back on the examination chair and rests until Tía Selena comes bursting into the nurse's office, every bit the colorful blur of chaos that Jasmine loves. "Pobrecita," she coos, and rushes over to Jasmine. "Let's get you out of here."

Of course, that same blur of chaos is a little much for her that afternoon, and she groans when she sits up. "Can we lower the volume like . . . a lot?"

"Ay, lo siento," she whispers and steps back. "I talked with your mami. She'll meet us at the house."

"No, no, tell her to stay at work. I'll be fine."

Tía Selena helps Jasmine off the chair. "She already left, so just accept that she's going to be all over you any moment now."

Jasmine waves at Nurse Simpson as they leave her office. "I'm sorry if I messed up your day," she says to Tía Selena.

"Nonsense. I'm glad I was able to come scoop you up."

Jasmine doesn't say it, but when they get out of the building, she's very happy that Tía Selena drove. Her house isn't *that* far, but her pounding head would have made it seem like it was a million miles away. Tía is quick to turn down the Café Tacvba blasting on the stereo, and Jasmine closes her eyes for the short ride.

Even though she doesn't fall asleep, she's groggy when Tía wakes her up down the block from her home. She trudges slowly down the sidewalk and offers up a lazy wave at Ina, who has a large swatch of canvas spread out on her driveway and is splashing paint all over it.

"I like her," Tía whispers. "Is she single?"

Inside, Jasmine cringes as she remembers Ina telling her about Fatima. "Technically, yes," she replies. "But uh . . . maybe not exactly available."

"Hmph. We'll see about that."

Jasmine ascends the front steps slowly. "Tía, please don't hit on my neighbor."

Tía sticks her tongue out. "You're no fun."

All hope Jasmine had of relaxing on the couch mere seconds after crossing the threshold evaporates when Mami comes rushing toward her. "Mija, mija, are you okay?" she says, and she's grabbing Jasmine's shoulders, then pulling her in for a hug, and Jasmine is trying to answer, but her mouth is smushed up against Mami's face, so she just makes a lot of grunting sounds.

"Breathing is important," she says when Mami finally releases her. "And I'm okay. Just a bad headache."

"That nurse at your school told me you passed out?" Mami says while rummaging through the cupboard for a mug. She turns on the gas burner on her way to the sink, then fills the kettle. "Ay, you didn't hurt anything else, did you?"

"No," says Jasmine, and she hops up on a stool at the island. "Just my pride."

"Hermanita, *please*," says Tía. "She's fine. Give her a chance to relax."

"With some tea," adds Jasmine.

Thus commences Mami's attempt to try to get Jasmine to explain everything that happened. At first, Jasmine resists because that's what she's used to. How long has it been since she last felt comfortable to be open with Mami about the world of the supernatural? Since this last apartment, Mami has been so closed off to what Jasmine is experiencing.

It takes her glancing over at Tía to remember that Mami *is* trying, that she wants to let go of ignoring their problems instead of dealing with them.

"Mami, I think my ghost is following me to school."

Mami nearly drops the mug of tea when she sets it down on the island. "Lo siento," she says, then frowns. "¿Qué dices? Porqué . . . I'm pretty sure you just said your ghost is following you."

Tía leans on the island with her elbows, her eyes alight. "Jasmine, you must tell us *everything*. What are we talking here? Is it like what happened here in the house?"

Jasmine takes a deep breath. Should she tell them *everything*? She isn't sure it's a good idea to share that she's been working with Bea and Jorge behind their backs, so she limits her story. She tells them about the library attack on Mr. Winters, then goes into greater detail about that afternoon's bizarre—and *very* public—display of activity in the cafeteria.

When she's done, Tía and Mami are silent. They're not even giving each other those all-knowing glances that seem to be their own form of communication. Would Jasmine be like that if she had a sister, too? But then their silence goes on for way too long, and Jasmine squirms on her stool.

"So . . . does that mean I have magic and it's broken?"

"What?" her mami says, her tone sharp. "Mija, why would you ever think something like that?"

"Maybe they're all trying to talk to me," she says, uncertain. "But I can't understand them."

"I don't think that's the case, mija," says Mami. "This isn't how the magic of the habladores works. There's no in-between or anything."

Tía Selena nods her head. "Your mami is right. This isn't something we're familiar with."

"It's just . . . it's the only thing that makes sense."

At that, Mami comes around from the other side of the island. When she hugs Jasmine, this one is much softer, and Jasmine can't help the tears that spring to her eyes.

"I got so overwhelmed," she says. "Everyone there saw it, Mami."

"That's probably why you passed out," Mami says, running her hand over Jasmine's back. "Your mind . . . it needed to shut down."

"Kinda like when you need to restart your phone if it gets too hot," adds Tía.

Jasmine pulls away and groans. "Great. So I'm like a broken iPhone, then."

"Mija, I don't want you to ever feel like you're broken," she says. "You're not. You're *amazing*."

"And that's not why we told you about Tunapa, Jasmine," Tía Selena adds. "It wasn't to make you feel bad or that there's something wrong with you."

Jasmine's eyes blur with tears again. "But it makes so much sense," she says. "Why won't this ghost leave me alone? It's made it hard for me to have friends. I don't feel like I'm good at anything, either. What if I'm stuck like this forever?"

"Oh, Jaz." Mami kisses the top of her head. "I don't think that's the case at all. But I'm sorry that you've also been keeping that in for so long. I know I haven't made it easy for you this last year."

"But know that both of us are here for you," says Tía Selena. "We are going to get to the bottom of this. En familia."

She likes that idea a lot. As a family.

"Can we do something about all this negative energy, though?" Tía Selena asks. Then she smiles at Jasmine. "Not that it's your fault. But I think having been here a few days, we need to celebrate this house instead of seeing it as an adversary."

"What does that mean?" says Jasmine.

"Well, *I* believe that energy matters, that what we put out into the world around us helps shape what we get back." Tía Selena stands up and waves her bangled arms about. "And my lovelies, the energy in this place needs a boost."

"Selena, you already saged the house," says Mami. "What else do we need?" Then she narrows her eyes. "Did you hide crystals everywhere?"

Tía winks. "An hour after I unpacked."

"Selena! Last time you did that, I stepped on one. It's worse than stepping on a Lego!"

She ignores that. "Creo que necesitamos una fiesta!"

"A party?" Jasmine frowns. "But our birthdays aren't until next spring."

"Oh, Jasmine," says Tía, twirling around once and then drifting over to her. "You and your mami have a house now."

"*Renting* a house," corrects Mami.

"Which means you get to have a *housewarming*. And let's be poetic about it, because the energy in this house is frigid."

Jasmine looks to her mami. "We've never had one before."

"Ay, mija, when you say it like that, I sound like the worst parent in the world. You've had birthday parties plenty of times."

"Not since . . ."

Jasmine doesn't finish. *Why did I have to go and kill the mood?*

"That's fair," Mami says. "So . . . let's do it. Let's have a party here. You should invite your friends and their families. I'll invite folks over from work!"

"And I'll invite some of my friends and regulars at the shop!" says Tía Selena. "It'll be good to get their take on this house."

"As long as they behave," says Mami, and then she turns back to Jasmine. "I haven't met Bea's parents yet. Would you ask Bea for the best way to contact them?"

"Yeah," she says. "I haven't met them, either, but I'm supposed to soon."

She hesitates, then decides to open up a little more.

"You know, Bea says they're actual supernatural investigators. Apparently, they get hired to deal with paranormal stuff all the time."

"Interesting," says Tía Selena. "Maybe they could help, too."

"Bea thinks so," says Jasmine.

"Are professional supernatural investigators even a thing?" Mami asks. "I always thought that was just in television shows and movies."

"Hermanita, we *did* just tell your daughter yesterday that our own mother could talk to the dead." Tía shrugs. "Who are we to say what can't exist in this world?"

"What if I just go to Bea's house and talk to her parents first before we invite them to a party?" Jasmine asks.

"What if *we* go," corrects Mami. "That's not something you need to do by yourself, okay, mija?"

"And I'd love to come as well," says Tía. "I need to make sure they're abiding by ethical spiritual standards, of course."

"I don't know what that means," says Mami.

Jasmine ignores that. "So . . . is that a yes?"

She nearly laughs when Tía gives Mami puppy-dog eyes.

"Of course," Mami says. "En familia, okay?"

The three of them join hands.

"En familia," Jasmine repeats.

19

It takes most of the next day to iron out everyone's schedules—Tía still has to run back to Pasadena a couple more times to take care of things at her shop—but on Wednesday night, Jasmine is standing in between Tía Selena and Mami outside the Veracruz apartment. It was a twenty-minute walk to 1243 N. Ardmore, which they did because Tía didn't want to lose her coveted parking spot outside the home. The duplex is an old but pretty building painted in a light blue, with ornate overhangs and huge windows on the front. After Jasmine knocks on the door, Bea arrives shortly after, dressed in their usual beanie and a jean jacket. "Welcome!" they say, stepping aside.

When Jasmine enters the Veracruz home, she is stunned into silence. Nearly every inch of every wall is covered with something. In the small entryway, there are two bulletin boards on either side, each full of notes, maps, and photos tacked to them, many of them overlapping one another. Jasmine slips out of her Chucks and leaves them by the front door as both Mami and Tía Selena marvel silently at everything around them.

"Come in, come in!"

Jasmine turns away from one of the boards to see a short, brown-skinned woman who is a near-spitting image of Bea. She comes over to the entryway and holds out a hand to Jasmine. "I'm Mrs. Veracruz," she says. "You must be Jasmine."

Jasmine shakes her hand. "Hi! Thanks for having us over."

She introduces herself as Helena to Tía and Mami while Bea

guides Jasmine deeper into the apartment. "Welcome," they say. "I know it's probably a lot."

Jasmine steps into what would probably be the living room in any other apartment, but she feels like she's just entered into a secret spy base. One wall has all sorts of instruments and weapons mounted upon it: something pole shaped with a sharp blade on the end, a wooden axe, multiple things that look like EMF readers but bigger. On another wall, there's a whiteboard listing ACTIVE CASES IN LOS ANGELES, and the names alone send Jasmine's mind into a tailspin.

BEAST MAN IN TUJUNGA?

KILLER BATS—PASADENA BRIDGE

SPIRIT ENERGY—BONAVENTURE HOTEL

EL CHUPACABRA IN EL MONTE

Next to each, there's a status that designates cases as IN PROGRESS, COMPLETE, or RESEARCH.

Mr. Veracruz sits in the far corner at a large desk with multiple monitors mounted on it. He's a burly man with broad shoulders and thick, curly hair, and when he turns around, his smile is warm and wide. "Bienvenidos, Jasmine," he said. "Welcome to the Home Base."

"That's what we call this place," whispers Bea. "I suggested a different name, but Dad thinks that's the funniest one."

But Jasmine's attention is on one of the monitors. One has numerous surveillance feeds on it, all playing at once. Another shows a map, and it looks as though Mr. Veracruz is tracking something: a small green dot flickers on and off, moving across some body of water. Another has a long thread in some type of forum, and Mr. Veracruz turns back to quickly finish what he was typing.

"Wow," she says. "This is . . . wow."

"A lot," says Bea. "Yeah, I don't really have people over much."

"Because you never know who you can trust," Mr. Veracruz adds, spinning back around. "We've had government agents try to illegally enter our home to get our documents and records before. Very *X-Files*."

"I don't know what that is," says Jasmine.

It's as if Bea's dad has seen a ghost, which . . . well, he probably has, Jasmine thinks. His face droops and she's certain she has never witnessed so much disappointment on one human's face before.

"Is he okay?" Jasmine asks.

"Let me give you a little tour," they say, spinning Jasmine away from their father.

Mr. Veracruz follows them, only to peel off at Mami and Tía. "I'm José," he says. "Have you really not shown your daughter *The X-Files* yet? It's one of the most important cultural documents we have in our community."

She has no idea what that means.

As Bea gives her a short tour, Jasmine is aware that the Veracruz home is jam-packed with things, and not just tools for supernatural hunters. In the kitchen, some of Bea's tests are stuck to the fridge with magnets, each of which is from a different national park in the US. And some of those tests . . . they're not even good scores. In fact, one of the spelling tests—which looks to be a few years old at this point—has a 40 percent grade on it. There's a small pile of dishes next to the sink, too.

"Ignore the mess," Bea says, seemingly reading her thoughts. "We do a big clean every Sunday. We're so busy with cases during the week!"

"It's all good," she says. "I really, really like your house."

Bea smiles at her. "Thanks."

From there, Bea takes her past the adults, all deep in conversation by the entryway, and down a short hallway where there's a bathroom and the main bedroom on the right and two closed doors on the left. The farther of the two catches Jasmine's eye. "Is that your room?"

"No!" Bea says, almost *too* quickly. "No, it's uh . . . a storage room. Mine is this one."

Bea's room is a little bit bigger than Jorge's, and unlike the rest of the Veracruz apartment, is exceedingly organized. To the right is a tall bookshelf stuffed with books and manga, and Bea has draped string lights and vines all over it. Their windowsill has numerous potted plants resting on it, and the bed is made so neatly that it looks like a hotel. The walls aren't bare, but the few framed pieces—some sort of anime fan art that Jasmine doesn't recognize and a couple posters of Paramore and a spooky-looking band called AFI—are placed perfectly on the walls. To Jasmine's left is a large electric bass with a red-and-white body.

"Wow, you play this?" Jasmine asks. "That's so cool."

"I want to start a band someday," they say. "But I haven't thought of a good name yet."

"I like your room even more than your house! The vibes in here are great. Especially that bookshelf."

"Thanks," Bea says, and then they shuffle from foot to foot.

Jasmine doesn't know what's going on, but her friend's energy has gotten really weird. Was it something she said?

"So, are you ready for tonight?" Bea asks.

"I guess," she says. "I don't really know what your parents are going to say. My tía is pretty into supernatural and spiritual stuff, so she's gonna help keep Mami's mind open."

"Yeah, that's good." Bea picks at the end of the comforter on their bed. "It'll be good for them to present their case."

"Well, I also want *you* to help explain stuff to my mami about what's been happening," she says. "Especially about school."

"Nah. I think it's best if my parents lead things."

Now Jasmine is deeply perplexed. This isn't the Bea she knows, the one who races from one thing to another, taking charge of investigations and spirit trappings. What gives?

There's a knock behind them, and Mrs. Veracruz is standing at the open doorway. "Bea, Jasmine, would you two like to join us now?"

"Of course," says Bea, and they rush out of the room without another word, following their mother down the hallway.

"This is weird," Jasmine mutters to herself. She expected weird because she knew she was going to meet people who called themselves "professional supernatural investigators," but this?

On her way out, Jasmine glances at the door at the end of the hallway and wonders what's behind it.

The Veracruzes have set up a couple extra chairs in the main room, and Bea taps a spot next to them on the floor for Jasmine to sit. All the monitors on the desk have been changed to a single image spread across the four of them, and that's when Jasmine realizes that they've prepared an actual presentation for her family.

There's a logo centered on it that says VERACRUZ INVESTIGATIONS. On one side of it is a stake—which makes Jasmine wonder if that means vampires are real, too—and on the other side is a stylized EMF meter.

"Thanks for joining us this evening," Mrs. Veracruz says, and she sits in the chair in front of the monitors. "Our daughter has given us an update about your situation, and we would love to provide you some information, guidance, and proactive measures to ameliorate what's happening."

"Amelia-who?" Jasmine says softly. "Wait, are we jumping into this now?"

"I'm also a little surprised," says Mami. "We just wanted to meet you and invite you to the party we're having this Saturday."

But Bea's mom seemingly ignores Mami. "My husband and I have been in the field of supernatural investigations for nearly two decades now, and our most requested issue is with hauntings and poltergeist activity."

"If it's all right," says Mr. Veracruz, placing a hand on his wife's shoulder, "we'd love to hear a little more from you about what's been happening in your home."

"A lot," says Jasmine. "But, it's not just at home. There's also—"

Mrs. Veracruz raises a hand to stop Jasmine. "It's okay. I think it would be best to just focus on one place, especially one that would be easiest to access."

"Access?" says Mami, alarmed. "Access for what?"

Mr. Veracruz smiles widely. "Nothing yet, and certainly nothing without your permission. Our daughter gave us lots of details, but we want to hear them from a primary source, if that's okay."

Jasmine feels Bea flinch next to her, so she glances at them. Their mouth is pressed closed so that their lips are a single line across their face. She vaguely recalls something Bea told her about her parents and wanting to be a good hunter and investigator, and she wonders if she's seeing one of the reasons why. They're so *official*.

"Jasmine, would you like to start?" Tía Selena asks.

She looks to her mami, who nods. Deep breath in, deep breath out. Then she turns her attention to the Veracruzes and starts talking.

She gives them many details about her spirit. She starts with its first appearance back in Westlake, then quickly summarizes their other apartments until she gets to the present home. At that point, she pulls out the notebook that has all her haunting observations in it.

"You actually kept track," Bea says.

"Yeah," she says. "I think it was a good idea."

Jasmine thinks she catches a redness spreading over Bea's face. She looks back to her notes and starts reading. She doesn't get far. After reciting the first entry, Mami gasps.

"I'm sorry. There was a cell phone floating above my head?"

Jasmine grimaces. "Yeah. Sorry for not telling you about that. I didn't know when was a good time!"

"Don't worry, mija," she says, reaching over and squeezing her leg. "I get why."

Jasmine continues, but falters when she gets to the shadow appearing behind Mami in the kitchen. She never got to tell Bea about it. She wonders if knowing about it is going to help. Does she also explain that she should be an hablador?

Bea nudges her with their shoulder. "Go ahead," they say. "Whatever it is."

With her friend's support, Jasmine tells them about the shadow in the kitchen. All the while, Mr. Veracruz types away at his computer; Bea's mom listens intently, never breaking eye contact.

When she finishes, both Mami and Tía Selena seamlessly pick up the story, telling the Veracruzes about Tunapa, habladores, and the long-gone magic.

"So, I know it's hard for me to hear all this," Mami says at the end. "I've tried to put aside my own anger and sadness, but . . . this isn't fair. For any of us, but *especially* for Jasmine. She's been going through all of this . . . alone."

Jasmine reaches over and holds Mami's hand. "Not anymore," she says.

Mami wipes a tear from her eye. "I'm genuinely going into this with an open mind. I want to help Jasmine, no matter what it takes."

"That's a good attitude to have," says Mrs. Veracruz. "Keeping an open mind is important."

Mr. Veracruz brings a hand to his chin. "And this spirit . . . it's been escalating."

"Definitely," Bea says, speaking up for the first time since Jasmine began her story. "And at school—"

"Hold on, mija," their dad says. "I think we've got it."

Bea grunts. When Jasmine glances at them, their brows are stitched together, and it's clear they're irritated.

A puzzle piece falls into place, but before Jasmine can react to it, Mami clears her throat. "So . . . what is it that you think you've figured out?"

Mr. Veracruz gazes at his wife. "Nexus," he says.

"Nexus," she echoes, nodding.

"What is a nexus?" asks Tía Selena. "I don't know that I've come across that word in my work."

"We had a theory after Bea told us about your case," says Mr. Veracruz. "We don't think you're experiencing a traditional haunting."

"Yes," says Mrs. Veracruz, "because we think there are *multiple* spirits haunting you at once."

"What?!" says Jasmine, shooting up from her chair.

Mami gasps. "You're saying there's more than one ghost in my house?"

"A nexus is a highly concentrated area of spirit activity," Mrs. Veracruz explains. Then she turns around and hits a few keys on the keyboard. The monitors flash and change to a crude diagram of a house, and Jasmine watches as an animation shows multiple "spirits"—which are drawn to look like flying sheet people—all move toward the house and begin to fill it up.

"There are places in this world that are highly attractive to lost spirits," says Mr. Veracruz. "So we did some digging, and we found something important."

He hits another key, and the slide changes to some sort of official document that Bea can't really read. Bea sighs, and when Jasmine looks at her, they say, "I actually found that."

"This is the property record for your address, but from nearly eighty years ago," Bea's dad says. "That neighborhood used to look very different, and at that exact spot, there used to be a mortuary."

Tía Selena actually chokes at the mention of that. "Ay, no," she manages to get out. "You're joking."

"We are not," says Mrs. Veracruz. "So you are living in a place that is prime for multiple hauntings."

"But that doesn't make sense," says Jasmine. "Because this spirit—or spirits, I guess—has been around for years. In different locations!"

"Exactly," says Bea's dad. "Traditional scholarship focuses on a nexus as a physical location. But given what we've heard from you and your family, as well as Bea's testimony regarding the school, we think we've stumbled on something *new*."

He taps at his keyboard to advance the slide.

Her name appears in the center: JASMINE. She watches as the same animated ghosts flutter and float around the screen until they cover her name completely.

Both of Bea's parents look at her, expectant and excited.

"I don't get it," she says.

"Ay, Dios mío," Tía Selena says under her breath. Then, much louder: "It's Jasmine."

"Jasmine is a nexus," announces Mrs. Veracruz, nodding. "Perhaps the first human nexus in history."

"Meaning *what*?" says Mami, her voice pitching higher on the last word.

"Ghosts are drawn to her," says Mr. Veracruz, tapping the swarm of ghosts in the center of the screen. "We can't explain why or what they want, but we are certain you've been attracting them for years."

Silence fills the room until Mami says softly, "What do you think, Selena?"

Jasmine watches Tía, sees the gears turning in her mind. "It would make sense, actually."

Mami groans. "I was worried you would agree with them."

"Well, what am I supposed to say, hermanita? I know you

don't want to believe in most of this stuff, but we know spirits are real. We know that there's often something they want."

"Exactly!" Mr. Veracruz claps when he says the word. "And these spirits are bothering you because they have some great need unfulfilled; maybe they need to say something before they move on."

Jasmie's heart flutters at that, and she can't help that she looks to Mami and Tía. The thought must have occurred to them, too: there are three people in this room, all who could have been habladores, but none of them are.

Is she still attracting ghosts like her own abuela? What is she supposed to do if she can't talk to them?

She's never wished for Papi more than this moment. An unbearable desire to blurt this out nearly overwhelms her, but then bumps rise on her arms, and the hair on the back of her neck stands straight up.

Oh, no! she thinks.

There's someone else in the room.

She tries not to panic. As the adults discuss the idea of a nexus and Mami expresses her skepticism, Jasmine gazes upward. There's nothing on the ceiling—she half expects to see one of those weird shadow creatures there—so she turns around, her hand on the back of the chair. She bends her leg back and grabs her ankle.

"What are you doing?" Bea whispers.

"Just stretching my legs," she says.

Jasmine looks along the ceiling where it meets the walls. Nothing. She doesn't see any dark spots spreading out, but truthfully, there's so much stuff lying haphazardly in the room that she's not sure she'd be able to see a ghost if it *was* here.

She touches her charm. Sits down. Tries to listen.

The hairs on her arm rise again.

She peers over her right shoulder, and that's when she sees the darkness.

There's a shadow just at the edge of the wall that the room shares with the kitchen. It's low to the ground, almost like it's a pet trying to creep forth without being spotted.

Bea puts a hand on Jasmine's left arm with a gentle touch. "Jasmine," they whisper. "Is something happening?"

She turns back to Bea, and try as she might, she can't hide the truth.

Her ghost is here.

Except . . . that might not be true anymore! She gulps as Bea peers over at where she was looking. *Is* this her ghost? Is it a different one? A new thought occurs to her: If she's been attracting ghosts this whole time, who was the spirit in Jorge's house? His abuelo?

Who is *her* spirit?

Bea leans closer. "Is it still here?"

She glances back.

The ghost has moved a little farther into the room.

She nods at Bea.

"Don't say anything yet," Bea says.

Mami focuses on Jasmine a little too long. She puts a hand on her right leg. "Jasmine, is something wrong?"

She smiles wide. "Nah," she says. "Everything's fine."

Everything is absolutely *not* fine, but Mami buys the lie. Guilt tears at her stomach. Why doesn't Bea want her to say anything? Wouldn't this be the best time for it, especially with two professional investigators sitting a few feet from her?

Bea grabs a thermal imager from the side table sitting next to them and turns it on as quietly as possible. Then they set it down in their lap, pointed toward the kitchen.

Jasmine looks once more. It's still there, watching. She can feel it! She gulps her fear down. *This spirit won't hurt you,* she reminds herself. *None of them have before.*

When she turns her attention back to the group, Mami has her arms crossed over her chest.

"I don't know that I want to do that," she says.

"Aida, please listen," says Tía. "It's an opportunity to do something!"

"We are not going to endanger your home," says Mrs. Veracruz. "We'll take every precaution."

"You don't know that," Mami shoots back. "You don't know what could happen. This isn't my first time dealing with spirits, remember? I saw what they did to my mami."

"But this isn't that," chides Tía.

"And making contact is only a first step," says Mrs. Veracruz. "We are not proposing anything further. We just want to gather more information."

Jasmine understands now why Bea talks like they do when it comes to ghosts; it's how their parents speak, too. Still, she can't disagree with either of them. She wants information as well! Why are these ghosts following her?

Once more, she glances at the shadow, which has barely moved. What is it doing? Why is this one so hesitant?

Bea discreetly points at the thermal imager, then gives Jasmine a thumbs-up. "I see it," they whisper.

"Just one ritual," says Bea's mom. "Just to see if we can get in contact with something, Aida."

"Ritual?" says Jasmine. "What do you mean?"

"Baby, you have to pay attention," says Tía. "Where's your mind at?"

"Sorry," she says, and then she can't help but peek over at the shadow—

Which has now moved fully into the room.

She can feel her heart in her throat. The spirit shadow doesn't look like the one that she saw in the library, though. This one's more like a large wisp of smoke, fainter than she expected.

The shadow drifts forward.

She controls her expressions as the adults keep talking. There's a new diagram on the screen. The Veracruzes are showing how they'll summon the presence—"Or *presences*!" Mr. Veracruz adds excitedly—in the house, how there will be protections in place to keep the spirits from running rampant, how this will all be foolproof. Jasmine recognizes the circle of salt from Bea's own trap, and it doesn't exactly make her feel better about what they're proposing. Did that circle ever actually work?

"Salt is often revered as a fierce protective agent," says Tía, nodding. "I think this might be worth pursuing."

"Jaz, you okay with this?" says Mami.

She tries her best to ignore the spirit, even though she can now see the darkness out of the corner of her eye. "I think it's a good idea," she says, then looks over at Bea and smiles. "I trust them."

Bea's cheeks flush red. "Thank you."

Mami hesitates for a moment. "Gimme a night to sleep on it," she says. "José, Helena, I really appreciate this. I won't waste your time, I promise."

She stands, and as soon as she does, the shadow rushes out of the room like it was blown away by a fan.

Mr. Veracruz ends the presentation and immediately begins typing furiously on the keyboard, while his wife walks them toward the front door. Bea and Jasmine trail behind the others.

"Was it your ghost?" Bea asks the second the others are out of earshot.

"I don't know," she says. "This one . . . this one looked different."

Bea gulps. "Really?"

"I'll write it down," she says. "Shouldn't we tell your parents?"

"No," they say quickly. "I'll take some measurements after you leave, though I'm not sure I'll find anything. You know, given that they think you're a nexus or something."

"Do *you* believe that?"

"Maybe," Bea says. "Need to do more research. I hope my parents weren't too weird."

"It was good," she replies. "Informative. I'll help convince Mami to do the ritual, too."

"Cool." Bea shoves their hands in the pockets of their jean jacket.

Jasmine doesn't know what to do with this. Why does Bea seem so unsure of themselves now?

Bea is curt when saying goodbye, then runs off toward their room. Light spills into the hallway for a moment, and then their bedroom door closes.

For a moment, Jasmine sees it, right outside Bea's door: the shadow.

She steps forward, but the shadow darts away, like they were sucked into the storage room across the hall.

Gone. Just like that.

Unnerved, she follows her mami and Tía out the front door, and they spend the twenty-minute walk home arguing. It's not an intense thing, and Jasmine senses that her mami *is* actually open to letting the Veracruzes help.

"I just don't want the same thing to happen again," Mami says.

"Hermanita, this isn't the same situation," says Tía. "You know that."

"My head knows that. My heart doesn't."

Jasmine likes how Mami puts that. She thinks that's what is going on with her as well. Her head and her heart want two different things. These hauntings have to stop. She cannot be known as the spooky girl at school. Life *must* become normal for the Garzas!

By the time she gets home, though, the feeling in her heart is growing. What if they succeed? What if they actually manage to get these spirits to go away, and they never, ever return? Does that mean she will be closing off the possibility, no matter how slim, that Papi will one day reach out to her?

Jasmine slips away from Mami and Tía when they go to the kitchen, and she heads to her room. Soon, she's got her notebook in her lap while sitting on the floor, and she writes:

#7

Saw a possibly new ghost today at Bea's. Or maybe it's mine. I don't know. This one looked like smoke. Is the Veracruz house haunted, or am I a "nexus"?

I still don't know what's going on.

Jasmine closes her notebook and sets it next to her. She stares up at the ceiling.

"Are you there, ghost?" she asks. "Do you hear and see all of this? Is there more than one of you?"

There's no response.

"Are any of you trying to tell me something? If so, could you, like, write it down instead? Letters are pretty cool."

Nothing.

She knows what will happen, but she does it anyway.

"Papi, are you out there?"

Silence.

Deep in the house, she thinks she hears a creaking, but it ends up being Mami, who comes to stand in the doorway.

"Well, that was an experience," she says.

"Yeah," says Jasmine. "You saw the wooden axe, too, right?"

Mami laughs. "I don't even want to know."

Jasmine narrows her eyes. "You *do* want to know, don't you?"

"I mean . . . yes, of course I do. Why was it made out of wood?"

They both fall into giggles, and Mami comes to sit on the bed next to Jasmine. She starts running her fingers through her hair and lightly scratching her scalp with her nails, and it relaxes Jasmine so quickly.

"I don't need a night to sleep on it," Mami says, her voice low and confident. "I've already called the Veracruzes and said yes."

"I think it's a good start," says Jasmine. "We'll figure this out."

"And do it together. No more ignoring our problems. And they want to do it after our party, so we'll have our next step soon enough."

"The party," Jasmine says. "Right! I'm glad we're still having it."

"Maybe your tía has some good ideas in that wacky head of hers."

Jasmine snuggles up to Mami for a while, her brain whirring with thoughts. She still can't piece this all together, but *some* things make more sense. She gets why Bea is the way they are. It makes sense that all these weird hauntings are the work of multiple ghosts instead of one very determined one.

But why doesn't she feel better about it yet?

Her mami helps her up when she gets sleepy so she can brush her teeth and wash her face. She climbs into bed and sleep finds her faster than it ever has. She dreams of only one thing that night: a room full of shadows.

And none of them talk to her.

20

Jasmine's morning ends up being more chaotic than she wants it to be. Because her mami had to be on set earlier than usual, Tía Selena is the one to wake her up. Unfortunately Tía has a very fascinating concept of time, so she somehow thinks that giving Jasmine only twenty minutes to get ready *and* get to school is ideal.

It's not. Jasmine rushes through the house, trying to get some form of a breakfast into her stomach while getting dressed. Tía follows her, convinced that Jasmine is panicking for no reason.

"Can't I write you a pass or something?" she calls out to her while Jasmine brushes her teeth.

"Not how it works!" she screams with a mouthful of toothpaste, which then dribbles down her shirt, so she has to change that before she leaves. In her room, she sees her notebook is still on the floor instead of tucked away where it should be.

Tía appears at the doorway. "¡Apurate!" she says. "I'll drive you to school, and then bring you some Thai takeout for lunch as an apology."

That does win Jasmine over. "I will accept that," she says with a grin, then stuffs her notebook back in her drawer.

After getting dropped off, there are only a few minutes left before Jasmine's first class starts, so she hopes that the Gay Supernatural Alliance is in the library. She gives Mr. Winters a brief hello after pushing through the double doors, then speed walks to the rear tables. A burst of relief hits her when she sees Jorge and Bea huddled over a book.

"Did your parents tell you yet?" Jasmine says to Bea.

Bea is all smiles as they close the book. "Yes!" they say. "We don't have a date yet, but they're already starting to prepare for it."

"Bea told me about it all," Jorge says. "And I think I'm gonna ask my dads if we can come, too. Not just to the party, but whatever Bea's parents are planning."

"I think Mami would like that support," says Jasmine, nodding. "And your papi needs to meet my tía! She's from Tunapa, también."

"So . . . a nexus?" Jorge looks worried. "How does it feel, Jasmine?"

The bell rings out loudly, and Jasmine sighs. "Never enough time," she says. "Can we talk more at lunch?"

"Perfect," says Jorge. "Can't wait."

Her heart swells. "And thank you. I really appreciate both of you doing all this for me."

"Of course," says Jorge. "I feel the same."

"The Gay Supernatural Alliance is alive and well," says Bea, and then they dramatically salute.

Jasmine feels more hopeful as she runs off to class than she's felt in a long, long time. She expects that it will be hard for her to concentrate during classes, but the day passes in a breeze. She stops by the front office to pick up the pad thai that Tía Selena dropped off, then heads to the cafeteria.

She hesitates at the entrance, though. It's her first time back since . . . since the incident. She weaves expertly away from a couple trash cans, hoping they don't magically scoot in her direction. Some of the students gaze her way, but Jorge and Bea are waving at her obnoxiously on the other side of the room, so it's the perfect distraction. She avoids the looks the other students give her and takes a seat with her friends.

"Lucky," says Jorge when she opens the to-go container and

the sweet/savory smell wafts over the table. "Much better than our lunch."

"Are you excited for the party?" Bea asks.

"Definitely," Jasmine says, then blows on the noodles dangling from her chopsticks.

"Your house is actually really cool," they continue. "I bet when you and your mami finish decorating, it's going to look amazing."

"Whose room do you think yours will look more like?" Jorge asks. "Mine or Bea's?"

They both promptly start arguing about their styles, and Jasmine notices how much more animated Bea is than they were the night before. *Maybe they just feel more comfortable with us,* she thinks.

But it does feel like there's something going on under the surface that she can't see. She hopes that someday Bea feels comfortable enough to share it with her.

○   ○   ○

Saturday also arrives quicker than Jasmine expects it to. She's grateful for that because between school and prepping for the party, she hasn't had much time to think about ghosts, being the first possible human nexus, or any of the other things that have been stressing her out. She even forgets that she passed out at school earlier that week until Mami tells her to sit down and take a breath that afternoon.

"You've been running around the house for hours, mija," she says, filling up a glass with water and passing it over the island to Jasmine. "Take a breath. I don't want a repeat of Tuesday."

"I'm just so excited," she says, then gulps down the water. "We've gotten a lot done."

Mami puts her hands on her hips and looks around. "We have."

There are no longer opened boxes tucked in the corners. While they didn't get everything put away, Mami and Jasmine agreed they wanted to at least look moved in by the time guests arrived. Some of the more complicated boxes were stacked in Mami's closet, and the rest were emptied out, their contents neatly organized in cupboards and cabinets. Jasmine even found an old stuffed animal of hers: Hiram the cat. She'd forgotten about it, but the sight of him filled her with joy *and* sadness. She remembered picking Hiram out at the toy store in the mall in the Valley with Papi.

Jasmine greets Hiram with a gentle pet as she enters her room and pulls out the dress she's going to wear at the party. She decides to dial up the femme when she thinks of Bea's beanie, so she lays a bright pink dress over her bed and smooths it out.

Perfect.

Savory smells waft through the house by the time Jasmine is out of the shower. After getting dressed, she heads to the kitchen, where Mami takes a brief break to braid Jasmine's hair.

"You look very gorgeous, mija," she says upon finishing. "And I'm so glad we're doing this together."

"Me, too," she says. "I can watch the pot while you get ready."

Mami winks at her, then heads off to the back of the house.

Today is going to be great, Jasmine tells herself as she stirs her mami's famous pozole. She sneaks a quick taste after blowing on the wooden spoon. It tastes *perfect.*

Everything is exactly as it should be.

Tía Selena returns from an errand, and she comes stumbling into the house with a large silver container wrapped in foil. "Almost dropped them!" she says.

When she sets the container on the island, Jasmine peels back the edge of the foil. Steam hits her face, as does the delicious scent of tamales.

"Did you make these, Tía?"

"Oh, absolutely not. Your mami is the cook, not me. I picked these up from my favorite carnicería over in Highland Park."

Then she gently swats at Jasmine's hand when she tries to pull one out. "Not yet!"

After that, it seems like there's an endless wave of people coming into their home. The Barreras are next, and Mustache Papi heads straight for the tamales when he sees Mami unwrapping one. As they fall into rapid Spanish, someone knocks on the door. When Jasmine answers it, there are two strangers standing there. One is a tall Black man with dark brown skin and a big Afro. He has multiple pieces of jewelry all over his face, and his arms are covered in intricate tattoos. The other person, a Black woman with long box braids, gold hoop earrings, and wearing a monochrome black suit, smiles down at Jasmine.

"Is this the Garza residence?" she asks. "Selena invited us."

Before Jasmine can even say anything, Selena is practically howling at her friends. "Justice! Samira! So glad you could make it!"

She kisses them both on the cheeks and steps aside to let them in. Samira winks at Jasmine. "Love the dress."

Jasmine blushes. She's not sure she's ever gotten a compliment from someone so *cool* before.

Bea arrives next, and she is dressed up in a checkerboard dress and black Doc Martens. She curtsies dramatically, which is when Jasmine spots a pin on her black beanie that reads SHE/HER.

"Welcome to the party," Jasmine says. "I wore this dress in honor of you."

Bea marvels at it. "It's so bright," she says. "You thought of me when you chose this?!"

"Absolutely. Your style is kinda rubbing off on me."

Jasmine can see the redness on Bea's cheeks. "Wow," she says. "That's . . . that's really cool."

She kneels over to untie her Docs, then glances up at Jasmine. "Okay, only time I'll ask this," she says in a hushed voice. "Anything new happen?"

She shakes her head. "It's weird. Not a thing. No weird shadows or sounds or anything."

"Huh." Bea stands and slips out of her shoes. "That is strange."

"Any new theories or discoveries?"

Bea frowns. "Can't say I found anything on my end, but . . . I'll keep trying."

She sniffs in the air. "Did your mom actually make pozole?!"

Jasmine takes her into the kitchen, where they find Jorge listening intently as Tía Selena explains the way she makes her tamales.

"Tía!" Jasmine says, pretending to be scandalized. "¡Qué mentirosa!"

"She's *lying*?" Jorge's mouth drops open, and a little piece of tamale falls out, which sends three others into a fit of laughter.

More and more people arrive. Jasmine meets the famed Lara, who lived in the Crenshaw apartment before she and Mami did. She has pale skin covered in freckles, and her hair is bright red, perhaps the brightest Jasmine has ever seen. Then there are more people from the crew Mami works with, like Salazar, who goes by his last name, wears overalls all the time (according to Mami), and pops gum every few seconds. He has his hair cut in a smooth high fade, and she can see a tattoo of a snake crawling up the back of his head.

There are people from Tía's circle of friends who look like they could be in punk rock bands, a coven of witches, or both. Within a couple hours, Jasmine's home is so stuffed with people that it actually feels small. She can't seem to remember the names of anyone she meets after a while, but she loves the warmth in her home, how cozy it feels, how much it really looks like she and her mami have been living there for a while.

She mostly sticks with Jorge and Bea in the living room on the green couch, only occasionally getting up to meet some new person that Tía or Mami has invited over. Each time she plops back down on the couch between her friends, it squeaks at her.

"How long have you had this couch?" Jorge asks. "I've never seen one this color."

"A while," she says. "I was pretty young when it was new."

"Looks like your parents bought it in the last century," jokes Bea.

"It's ancient history," adds Jorge. "Maybe you should put it in a museum."

"Well, *I* like it," says Jasmine. "My papi picked it out, so I think that's why we don't get rid of it."

She pushes away the sadness that threatens to weigh her down. *Not now,* she tells herself. *It's a party!*

The three of them fall silent for a moment amidst all the adults talking loudly around them.

"We keep Abuelo's room mostly the same," says Jorge. "Kinda like how Bea—"

He stops. When Jasmine looks at him, he looks horrified.

"Jorge." Bea merely says his name, but Jasmine can tell she's angry.

"What's wrong?" she says.

"Nothing," Jorge says, and he stands up. "I am going to get some more tamales!"

Then he darts out of the room.

Bea, meanwhile, is scowling.

"Did he do something wrong?" she asks. When Bea doesn't respond, Jasmine's blood pumps loudly in her ears. "Did *I* do something wrong?"

"No, you're fine," Bea finally says, then pulls her beanie down a little farther. "Jorge's just being weird."

In an instant, Jasmine is taken back to the first day she met the other members of the Gay Supernatural Alliance. She remembers sitting at that table, feeling like she'd walked in on a party she hadn't been invited to.

But Jasmine did invite these two to her party. So what gives?

"Is this another secret?" she asks. "Clearly, Jorge was talking about something."

"Drop it," says Bea, her voice cold.

Drop it? Now, Jasmine is the one scowling. "I don't get why you're mad at me, Bea. I thought you said I didn't do anything!"

"I don't want to talk about it," she says through gritted teeth, and then she's on her feet, heading off toward the kitchen.

When Jasmine looks up, two of the adults—and she honestly can't tell if they're Mami's friends or Tía Selena's friends—are watching her.

Her head buzzes. Were they eavesdropping?

She pushes herself up and—

No.

No!

Her stomach sinks when she feels it all over her body.

Her ghost is here.

Ghost. Ghosts. She doesn't know. She doesn't *care*. This is the worst time for this to happen!

She keeps her head down as she weaves around people holding drinks in their hands, chatting with one another, oblivious to what's happening. In the kitchen, she sees both Jorge and Bea tucked in the far corner, clearly arguing in hushed voices. She storms over to them.

"None of this at my party," she says. "What's going on?"

"I shouldn't have said anything," Jorge says. "I made a mistake."

Bea stands up straighter. "It's all fine, now."

"It's *not!*" Jasmine hisses.

She raises her arm up. It's covered in goose bumps.

"No," Jorge says. *"Now?"*

"Should I get my EMF—" Bea begins.

"NO!" Jasmine yells.

Too loud. She's aware of how quiet it just got in the kitchen, and she turns to find all of them looking at her.

And there, dripping down from above the stove, is a shadow spirit.

"Jaz?" Mami says. "Everything okay?"

"Yes," she says, but it sounds like she's choking when she speaks.

"I can help," Bea says.

"Not tonight," says Jasmine. "We have to ignore it. This is supposed to be a party."

"Jasmine," Bea says softly, "you can't keep ignoring the ghosts in your life."

"Like the one we ignored at your house?"

Jorge actually gasps. "What? What ghost?!"

"Nothing," says Bea, but her wide eyes tell the truth. Jorge hit a nerve.

"There was a ghost in your house?" Jorge grabs Bea by the shoulders. "You told me Jasmine might be a nexus, right?"

"So?"

"Bea, *you know who that ghost might be.*"

All the color drains from Bea's face. "Stop it."

Jorge lets go of her and stares at Jasmine. "The shadow at my house. This proves it. That had to have been mi abuelo."

"Hold on," Jasmine says. "Let's not assume that!"

The sensation hits her so hard then that she feels the breath knocked out of her. She doubles over, and Jorge grabs one of her arms.

"Jasmine?" he says.

She uprights herself. Spins around.

The shadow has covered the entire ceiling.

"No, no, no!" she cries, then wobbles.

"Jaz, what is it?"

Mami rushes to her side as the conversations in the kitchen all die out.

"Not now," she says forcefully. "Please go away."

Mami grabs Jasmine's face in her hands, stares into her eyes. "Mija, is it happening right now?"

Tears fill her eyes. "Yes," she says. "And it's *huge*."

She hugs her in a tight embrace. "I'll call the party off," she says. "Send everyone home."

Jasmine yanks away. "No! Please don't do that!"

"Jaz, no," says Mami. "You're in distress. I can see that. It's just a party."

She looks back up to the ceiling, to the growing pool of darkness that seems to be stretching toward her.

"We don't *get* parties!" she cries out. "And I'm ruining the first one we've ever had!"

"It's not ruined," says Bea.

Jasmine whirls on her. "What won't you tell me?" she sneers. "Why do you always have some secret you're keeping from me?"

"Jasmine, please," says Jorge, and he shivers. "I really shouldn't have said anything."

"Are you scared?" she screams, then points up at the ceiling. "You can't even see what I'm seeing. Why are *you* afraid?"

"Jaz!" Mami yells.

But the blood is thumping in Jasmine's ears, and she can't stop. She glares at Bea, who shrinks away from her.

Tears spring to Bea's eyes. "Fine," she says as they spill down her cheeks. "If you have to know, my brother died."

Bea pushes past Jasmine.

"I'm sorry," Jorge says, and he spits out the next words. "I'm sorry for being so scared, Jasmine."

He chases after Bea, and Jasmine stands there, her head spinning, her mind reeling. What? *What?* Bea had a brother?

She doesn't know how to handle this. She hears Mami talking to her, saying something about her head, but she swats her away.

"You're not ruining this party!" Jasmine yells up at the ceiling. "Go away, ghost! Go somewhere else!"

"Ay, Jasmine, is it here?" Tía Selena is in front of her, her eyes wide in alarm. She gazes up. "Talk to us, spirit!"

The adults in the living room are now trying to push their way into the kitchen to see what all the commotion is, while Mami's and Tía's friends watch in horror from the dining room.

They're all watching her. Just like the kids in the cafeteria.

The shadow stretches one appendage down. Then another. Then another. Reaching for her.

The Veracruzes were right. Jasmine knows this now. That's not one ghost; it's a bunch of ghosts.

Her vision blurs again. Her head pounds. Mami is trying to tell people to leave, that the party is over, and Jasmine wipes away tears. Makes eye contact with Bea.

Whose face is red and puffy from crying.

Jasmine bolts away from it all, running down the hallway to her room. She slams the door hard and curls up on the bed, sobbing. She wills the ghosts away, begging them to leave her alone.

Unfortunately, they follow her.

She watches in disbelief as the shadow spirit pours all around the edges of the door, spreads across the ceiling, and then the spirits reach for her again.

"Go away!" she screams. "You're ruining my life!"

The oily appendage stills.

Shrinks.

And the whole thing disappears.

Yet despite the relief she feels that it's gone, Jasmine falls into a deep, shuddering cry.

Jasmine isn't just haunted.

Her life is ruined.

21

Jasmine doesn't come out of her room for the rest of the night.

She isn't crying anymore, but she feels no better. She replays what happened, and every decision she made feels like someone else did it. How could she yell at her family? At her friends? Why did she make such a spectacle?

Why won't her ghosts leave her alone?

She can't face Bea. She won't be surprised if she'll never speak to her again, and there's a whole new hole opening up in her heart. Jorge probably hates her, too. Why, *why* was she so mean?

It's like her whole life is falling apart. Like she's never going to get past this moment. Like her chest will split open and she'll turn into a human volcano, and there will be newscasts about how dangerous she is and how no one should approach her because they'll get hurt. She's never, ever felt like this before.

o o o

But . . . no.

No, that isn't true.

Jasmine has felt this way before, but she hasn't thought about that specific moment in a long, long time.

Because it hurts too much.

o o o

She's in a hospital. The lights are too bright, too fake, and as Mami squeezes her hand harder, it all makes the dull headache behind her eyes even worse. It doesn't help that she has no idea what she's about to experience. All she knows is that there was an accident, Papi is in the hospital, and Mami plucked her out of school to get here as fast as possible. She's practically pulling Jasmine along, and she's struggling to keep up.

Jasmine doesn't want to do this.

It's a very sudden feeling that comes over her. She doesn't want to walk into this room at the end of the hallway, she doesn't want to see what's in there, she doesn't want *any* of this.

Mami slows before they reach it, and Jasmine wonders if she's thinking the same thing as her. What if they just don't go in? What if he isn't in that room, and they just go home, and there's Papi on his green, squeaky couch, and everything is fine?

There's a small whiteboard on the door. She sees Papi's name: GARZA, EDGAR. Mami knocks, and it swings open.

There's someone in the bed, but Jasmine doesn't recognize them. She sees tubes. Bandages. There's a constant beeping nearby, and the nurse—a tall Filipina woman who will later introduce herself as Yolanda—is examining something on the person's arm.

That's not Papi. It can't be.

But the head turns, and Jasmine sees his bloodshot eyes, and then he laughs, weakly, and that's him. She would know that laugh anywhere.

"Sorry you have to see me like this," he says, and his voice . . . it's so quiet. Soft. Like breathing is hard.

"Mr. Garza, please," says Yolanda. "We talked about this. Your ribs—"

He grunts. "I can deal with the pain if it means getting to talk to mi amor." When a smile grows on his face, she can see something else there: a small grimace.

Whatever happened, it has to be hurting him.

She steps closer, and she sees bandages everywhere. His forehead, his arms, the fingers on his right hand. She can't stop staring, even when Papi clears his throat and says, "Jasmine, look at me."

She gazes down his right leg. Something is wrong. Part of it . . . part of it is missing.

"Up here," he says.

She obeys, finds his eyes, and there are glassy tears in them.

"You should have seen the other guy."

Jasmine grins at that. *That* is her papi. She moves closer quickly, her impulse to hug him, but then she stills. How? How can she hug him like this?"

"Ay, Edgar, ¿qué te pasó?" Mami asks, her words quivering.

This time, he glances over at Yolanda, then nods. She smiles. "Thank you, Mr. Garza," she says. "Let me help you."

Then she turns to Jasmine and Mami. "He was rear-ended on the highway while at a complete stop. There's a lot of damage, and we'll be prepping him for surgery soon for . . ."

She stops. Looks down at his leg—or where his leg should be—and then presses her lips together.

But Jasmine is observant, just like her papi, so she already knows what has been left unsaid.

"I'll be okay," says Papi. "They're coming to take me soon, and the doctors are going to fix everything up, I promise."

There's a stone in Jasmine's throat instantly. "Papi," she says. "Are you sure?"

He nods, then looks over toward the far corner. "La chaqueta, Aida," he says.

Mami rushes over to the blue denim jacket draped over a chair, and Jasmine tries not to pay attention to the red stains all over it.

"The front pocket," he says. "Dámela."

She reaches in and pulls out a gold chain, and it glitters in the bright lights of the room. Mami then turns to hand it to him, tears streaked down her face, and he shakes his head.

"Es para Jasmine," he says.

"What?" She wipes at her face. "For me?"

"I've been meaning to give it to you, and why not now? It'll give you strength and protect you, and it will help us both."

She reaches out, and Mami places it in her hand. There's a small heart charm at the end of it.

"I don't understand, Papi," she says. "Why are you giving this to me now?"

"Soon," he says. "This protected people in my family for generations. It's helped me, and now it's your turn. I want you thinking only of my own healing, okay? We'll get through this."

Mami helps Jasmine fasten it around her neck, and she touches the charm after it falls against her chest. It looks old, despite that it still shines. "Thank you, Papi," she says. "I like it."

He smiles through another grimace, and then the nurse says it's time. They have to get him prepped, but Jasmine doesn't want to leave the room. She doesn't want Papi out of sight, and dread stitches itself to all the bones in her chest as Mami tries to lead her away.

"Go, mi amor," Papi says. "I'll be done soon. I promise."

At the doorway, she looks back at him one more time, and he closes his eyes, lies back into the pillow. He looks so very, very tired.

○ ○ ○

They wait in a room for hours and hours.

There are a few other families there. Too many pacing people who make Jasmine nervous. There's a water fountain and a vending machine, and then a bunch of posters about different wards in the hospital, and the lights are giving her a headache.

Her heart races faster than it ever has. Time is crawling by, and every time she glances up at the clock, only a couple of minutes have passed. She just wants to *know*. And when she thinks about Papi—and particularly what he looked like in that bed—her mind spirals from one thought to another. Why is he even in surgery? What are they doing to him? How long is it supposed to take? Why isn't anyone updating them?

What if it doesn't work?

Why did Papi choose this moment to give her the necklace and the charm?

Did he know he wasn't going to make it?

Her thoughts burn in her head, and she hates every second of it. That flame spreads through her, especially in her chest, and she wonders if this is what a heart attack is. It hurts so bad, so she stands up, takes a deep breath, and then *she* is the pacing person in that waiting room.

"Jaz, come sit down," Mami says.

She's going to explode if she sits down. Sweat pours down the back of her neck. There's no end to this, is there? Not until she knows, and she doesn't know.

"Jaz, please," Mami says, and she pats the chair next to her. "I'm sorry we've been waiting so long."

A door opens down the hall. Jasmine turns toward it, and there's a doctor coming her way, his long white coat flowing behind him, but he's got his eyes trained downward. She can see his pale skin and his brown hair, but she can't see his face. When he's close to the waiting room, Jasmine stops.

He looks up at her with green eyes.

A downturned mouth.

Sorrow all over everything.

That's when she knows.

And Jasmine's whole life explodes.

22

When Mami comes to check on her, Jasmine is still curled up in the same spot on the bed. Without a word, her mami helps her up and out of her bedroom. The house is still warm, but it's silent. Tía Selena stands at the opposite end of the hallway, wrapped in a colorful shawl. She leans against the wall, sadness in her frame.

Jasmine ducks into the bathroom because she can't bear to see it anymore. There, she washes her face, then brushes her teeth. When she comes out, Mami is standing off to the side.

"We don't have to talk about anything tonight," she says, her voice gentle like her hugs. "Sleep. Tomorrow will be here, and Selena and I . . . we love you, Jasmine."

"I love you, too," she says, then glances at Tía. "Both of you."

"If anything happens, come get us. We'll deal with it together. En familia."

Jasmine turns away and heads to her room. She changes into some pajamas, then returns to her bed. She pulls her cobija over her head and surrounds herself with darkness. If her shadow ghost thing shows up, she simply won't acknowledge it.

Ever again, if she can help it.

º º º

She sleeps for nearly ten hours, a deep, dreamless rest that she eases out of in the morning. She lies in bed for a while, though, even though she has to use the bathroom, because she's not sure what she'll find in the house.

Are they mad at her?

Will they forgive her?

Has she ruined everything?

She finally pushes herself to her feet. Relieves herself in the bathroom. Washes her hands, then splashes water on her face. When she glances at herself in the mirror, she looks like she hasn't slept at all.

When she walks into the kitchen, Mami and Tía Selena are sitting at the island, both of them sipping at their cafecitos. They glance up at Jasmine, and she expects them to leap up and come to her, but she's pleasantly surprised when they just bid her good morning.

"What time is it?" Jasmine asks.

"Nearly ten," says Mami. "You slept awhile."

"I still feel tired," she says, approaching the island. Tía has an unwrapped tamale in front of her, and Jasmine's stomach rumbles.

"You want one?" Tía asks.

She nods.

Tía gets up and moves her plate to the dining room table. Jasmine shuffles over to it and sits in an empty chair, and Mami sits across from her.

"So," she begins. "Last night. We don't have to talk about it."

"I think I have to," Jasmine says. "I don't know how to fix this."

"Fix what, mija?"

"Everything I broke."

"You didn't break anything, Jaz."

She gives Mami a doubtful look. "My friendship with Jorge and Bea."

"Well, I can't speak for them, but you don't know what they're feeling, do you?"

Jasmine realizes then that she didn't even think to check her phone or plug it in to charge. What if they texted her?

She starts to get up, but Tía places a steaming tamale in front of her, and the smell . . . oh, it's too good to leave this behind.

Tía Selena sits down, then puts a piece of her own tamale in her mouth. She chews for a second. "By the way, my friends think you're amazing."

Jasmine stops blowing on her food. "What? Why?"

"You spoke to a spirit in front of them," she says. "They think you're bold. Unafraid. Both Samira and Justice in particular were impressed."

"Unafraid?" Jasmine scoffs. "I don't know about that."

"You *did* confront a spirit last night," Mami says. "In a room full of people. Maybe you were afraid, mija, but that's still a courageous thing to do." She sighs. "More courageous than I've been the last few years."

"What about your coworkers?" Jasmine asks. "They must think I'm a weirdo."

"I told a little white lie," she says. "Said that despite me warning you not to, you decided to practice your monologue for the school play."

Jasmine is about to put a bite in her mouth when Mami says that. She drops her fork. "Mami, *what?*"

"They think you're a better actor than the leads on our project," she says, a smirk spreading across her face.

"But I don't want to be an actor!"

"They don't need to know that!" Mami crosses her arms. "I know lying can be a bad thing, but I chose to protect you in that moment. Most of those people won't ever see you again, so what does it hurt them?"

Jasmine flushes red. "Mami, you didn't need to do that."

"No, I did," she says. "I need to do more than just listen to you, Jaz. I need to *fight* for you."

"Thank you," she says sheepishly. "But . . . what am I supposed to do?"

"With what?" Tía asks. "The ghosts or your friends?"

She shrugs. "Both?"

Mami stands and heads to the kitchen to get some more coffee. "Well, I think last night was a clear sign we need to be proactive. I already spoke to the Veracruzes. We have to move forward with something because . . . ugh, Jasmine, I never want to see you like that again."

"Okay, but . . . that doesn't help me with Jorge and Bea."

"I know," she says, and she returns to the table. "What part is the hardest? Or makes the least sense?"

Jasmine eats some of her tamale while she thinks. It all feels hard. But then she sets her fork down.

"Why did I say all that?" she asks. "I want to apologize to them—especially to Bea. But . . . why would I be so mean? It's like I became a different person last night. I don't even agree with what I said!"

Mami and Tía exchange a look, but it's not like the secretive one from before. It's almost as if they're asking each other who should answer Jasmine's question.

"Well," Tía says finally, "what do you mean that you don't agree with what you said?"

"We've had parties before," Jasmine says. "You even pointed that out, Mami. Yet last night, I was convinced that was the first party ever, and that I ruined it. I was so sure of that."

Mami rests her chin on her right hand. "You know, sometimes, when we're scared or angry or hurt or sad—any of those emotions, really—it's like our brains can't see anything else. Or it's like our minds are one of those twisted mirrors we used to visit on the boardwalk out in Santa Monica."

Jasmine isn't really sure she understands. "So . . . I couldn't see the truth?"

"Not literally, Jaz." Mami sighs. "Do you remember years ago when I would sometimes lock myself in my bedroom? Right after Papi died?"

Jasmine's heart skips a beat. "Yeah. Of course."

"At the time, I thought I was protecting you. Like so many things, I thought if you weren't exposed to it, you wouldn't experience it. But during those moments, my sadness over Papi was so immense, Jaz, that it was almost like *you* weren't there."

A stone forms in her throat. "How is that possible?"

Mami's crying is soft and quiet. "Oh, mija, it was like . . . losing him so suddenly clouded my everything. It took me months to be able to remind myself that I still had *you*. That I still had something to live for."

Tía reaches over and grabs her sister's hand. Jasmine sees the wetness running down her cheeks. "I remember that," she says. "And I remember how I used to tell you that your life wasn't over, and it was like . . . you literally couldn't believe me."

"But it wasn't over!" Mami says, smiling. "And until I broke through to the other side, I didn't think it was possible."

"This might help you understand, Jasmine," Tía says. "I once had a therapist who said something very profound to me: sometimes, the narrator in our minds isn't telling us the truth."

The words hit her like a truck speeding through The Intersection. She leans back in her chair, and all the thoughts she had last night come spilling back. She thought her world was ending.

"Why, though?" Jasmine asks, choking back tears. "Why would I lie to myself?"

"I don't think it's quite that," says Mami. "Though, to be fair, you probably learned that from the best."

She frowns. "Huh?"

"Me, Jaz. You've watched me lie to myself for *years*. And I feel terrible about it."

"Both of you, stop it," says Tía Selena. "Honesty is good, but we don't need a pity party."

"Selena!"

"Bah!" she spits. "Jasmine, your mind told you what it did because it was trying to protect itself. We all do it, me included!"

"Protect me from what, though?"

"From being hurt again," says Tía. "There's a reason I haven't dated anyone in a long time, amor. I got hurt by someone, and every time I see a gorgeous woman, my mind freezes. It reminds me of what that horrible person did to me, and it puts up all these walls. I only see all the things that once injured me."

"You never told me that," says Mami, her voice low.

"I'm working on it," she says dismissively. "Please don't be hard on yourself, Jasmine. You've been dealing with these ghosts all by yourself, and it happened after you lost your papi. Nothing about your grief is strange or terrible or weird. It's just . . . different. It's always different for everyone."

"I guess," she says. The hole inside her heart grows then. Has she really been that sad all this time?

She thinks about how often she's wondered when she'll get over her papi's death.

She thinks about all the times her sadness felt like a bag of concrete on her chest.

She thinks about the hauntings and how they—

"Oh, my god," she says, and she bolts upright.

"What, Jasmine?" Mami says, and both she and Tía shoot up as well. "Is it happening again?"

"No," she says. "Wait here. I just realized something!"

She tears away from the table, down the hallway, into her bedroom. Rips open the drawer where her notebook is, and then she's holding it high when she returns.

"I wrote it all down," she says, breathless, flipping the cover open. She hasn't written much, so most of it is on the front page.

She reads each entry aloud, even though she can feel Mami's glare when she shares the things she's done at school with the GSA. She has to, though.

Because the truth is staring her in the face.

"Okay," says Mami. "That's a lot. But I knew most of that. Except for that library thing."

"It's fine," she says. "My teachers are okay, and I didn't get in trouble."

"Not my main concern, but sure. So . . . what are you getting at?"

"I'm not following it, either," says Tía Selena.

Jasmine dramatically places her finger on the addition she made to her second entry:

I miss Papi.

They both crowd around her and look.

"Oh, Jaz," says Mami, "I miss him, too."

"No!" she says excitedly. "I took Bea's suggestion seriously, but I didn't *actually* do what she asked me to, which was to record *everything* about each haunting."

She taps the sentence. "Except this time!"

Mami narrows her eyes and tilts her head to the side. "And that means . . . ?"

"Every single time I got sad or thought about Papi, *the ghost showed up*."

Tía Selena clutches her heart. "No," she says. "¿En serio?"

"Every time," says Jasmine. "And I was so lost in my own head, I couldn't see it!"

"Now, Jaz, don't get ahead of yourself," Mami says. "I know that seems like an explanation, but . . . oh, mija, I don't want you to get your hopes up. Papi is *gone*."

"I know," Jasmine says, deflating a bit. She pushes past it, though. "So, let's contact the spirit. Let's find out if it's him or if it's someone else. Either way, I think it can hear me or sense my feelings. It has before, and it definitely did last night."

Tía Selena perks up at that. "¿Qué significa eso?"

"When the spirit shadow followed me to my room, I told it to go away. I said it was ruining my life. *And it listened to me.* It went away immediately!"

"Ay, Dios mío," says Tía Selena. "Aida, what if we have this wrong?"

"Not you, too!" says Mami. "Please, no wild conspiracy theories."

"Not a conspiracy, hermanita. Think about it. What if Jasmine's magic *is* there? What if it just looks different than what we're used to?"

To that, Mami doesn't have a quick reply. She turns and stares at Jasmine for a moment.

"I don't know what is happening to you, mija," she says. "And it's hard. I don't think this is hablador magic, and I hope it isn't the same darkness that took your abuela from me and Selena. Not knowing what this is . . . it scares me, Jaz."

"All the more reason to find out what this ghost or these ghosts want," says Jasmine. "Please. I know you said you already talked to Bea's parents, but I think we need to do this."

She smiles at herself. "En familia."

"Oh, gross," says Mami. "You can't use my line against me! I'm the parent here."

Jasmine sticks her tongue out.

"I'll call them again," she says. "In the meantime, think about what you want to say to your friends."

Jasmine's heart drops like a stone. Right. They're probably still mad.

Or are they? She doesn't know. And she can't know unless she talks to them.

"Okay," she says. "I'll probably wait until tomorrow, though."

"That's a good idea, Jaz," Mami says. "I'm very proud of you. I hope you know that."

And with that, Jasmine decides to wolf down her lukewarm tamale. She'll send a text to the group chat later. But for now, she needs to be with her family.

23

Courage isn't always easy to come by. Despite feeling energized by her time with Mami and Tía Selena, Jasmine stares at the group chat with the GSA while in bed. It hasn't been updated in over a week, and somehow, that makes the task even harder.

But she has to do this.

> Hi, guys. If you're around tomorrow, I would like to talk to you and apologize. I'm really sorry for what I did.

She hits send.

Her heart rate skyrockets.

Seconds later, she sees the three dots—someone is replying—and she panics. She sets her phone to airplane mode.

At first, she's ashamed. Why is she being such a coward about this?

But then she breathes deeply. She's taking one step at a time; she doesn't have to feel everything all at once, and she doesn't have to solve this all at once.

She sets her phone to charge, then pulls her cobija over her.

She'll deal with her friends tomorrow, no matter how they feel. As she struggles to find sleep, she wonders if her theory is real. Does her ghost (ghosts?) actually hear her? Can they sense her? Her moods? Her feelings? Her desires? Is it possible that she *can* communicate with them in some crude way?

Now is not the time to test it, though. As hard as it is, she tries not to think about Papi, tries not to bring on her sadness. She tries to be in this very moment.

And not long after that, she falls into a dreamless slumber.

∘ ∘ ∘

Jasmine doesn't find Bea and Jorge before school.

They're not in the library, and Mr. Winters is so busy that he barely acknowledges Jasmine when she rushes in. She suffers through her first four classes before the lunch bell for eighth graders rings.

The cafeteria is a quick jaunt away, and Jasmine stands at the entrance. Somehow, she doesn't care if the other kids look her way or make comments. Turns out that when you hurt your friends, *that* pain stings more than any social anxiety could.

She sees them in the usual spot on the other side of the room.

And it looks like Jorge left a spot beside him.

Even though her heart leaps at the sight, she doesn't stop. She strides over to the table and sits with her friends who both look . . . well, a little sick. Jorge appears to have put on the first thing he found that morning. She hasn't ever seen him wear sweatpants to school. His oversized Lady Gaga shirt is wrinkled on the front. Bea has her SHE/HER enamel pin on the lapel of her denim jacket, and it's the only bit of flair she's wearing. Her normally bright hair is tucked completely under her beanie, and she has no dramatic makeup, either.

It's enough to confirm Jasmine's worst fears, but still, she presses on.

She has to.

"Hi," she says, knowing that this isn't going to be easy. "Thank you."

"Okay, so we forgive you!" Jorge blurts out.

"Jorge!" Bea says, scowling at him. "You couldn't wait a second to let her talk?"

"Forgive me?" she says. "I wasn't even going to ask for that. I just wanted to say I'm sorry."

Both of them look away from her for a moment, and Jasmine decides to keep going.

"I don't want to make excuses for being so mean to both of you," she says. "It didn't matter that I was scared and overwhelmed. I shouldn't have made fun of your fears, Jorge, and I shouldn't have pushed you so hard, Bea. I'm so sorry."

"I know," says Jorge, sighing. "Me and Bea . . . we talked about something you said."

"You said I always have some sort of secret I'm keeping from you," says Bea. "And . . . we did treat you like that at the start. And then I kept treating you that way."

"We didn't know if you'd think we were a couple of weirdos," adds Jorge.

Jasmine raises an eyebrow. "I mean . . . you *are* both weirdos."

"I accept that," says Bea. "Proud weirdo."

"Me, too," says Jorge.

"The thing is . . ." Bea hesitates, then takes Jorge's hand across the table. "It's not that I didn't want to tell you about my brother. In fact, Jorge started pushing me to right after you told us about your papi."

She gasps. "Really?"

"I thought you might like knowing," Jorge says.

She lowers her gaze. "I would have," she says softly.

"But . . . can you understand that it's hard to talk about him?"

"Of course!" Jasmine says, looking back to Bea. "I'm not mad or disappointed in you. Again, I shouldn't have pushed you to tell me a secret. It isn't fair. I only told you mine when I felt comfortable."

"I won't let Mom change Ramon's room."

Bea says it in a rush, then wipes at her face. "That's what the room is in my house. The one with the closed door. I keep feeling like if we change it, then he's really gone. He'll never come back."

"We kept a lot of my abuelo's stuff," says Jorge. "It makes my papi feel closer to him."

Then he sighs. "And me, too."

Jasmine pulls the charm out from under her shirt and holds it up delicately. "I keep this on all the time. Papi gave this to me the day he passed. I haven't taken it off since, even when Mami says it's getting gross. I just . . . can't."

"Look at us," says Bea. "Three eighth graders, one big mess."

All three of them burst into laughter. "That should be the tagline for the GSA," says Jasmine.

"Which is still on the case," says Bea. "You know, if you still want us there this upcoming weekend."

"Do you think we can do it by then?" Jasmine asks. "I had an epiphany, and I think making contact is the best way forward."

She tells them about her notebook and how she realized that she'd been leaving her emotions out of the descriptions. Bea is practically floating by the end of it.

"Wow, don't be too proud of yourself," Jorge says.

"I mean, when I'm right, I'm right!"

"You definitely suggested the best thing for me," says Jasmine.

Bea's joy evaporates. "I wish my parents knew that," she grumbles.

Jasmine glances at Jorge. "Can I ask about them? Because I noticed something weird when I went over there."

"Oh," says Jorge. "They can be . . . kinda intense, right?"

"Yeah. And they talk over you a lot, Bea."

Bea nods. "My parents have always believed in the supernatural," she continues. "But after Ramon died, they threw themselves into it. Formed their company. Started taking clients. And . . . it feels like they forgot about me."

"Forgot about you?"

"I can do all this, too," she says. "I can contribute. I was the one who found out what used to be on the lot your house is on now. But they still see me as, like . . . an assistant. Not a daughter."

"Honestly, I think they're sad, too," says Jorge. "Papi started going to church more after Abuelo died, and sometimes, me and Dad wouldn't see him for days. So maybe that's why they focus so much on work."

"Ugh," Jasmine groans. "Why don't we ever talk about this stuff? Secrets only make it worse."

"Because it hurts," Bea says plainly.

It's all the same problem, isn't it? Jasmine thinks. No one says what they're really feeling. No one talks about what's really happening.

Has it ever helped any of them?

"Well, then let's stop hiding stuff from each other," says Jasmine. "I promise not to again. It made me resent you, too, and I don't want that."

"Deal," Jorge says, extending a hand to the middle of the table.

Bea puts hers on top of it. "Deal."

Jasmine is last. "Gay Supernatural Alliance, back in business."

There's not much time left in lunch, so the three of them dart over to the serving counter to get food. She is thankful at how great the relief feels. It's as if she's been plucked out of a terrible darkness, one she could not see a way out of an hour earlier.

She sets her tray down on the table, but before she eats, she watches Bea and Jorge argue over whose dad has the worst jokes. One thought of many swirling around in her head feels the biggest: Jasmine Garza actually made some friends.

○ ○ ○

Even though Jasmine is eager to update Mami and Tía Selena about her apologies to Jorge and Bea, she attends one last emergency meeting of the Gay Supernatural Alliance in the library after school on Monday. Bea thought it best they go over some things a final time. However, she's met with a surprise once she gets there.

"I want to sit in on your meeting," Mr. Winters announces, coming out from behind the circulation desk. "I think I'm allowed to, given that you keep using my library."

Jorge and Bea stare at the librarian with mouths wide open. Jasmine, however, is smiling. "I'm down if y'all are," she says. "The more, the merrier."

"Besides," Mr. Winters adds, pulling up a chair, "I am also very, very gay, so I definitely belong here."

Jorge snaps a finger. "Yaasss! We love that."

"I don't know," says Bea, narrowing her eyes at him. "How can we trust you?"

"Well, I haven't reported you for dumping salt all over one of my rooms. Or recording in here without permission. Or for whatever weird, chaotic rituals you all seem to be conducting in here every week. That sounds pretty trustworthy to me."

Jasmine actually laughs at that. "Oh, you're fun, Mr. Winters."

"Plus, I've never actually eavesdropped on any of your meetings because I'm a good librarian. So . . . what exactly do you talk about?"

Bea still has suspicion all over her face. "Uh . . . you know. Typical GSA stuff."

"Like what?" He smiles wide.

"Like . . ." Bea looks at Jorge in panic. "Why don't you read back some of the notes from previous meetings, Jorge? He's our secretary."

He frowns at Bea. "I don't actually take notes."

"Well, can't you all remember one thing you normally talk about?" the librarian asks.

"Ghosts," Jasmine blurts out.

"Ghosts?" says Mr. Winters.

"Ghosts," confirms Jorge, smiling awkwardly.

"We're the Gay Supernatural Alliance," explains Jasmine, and she pushes on because she doesn't feel nervous about this anymore. "Kind of a dual-purpose club."

"I remember ghosts coming up the other week when things went haywire, but we didn't really talk about it." He crosses his right leg over his left, then places his hands atop his knee. "Well, let's chat, then."

"Are you serious?" asks Bea.

Mr. Winters throws his hands up. "Something has been happening in my library, no?"

"It might be haunted," Bea says cautiously. "Depends on your definition of haunted."

"Are there *other* definitions?"

Bea lays the suspicion on thicker. "How do I know you aren't working for any anti-ghost groups?"

"Those exist?" asks Jasmine, and Jorge shrugs at her.

"Well, I have a personal stake in all of this," says Mr. Winters, and he uncrosses his legs and leans forward. "I think I know who is haunting this place."

"Impossible," says Bea. "Our rigorous investigation has produced no conclusive information!"

"Plus," says Jasmine, "we kinda think that places might not be haunted. People are."

"And that person would be Jasmine," adds Jorge. "Cuz . . . well, *she's* haunted."

"I . . . don't understand that," says Mr. Winters.

"Wait." Bea leans forward. "You said you knew who might be haunting this place."

Mr. Winters sighs, and Jasmine watches his body change. He leans his head back, and when he looks at the three of them, his eyes are red.

"It might be my husband," he says. "He died a few years ago, and I know this sounds silly—"

"Nothing in the realm of the supernatural sounds silly," Bea says.

He smiles. "Fair. But . . . that thing with the bookshelves and Mx. Chen. *That* felt like something he used to do."

Bea reaches into her jean jacket for her notepad, then hesitates. She glances over at Jasmine and smiles, and Jasmine gets it: Bea is choosing to be in the moment, rather than perform the role of investigator.

It's a start.

"Why do you say that, Mr. Winters?" Jorge asks.

"He was always so clumsy," says Mr. Winters, and he gazes upward. "Running into counters, dropping mugs and plates, and once, he knocked one of these bookshelves clean over. Thankfully, it didn't cause a domino effect, but it was a disaster. It was like he had no idea how physical space worked."

Jasmine gulps loudly. "But what if it *isn't* him?" she asks.

The side of his mouth curls up in a short, sad smile. "I think I choose to believe that's what is going on because it means he's still here in some way. Even if it's just him running into shelves or dropping books, maybe that's his way of letting me know I haven't been forgotten."

"That sounds nice," says Jorge.

"But what if—" Jasmine begins.

Mr. Winters raises a hand. "Like I said. Sounds silly."

"It doesn't," she says quietly.

"Well, think of it this way. We all have to lose the people we love in our lives. There's no way around it. So we develop stories or habits in order to make peace with that. Do any of you do something like that?"

The three of them are quiet, despite sharing a pained look with one another.

Mr. Winters nods. "Sounds like that's a yes," he says. "This is my thing, then. When I find a whole stack of books toppled over, or when the entire roll of paper towels has been unrolled, I think it's Keondre. And it allows me to keep living and not spend all my time sad about losing him."

Heat rises to Jasmine's face. Is that what she's been doing all these years? Spending time being sad and refusing to move on? How many times has she refused to try to make a friend? How many times has she kept the truth to herself to not upset others? How often does she beg her papi to talk to her again?

Maybe Mr. Winters is right. Maybe he's been talking to her in his own way.

"Enough of my little therapy session," says the librarian, standing up. "I should actually leave you alone to conduct your meeting. I'm closing up at four thirty, though, okay?"

They all agree to be out by then, and then Mr. Winters heads to the front of the library. Jasmine can hear him organizing books as the group sits in silence.

"No more secrets," Jasmine finally mutters. "I know we agreed on that before, but I think we really can't bottle this stuff up anymore."

"Amen," says Jorge.

Bea rubs her hands together. "So, let's go over the ritual one more time . . ."

24

The one thing that makes Jasmine more nervous than anything else is how quiet her home and school are.

After such a relentless stream of hauntings, Jasmine's ghosts do nothing for the remainder of the week. No trash cans vaulted her way. No creaking in her house. No objects spilling out of cabinets and closets.

No horrifying shadow spirits spilling out of the walls.

She thinks she should be comforted by this, but it only sets her on edge. Why is the silence happening *now*? Why have her ghosts chosen to go away?

Doubt creeps in. Maybe she isn't a nexus. Maybe she doesn't have magic at all. Maybe this attempt at communicating with the spirits isn't going to work.

Maybe maybe maybe maybe.

○ ○ ○

Tía Selena catches her zoning out on the green couch after school in the middle of the week. She plops down next to her. "What's on your mind, Jasmine?"

She sighs. "Everything."

"Okay. Share one thing with me."

"How do you still believe when you don't have magic?" she asks.

"Well." Tía shifts on the couch. "Coming in fast and hard today."

"Sorry!" Jasmine exclaims, then curls up next to her. "My

brain feels like it's being shaken every five minutes, Tía. I should be excited about this weekend, but instead, I'm questioning everything."

"Ask the questions, then! Let's find out what the answers might be."

"What if I'm not a nexus?"

"Did you think you were a nexus before a week ago?"

She frowns. "Well . . . no."

"So you already know how to live life *not* as a nexus, right?"

"I feel like that was a trick question."

"You asked it, not me!"

Jasmine grumbles. "Fine. What if I don't have magic?"

"Well—"

"You're gonna say, 'Well, did you think you had magic before?'"

"Your words, not mine."

"Oh, I don't like this game."

Tía Selena laughs. "It's not a game. But I am trying to get you to see how your mind might be overstating how big all of this feels. Your world isn't going to end this weekend, Jasmine. It might change, but hasn't it changed a lot already?"

"Yeah," she says. "Maybe too much, though."

Tía loops an arm around her and pulls her closer. "I understand that. I think you and your Mami have had a lot of change since Papi died. So it makes sense you want things to calm down."

"Exactly!" Jasmine says. "Could everything pause for like a decade? That would be nice."

"But change can be really fun and exciting, right?"

"Nope. Never is."

"Well, you made two new friends, didn't you?"

Jasmine squirms in Tía's embrace. "I mean . . . yeah."

"And you had the courage to tell Mami and me about what you're going through."

"Sure."

"And I'm here now, and that's a big change."

"Ugh!" she groans. "How did this end up being one of your traps *again*?"

Tía's laughter fills the living room. "You must always be on guard around me!"

"Canceled! I cancel you!"

"That's my answer, by the way," she says. "To your question about belief."

"That you're a trap?"

"No, Jasmine," Tía says, feigning irritation. "It's that the world is constantly changing. For me, belief is a choice. I choose to believe in spirits, in the power of crystals, in sage, in practices not just from the village I came from, but that I've learned since moving here to California. It makes the world richer. It makes it easier to deal with change."

"But why is there so much change in my life right now?"

Tía shifts in place. "Are you familiar with how sacred a crossroads is?"

"A crossroads?" Jasmine shakes her head. "I don't know what you mean."

"A crossroads can be literal—a place where important avenues and ways meet—or it can be metaphorical. It sounds like you have a lot of big choices to make that could change your life again. But the crossroads . . . it's powerful. It's a chance for you to take control of your life and twist it into what you want."

"I guess," she says, not certain she understands.

"I think after this weekend, you'll get to decide what to believe about your ghosts and what magic means to you. Even if you don't have any literal magic."

She boops Jasmine's nose. "Because you're magical to me, mija."

Jasmine groans again and slides out of Tía's arms. "Why are you and Mami so cheesy?"

"Deal with it!" Tía says. "It's not going away anytime soon, and neither am I."

"I'm glad you're here," Jasmine says softly.

"Me, too, Jasmine."

Jasmine rests her head on Tía Selena's shoulder. She makes a choice then, that, at the very least, she can choose to believe in her family.

25

Early on Saturday morning, the day they're supposed to contact Jasmine's ghosts, the peace ends. Jasmine wakes up to a torrent of noise. She bolts upright in bed and hears a persistent but irregular knocking. There's some light spilling in through the window, and she rubs her eyes so they adjust faster.

The knocking becomes a pounding.

"Jasmine?" Mami's voice is pitched high. "Jasmine, is that you?"

"No!" she cries out, then throws her cobija off her. "Please, would I ever be that loud?"

She rushes to her door and flings it open. Mami is there, her hair wrapped up above her head and her eyes wide.

Something pounds on the wall toward the kitchen.

"Mija, have you ever experienced this before?" Mami asks.

"Not since Samantha," she says.

"Ay, que ruidosa!" Tía Selena calls out from Mami's bedroom. She emerges and Jasmine clamps a hand over her mouth to stop a gasp.

"What?" says Tía.

"Tía, what's going on with your hair?"

It appears to be standing out in every direction, which Jasmine hadn't known was even possible. Had Tía been shocked during the night?

"Selena, are you feeling okay?" Mami asks.

The knocks ring out again.

Tía reaches up and gingerly touches her hair. "Oh, no," she says. "That's not supposed to do that."

And then she reaches over and lays her pointer finger on Mami's arm.

A small spark leaps from one woman to the other and Mami yelps. "Selena, stop!"

"Oh, this *energy*," says Tía, her voice far too gleeful for this early in the morning. "Something is happening now!"

KNOCK KNOCK KNOCK KNOCK KNOCK

"Something?!" says Mami. "Meaning what?"

KNOCK KNOCK

Suddenly, the pounding on the walls races toward the three of them, and Jasmine can't help screaming as it passes all around them, a fury of sound. Mami clutches her and—

It's over.

Mami huffs and puffs next to Jasmine. "What was that?" she says.

"Hmph." Tía crosses her arms. "Guess the spirits are getting excited. Wish they would leave my hair alone!"

She trudges back into the main bedroom. Mami shakes her head, then clicks her tongue against her teeth. "I don't like this. Not one bit."

After planting a kiss on Jasmine's forehead, Mami heads back to her room to continue getting ready. Jasmine lies in her bed, wide awake, waiting.

"Is that you, Papi?" she asks, her charm cold against her neck. "Are you behind all of this?"

Nothing happens.

o o o

But it continues.

o o o

Mami is making huevos rancheros—the real kind, not the ones with no flavor that are in the trendy restaurants in

Hollywood—when one of the cabinets flies open. Thankfully, Mami isn't in front of it when some of the plastic tumblers fall out and bounce along the floor. She darts over and shuts it, and Jasmine's heart leaps when she hears more cups and plates banging against the inside of it.

Like they're trying to get out.

Tía Selena merely seems pleased. "It's almost time," she says, grinning.

Jasmine isn't comforted by that. But she heads to the bathroom to get ready, hoping that her ghosts at least leave her alone while she showers.

○ ○ ○

The sounds continue: Pounding. Creaking. Groaning. Doors slamming shut or flinging open so fast they bang. There's no pattern to them throughout the day, but Jasmine finally can't take it anymore. The front door flings open at one point, and she groans.

"That's enough," she says. "Mami, I'm going for a walk, okay?"

"Don't go far," Mami says.

Jasmine heads outside and feels instant relief in the warm sunshine of Los Angeles. Her mami stands on the stoop behind her.

"If anything gets weird, come right home."

Jasmine holds up a peace sign in response.

Her head is overflowing with thoughts as she walks down the sidewalk. She sees a couple on the other side of the street, walking hand in hand with a border collie leading them on a long leash. She wonders if anyone else knows how strange the world is. Is it just her and her friends and her family?

She thinks of her conversation with Mr. Winters from Monday.

Do any of them talk about how hard it is to lose someone?

She doesn't realize it until she is a block away from Carl that she's been walking the exact path to school. His playing is slow and mournful that morning, and she's never heard this particular melody before. She stands and watches him for a while before he lowers his saxophone and bows at her. "Good afternoon, young lady," he says. "It's a beautiful Saturday, isn't it?"

"Yeah," she says, not sure she wants to agree given what her morning has been like. But she does look around at the neighborhood—at the people rushing in and out of the hospital across the street, at the butterflies that fly by, at the sun that beams down on them—and it *is* a beautiful day.

"That was yours," Carl says.

"What was?"

"The song," he explains. "A fair trade, remember?"

Her face flushes. She'd forgotten about that! "Thank you, Carl," she says. "It was gorgeous."

"Where you headed?" he asks while polishing his sax. "And where's your momma?"

"I'm just on a walk. Tryin' to clear my head."

"I feel that." He puts the saxophone up to his lips and blows out a long, sweet melody. "This helps. It's my walk, so to speak."

He returns to playing, and Jasmine marvels at how quickly he appears to get lost in his music. It's not just that he doesn't seem to notice her standing there anymore; the whole neighborhood has slipped into the background. All that matters is what he's playing.

She is about to turn back when she sees a flicker.

A flicker of darkness.

Jasmine nearly stumbles as a shadow spirit slowly pours out of the end of Carl's saxophone. He plays harder, faster, deep in the melody, and it oozes forth.

"No," she mutters under her breath. "Not now!"

She turns and runs back to her house. She's breathless when she bursts in the front door, and both Mami and Tía Selena stare at her with wide eyes.

"Mija?" says Mami. "Did something happen?"

She nods then quickly explains what she witnessed.

This time, Tía doesn't grin. "This is escalating," she says, her tone grave.

"Do you think they know?" Jasmine asks. "That we're going to try to talk to them tonight?"

Mami throws a dishrag into the sink forcefully. "Well, then I hope they actually speak up this time! Because this is getting out of hand."

She looks upward. "Do you hear that, spirits? This is the Garza household, not yours! Go somewhere else!"

There's a creak in the back of the house, and then . . . nothing.

"Period," Jasmine says.

The sisters laugh, but Jasmine's nerves flare. She really hopes Mami is right.

26

If Jasmine didn't know better, she would think the gathering at 4678 La Mirada Avenue was another big party, not a séance.

That was the word Mrs. Veracruz used when she arrived with her daughter and husband in tow that evening, both of them carrying large plastic containers overflowing with supplies. The Barreras followed after them moments later, all three of them carrying glass dishes and plates covered in aluminum foil. Jorge had a Ziploc full of cookies that he said would need a few minutes in the oven before they were perfect.

The kitchen comes to life as Jasmine's family and Mustache Barrera fall into Spanish. Jasmine is mostly fluent, but this is *way* too fast for her, and they also constantly speak over the end of one another's sentences. Who can even pay attention to that?!

She wanders over to the living room, where Bea's parents are setting up. She can't really grasp what they're saying, either. She hears that word again: "séance."

But what does that actually mean? She knows about the salt, the candles, the incense. Bea explained it all. She knows that they'll all have to unite their minds in one goal. She knows that sometimes, these things don't even work.

And yet, none of that provides any comfort to Jasmine's frayed nerves.

Jorge joins her, nudging her with his shoulder as he does.

"I talked to my dads about what I have been feeling about mi abuelo," he says.

"Really? What did they say?"

"It was hard," Jorge says. "Papi didn't want to admit how sad he's been, and it scared him how obvious it was to me and Dad. But we had a good conversation, and I told them about how you saw a spirit in the house, so there's a chance it might be Abuelo."

"Wow," says Jasmine. "That's . . . that's amazing."

"Thanks for giving me the courage, Jasmine."

She laughs. "Is this where I say something super corny about you having the courage inside you all along?"

Jorge sticks his tongue out at her. "I'm serious, Jasmine!"

"I know," she says. "And I'm proud of you. I really am. Is that why they decided to come?"

"Yeah. I don't think Papi has a lot of hope, but he didn't want to ignore the chance to speak with Abuelo in case it did work. He's the religious one, anyway. His church doesn't really like all this supernatural stuff."

"Wait. If your dad isn't religious, then why is he here?"

"He told me he wants to keep an open mind," says Jorge. "Said it couldn't hurt to at least try, you know?"

"I hope it doesn't hurt," she says softly.

He slips his fingers between hers. "We're all going to be here. No one is getting hurt."

"I know. I guess it's hard for me to not worry about this. What if it doesn't work? What if all these spirits keep showing up forever?"

"Let's not think of forever," says Mami from behind her, startling Jasmine when she speaks.

"Were you spying on us?" Jasmine asks.

"No, not at all. Just came to see the progress."

"Your mami is right," says Mrs. Veracruz. "I know this is very overwhelming, but the supernatural is not really something to fear."

"Well, not this kind," says Mr. Veracruz. "Those things out in Topanga we saw last—"

"Not the time, José!"

He smiles sheepishly at Jasmine and Mami. "You'll be fine."

"Truly not as comforting as you think, José," says Mami. "But I believe you."

Bea starts setting up candles around the room, lighting each one as she goes. "We have to get the space just right," she tells Jasmine. "The mood and energy are very important."

"Okay," she says. "I trust you guys."

"Plus," says Bea, "if anything starts to get weirder than usual, we're stopping it."

"What counts as 'weirder than usual'?" Jasmine asks.

"Pretty weird," Mr. Veracruz says gleefully.

Bea must get that from him, she thinks.

When the Veracruzes have assembled the space correctly, they invite everyone to sit in the Garzas' living room.

Their coffee table has been moved to the center of the room as a focal point. Jasmine, Mami, and Tía Selena decide to sit on the side nearest Papi's old couch. Mrs. Veracruz assures them that being close to something meaningful to the deceased can help.

All of the white candles are lit, and on the table are various items that are supposed to increase the odds of success; multiple sticks of incense are lit. A bag of salt sits next to a couple violet-colored crystals, and they're both alongside a spirit board.

"They usually call these things—" Bea begins.

"We think Ouija boards have a bad connotation," says Mrs. Veracruz, oblivious to how quickly Bea deflates with the interruption. "Spirit boards are used all over the world and in different languages to help act as a medium."

Jasmine nods at Bea, hoping she gets the message. *Speak up!*

Bea opens her mouth, but doesn't get a chance to talk.

"Normally, we ask for photos of the people who have passed on," says Mr. Veracruz. "But since we don't know the identity of any of these spirits, we have to use other means to connect to them."

"And the candles?" Mami asks.

"To provide something to guide the spirits to this place!" Bea spits out. Her mom glares at her, but she presses on. "It's light. Warmth. Something to remind them of the world of the living."

"Oooh, I love that," says Tía Selena. "We used candles a lot for funeral processions in Tunapa."

"I remember that," says Jorge's papi. "Those things used to last for hours."

"Well, we're glad you both decided to join us," Mami says to the Barreras. Then she looks around the room. "That goes for everyone. It's been a very strange journey for us, and I'm happy Jasmine helped push me into accepting your assistance."

She leans her head onto Mami's shoulder. "Thank you," she whispers.

"Te amo, mija."

Mrs. Veracruz asks to turn off all the lights and Tía hops up to oblige. The room is dropped mostly into darkness, but the candles provide a soft, soothing glow. Tía sits back down, and then silence falls.

Bea's mom clears her throat. "In order to help the spirits that reside in this place reach our realm," she begins, "it's imperative that we *all* open our minds. We are all from different belief systems. We all have different backgrounds and different experiences. But we need to be united now. Any negative or skeptical energy will just make it harder for the spirits to communicate."

Doubt floods into Jasmine. She wants to believe more than anything. Shouldn't it be easy for her? She knows ghosts are real. She's seen them! Heard them! Felt them!

But she still isn't sure this is going to work. What can candles, crystals, and a spirit board do that she hasn't tried? She's been begging the universe for help for years, and it's ignored her the whole time. Why would it suddenly grant her wish now?

Mami reaches down and grabs her hand. "Calmate, mija," she whispers gently. "I can feel you squirming."

Tía Selena's hand finds Jasmine's other.

"En familia," she says.

In the candlelight, Jorge and Bea, sitting alongside one another, smiling in her direction.

She's not alone.

And she has to *try*.

She imagines that her mind and her heart are a doorway, and she's turning the handle. Pushing the door outward. There is a darkness on the other side of it, but it's a darkness of unknowing.

She has to let it in.

"Good," says Mrs. Veracruz. "If everyone is ready, I'd like us all to join hands."

There's a rustling as the group moves to hold hands, and Jasmine squeezes her family's hands tighter.

"I'd like you all to imagine an energy," Mrs. Veracruz continues. "A ball of shadowy darkness, since that's what Jasmine has been seeing. Imagine that here. Focus on it."

Jasmine closes her eyes. She thinks about the shadows she has seen all over the neighborhood, and imagines them as one shifting ball, almost like a flock of birds.

"We welcome any and all spirits that might be close," says Mrs. Veracruz. "You are welcome here. You belong here. If you'd like to make your presence known, we will accept it."

The room is quiet, though Jasmine is certain they can all hear her galloping heartbeat.

She waits. Wonders if she'll hear the spirit in the home. Anticipates the creaking and the groaning.

Nothing.

More silence.

She opens her eyes. Everyone else has theirs closed, and she frowns. The spirit is choosing this moment to keep to themselves? She touches her charm and sends out a message: *Papi, if you can hear me, please. Please talk to us.*

○ ○ ○

There's nothing.

○ ○ ○

"Any spirits," Mrs. Veracruz continues. "Anyone who is here, you are welcomed. We will listen."

○ ○ ○

Nothing.

○ ○ ○

"If you—"

○ ○ ○

She feels them.

The hairs rise all over her body, along with the bumps. She sucks in a deep breath and her eyes shoot open.

"Someone's here," she says.

The others quickly open their eyes and look around the room. Jasmine lets go of Tía and Mami.

"Please keep the circle closed," says Mrs. Veracruz, but Jasmine ignores her. She stands up, and as soon as she does, the knocks return.

They're the same ones she heard that morning, though they're coming from the back of the house.

"Are you expecting anyone?" asks Bald Barrera, casting a nervous look upon his husband, who is now gripping a rosary and praying with his free hand. "Xavier, it's going to be okay."

"Yeah, Papi," says Jorge. "They won't hurt us."

Bea and Jasmine share a look of both shock and pride. *He's facing his fears!* Jasmine thinks.

There's a loud crash in the kitchen. Jasmine leaves the circle and darts to the entrance to the dining room. She watches in horror as multiple cabinets swing open in the kitchen. Another bowl falls from one of the cupboards and smashes on the floor.

"Mami!" she calls out. "It's happening again!"

The ceiling groans above Jasmine, and she freezes. She slowly looks up, half expecting to see a shadow, but there's nothing there. A long *crreeeeeeaaaakkk* rips out, and then it moves across the ceiling, as if someone is walking around above them.

Mustache Barrera prays faster and louder.

"Is this normal, Helena?" Mami asks.

"Normal?" Mrs. Veracruz scoffs. "Hardly anything is normal in the world of the supernatural."

"But no," adds Mr. Veracruz, his voice wavering. "The circle is broken. This shouldn't be happening."

The front door flies open.

A couple books from a shelf in the living room float off of it, then drop to the ground.

Jasmine looks to her family, but even Tía Selena looks freaked out.

"Maybe we should stop this," Mami says. "It's getting out of hand."

"Like I said, we *did* stop it," says Mr. Veracruz, and now he's standing, the bag of salt in his hand. "We could create a protective circle for us . . ."

"Leave it, José." Mrs. Veracruz rises and then pulls a digital camera from her pocket. "We need to document this."

Another crash rings out in the back of the house.

"Mom, maybe we shouldn't," says Bea. "I think we should help them first."

"It's a case, honey. This is what we do!"

Mrs. Veracruz raises the camera and switches it on, and then the house responds.

The knocking returns, and it races toward the living room. Mami yelps as the knocking swirls around them, and it turns into pounding, as if closed fists are being banged on the walls.

Everyone is wearing panic on their faces, except for Mrs. Veracruz, who spins as she films the candlelit room. "This footage is good," she says. "And the mic on this is very high quality, so we should pick up any ambient sounds we can't quite hear."

"Not if you're talking, dear," says Mr. Veracruz.

"Mom, Dad, please!" Bea yells.

All at once, the candles in the room go out, and silence falls once again. Jasmine steadies herself as dizziness sweeps through her.

Something is happening.

And a new thought appears, and it terrifies her: *Someone is coming.*

She turns and glances down the hallway. The whole house is dark now, but she can still see it. It's darker than darkness.

A shadow spirit.

They drift slowly down the hallway, and Jasmine's stomach drops. They look enormous, stretching from the floor to the ceiling, and then the spirit oozes forward.

Bea is at her side immediately. "You see something, don't you?" she says.

Jasmine nods, then points down the hallway. "One of them," she says. "They're here."

"Them?" Bald Barrera moves to stand behind Jasmine. "I don't see anything."

"Only she can see them, Dad," says Jorge. "We don't know why."

She takes a step toward the shadow.

"Jaz, what are you doing?" Mami says. "Come here."

"Mami, I have to find out," Jasmine says. "I have to know what they want."

"What they want?" Mami crosses the room, then flicks on the lights in the living room. "We don't know what this is. Let's not jump into anything."

Jasmine takes another step, and the shadow continues drifting closer. "It's not the same, Mami! This isn't what happened to Abuela Griselda."

"You don't know that. I don't want you to be taken like she was."

"Aida, she has to try," says Tía Selena. "What if this is our only chance to reach Edgar?"

"We're right here," says Jorge's dad, and he lays a hand on Jasmine's shoulder. "We can *all* protect her from . . . well, I don't actually know."

"We'll do it," says his husband. "Whatever it takes."

"I'll be fine," Jasmine says, more a message to herself than to her mami. She stands taller and stares down the hallway. "I'm ready to listen, spirit. Whoever you are, you're welcome here."

She's not sure that's the right thing to say, but maybe mimicking Mrs. Veracruz isn't such a bad idea. So Jasmine holds in place, opening herself to the spirit in the hallway.

"Please," she says, touching her charm, wishing so desperately for her papi's help. "Just tell me what you want."

It happens so fast that she barely has time to react.

The shadow rushes forward, no longer like they're a dark blob of maple syrup, but as if they're made of the wind. In the blink of an eye, they float directly in front of her.

It's just . . . *darkness*. Swirling, pulsating darkness. She sees no features, nothing to indicate that there's a human soul within this. The terror spikes again: What if she's got this all wrong? What if none of these shadows are human?

But she presses onward.

She *has* to.

Because even if her papi isn't here, he would want her to be strong.

"Hi," she says, and she can feel the eyes of everyone in that room on her. "I'm Jasmine."

The darkness doesn't move. But she knows this darkness—whoever they are—is staring back at her.

"I don't know why you're here, but . . . we live here. My mami and I. And Tía Selena for the time being."

She turns and waves both of them over. Tía joins her without hesitation, but Mami's steps are unsure and frightened.

"They're not doing anything," Jasmine says, glancing briefly at the shadow. "They're just . . . looking at me."

When Mami is on her other side, Jasmine turns back to the shadow. "This is us. We want to live here, and we want to *stay* here. But you make that hard for us sometimes. Is there something you want to tell us?"

The formless shadow moves, much like the one in the corner of Jorge's house did. She looks down and sees the protrusion. It reaches—like an arm without a hand—up and up and up.

And Jasmine's scream is cut off when it wraps around her throat.

27

Jasmine gasps for breath, and she can feel the shadow.

It's cold. Cold and empty and nothing about them feels like a person.

Because this isn't a person at *all*.

She lurches back, and Mami is screaming at her. "What is it, mija?! What's happening?"

Her hands go to her throat and she tries to pull the appendage off, but her hands go right through the shadow. It isn't solid!

There's whispering at her ears, but she can't parse the words. Who is that? What are they saying?

"Stop it!" Mami screams at Mrs. Veracruz. "Make it stop!"

Jasmine falls back, and it's enough to dislodge her from the shadow spirit. She hits the ground hard and her tailbone screams with pain.

All the while, the shadow looms over her.

"Leave us *alone*!" she screams. "If you aren't going to tell us what you want, then go somewhere else!"

Bald Barrera reaches under her arms and helps her upright, and to Jasmine's shock, the shadow doesn't move.

They—or it, she isn't sure anymore—just watch her.

"We can't live!" Jasmine screams, her breath heaving her chest up and down. "We move all the time. I can't make friends. I can't have anyone over. Nothing in my life is normal."

"Mija . . ." says Mami.

"I have to tell them the truth, Mami. Please!"

Mami nods.

Jasmine looks over at Jorge and Bea. Bea nods, too, and Jorge—oh, he's standing so tall. So unafraid.

"Tell them," he says. "Don't back down."

It is the boost she needs.

"Why aren't you my papi?" she says. "Why couldn't you be the one ghost I need?"

She doesn't get a response.

So she chooses to believe that this shadow is human, and that she has some ability to speak with the dead.

"I need you to go," she says, and her eyes fill with tears. "I can't move on. I can't live my life because I keep expecting one of you to be *him*. He's never coming back. Ever. I can't accept that if you stay here."

For a brief moment, the shadow drifts slowly backward. A new appendage grows from it, but this one is smaller, thinner, and it stretches to her, swirling, twisting.

It's a hand.

A hand!

"I see something," she tells the group. "Mami . . . this thing *has* to be a person. There's a hand reaching out to me!"

"Please, mija," Mami begs. "Please be careful."

The hand stretches closer to her.

And it stops just short of . . .

Her charm?

"What?" she says.

She looks down.

There is a finger *pointing at her charm.*

She reaches inside her shirt and pulls it out. "This?"

Mami gasps. "Edgar," she says, her voice light.

"Papi?" His name cracks in Jasmine's throat. "Is that *you*?"

The thread of a shadow drifts ever closer . . .

And then it pulls on the charm.

Jasmine swats it away. "No!" she yells. "It's the best thing I have of him!"

The reaction is instant. There is a horrible groaning in the house, and then Jasmine stumbles as the floor begins to move. Mami dives and catches Jasmine, and someone screams.

Jasmine glances down and can't believe what she's seeing.

There is an opening in the carpet.

Somehow, it has split, and there's a dark crevasse growing in her house, and it is deeper, more terrible than any of the shadow spirits.

"Ay, Dios mio!" says Mustache Barrera.

Jasmine's mouth drops open. "Can you see that?" she yells.

"Yes," he says.

"So can I!" Tía Selena lurches to Jasmine and grasps her. "Oh, *no*."

"What is that?" says Bea. "Mom, Dad, have you ever seen something like this?"

They don't answer. They both stare in shock at the same thing Jasmine is staring at.

From the darkness, multiple shadows are pulling themselves out and oozing onto the carpet. Jorge shouts nonsense and points upward, and Jasmine sees more shadows dripping from the ceiling into the space, each of them formless and always shifting.

"*Those* are what you've been seeing this whole time?" Jorge screams. "Please tell me you're kidding!"

Mrs. Veracruz's camera hangs at her side. "Xavier, this is . . ."

"I know, baby," he says. "We've never seen anything like this."

"It's happening again," Mami says, and she pulls Jasmine back. "Jasmine, stay away from it!"

"What's happening again?" asks Mrs. Veracruz.

"What happened to my mami," she says. "This darkness . . . it took her! I know it!"

More of the shadows spill from the chasm, and they begin to

press together, to merge, to form a much, much larger version of themselves. Mami yanks Jasmine to the right, aiming for the kitchen, but the darkness grows, blocking their path.

"What do we do?" asks Jorge.

The mass of shadows continues to grow.

"What do you want?!" Jasmine screams.

The shadows . . . hesitate.

She can feel them watching her.

And then a new appendage bursts from it, and it stretches toward her. Mami picks up the Ouija board and lets loose a cry as she tries to chop the appendage with it.

It passes right through the darkness.

Which reaches for Jasmine's neck again.

"Oh my god," says Bea. "I get it."

"What?" says Jasmine, panicked. "Get what?"

"Jasmine, they're telling you what they need. It's *you*."

"Me?" She puts her hands up as the arm inches closer. "No, I'm not what they think I am! I'm not an hablador! I don't have anything to give them!"

"It's you," Bea says again. "I've never been so sure of anything!"

"How?" Mrs. Veracruz asks. "If she's a nexus, it doesn't matter who she is. The spirits will simply be drawn to her."

"But it *is* her!" Bea screams. "Jorge and I never found evidence of anything supernatural at school until *she* showed up. She is the key to it all!"

The shadow is so close, and Jasmine's heart is thumping in her throat.

"What do I do?"

A thundering groan hits the house, and the chasm snaps shut. The shadow mass pulls away from her and shivers—

And then it bursts out of the window behind Jasmine, shattering the glass as it does.

28

Mami shields Jasmine from the broken glass as the others cry out. But Jasmine can't focus on that because Bea's words continue to echo in her mind.

It's you.

What if the ghosts know what she was supposed to be? What if they don't know the magic in her family died a long time ago?

Jasmine rears back, then breaks away from her mami. She runs into the kitchen, ignoring what the others are yelling at her, and she heads to the front door, wrenches it open.

She gazes out.

She sees the impossible.

There, sitting over La Mirada Avenue, is a massive, swirling ball of darkness.

Shadows swim within it, and to her horror, she sees more joining them, dripping out of the second-floor window of the house across the street, flying out of cars, floating like smoke up toward the others.

Bea and Jorge nearly collide with Jasmine, then they look up to see the ball of shadows.

"That's . . . terrifying," Bea says.

"What am I supposed to do?" Jasmine asks, stepping outside and onto the stoop. "I don't understand!"

"Bea, explain yourself!" Mr. Veracruz commands as he comes up behind them. "What are you talking about?"

Bea whirls around on her father. "Are you actually going to listen to me?"

He looks shocked. "Bea . . . of course I will."

"You barely do!" she says. "I've been trying to tell you about my theory in this case for weeks, but you and Mom are always interrupting me or putting me down!"

The rest of the adults arrive, but seem unsure what to look at: the darkness or Bea.

"What do you mean by that?" Mrs. Veracruz asks.

"Ever since Ramon died, it's like I don't exist," Bea sobs out. "And then here is this case that falls in my lap, and I do my research and I come up with a theory, and you two won't listen at *all*."

"Bea," Mrs. Veracruz says, her face falling. "Oh, my love, I'm sorry."

But Bea says nothing to her mother. She turns to Jasmine. "Jasmine, I get it now. I threw myself into this case to prove myself to them, and I didn't think how scary this was for you."

She glances up at the swirling shadows, which continue to grow. "But that thing? *You* can solve this. I know it. Because no one makes me feel better about being myself than you."

"What?" says Jasmine.

"You always compliment me," Bea continues. "You care about my pronouns and never make a big deal out of them. You even dressed differently because of me. Do you know how happy that makes me?"

"I always feel safe with you," adds Jorge. "Always."

Bea grabs Jasmine's shoulders. "Talk to them. You're so good at it, Jasmine. Let the shadows do what they need to."

"But what if they take her away?" Mami asks. "What if this is just history repeating itself?"

"Then we'll go, too!" Jorge says proudly. "They can't take all of us, can they?"

"I'm in," says Bea. "We're not afraid."

"Oh, I'm totally afraid," says Jorge. "But there's nothing wrong with that."

Jasmine grabs her friends' hands as her heart patters away in her chest. "Mami? What do you think?"

Tía turns to her sister. "Aida, if they were going to take her, *they already would have*. They haven't. She's right here beside us. And somehow, she's the key to why all these souls are here."

"I can't lose someone else!" Mami yells, then breaks into a sob. "I barely feel like a person after Edgar died. If I lose her, too . . ."

She doesn't finish it, but Jasmine doesn't let her. She lets go of her friends and plows into Mami, wraps her arms around her, her own throat heavy with sadness.

"I'm not going anywhere," she says. "I don't want to go anywhere. I want to be here with you."

She pulls away. "But we can't live like this anymore. We are nothing but secrets and sadness, and I'm so tired. I want something else, Mami. *Please*."

Mami wipes at her face. "Okay, but when did you start sounding like such a grown-up?"

"Los jovenes," says Mustache Papi, shaking his head. "They are way too smart these days."

His husband laughs. "I was fully a himbo as a teenager."

"What's a himbo?" Jorge asks. "Actually . . . never mind. Can we deal with the ghost thing first?"

Mami squeezes Jasmine's hand. "En familia," she says.

"Always," says Jasmine. "Me, you, Tía."

Tía grabs Jasmine's other hand. "You know I got you." Then she glares at Mami. "Both of you."

A peal of thunder breaks out, and Jasmine peeks out the door again.

The mass is bigger.

And she knows she has to do something, or this is never going to change.

With her mami, her tía, and all her new friends behind her, Jasmine runs toward the street.

As she approaches the spirits, the whispering returns. But this time, it's overwhelming, filling her ears so much that she presses her hands against them to shut it out.

She stands at the end of the walkway. "What do you want?" she screams. "I am listening. I'm *trying*. Why won't you tell me what you want?"

There's a clanging sound to Jasmine's left, and she turns to see Ina standing at the end of her driveway, headphones now hanging around her neck. She is cast in the light from the side of her house. A canister of paint rolls across the cement, leaving behind a bright purple streak, and it spins and comes to a rest against the wooden leg of an easel.

Jasmine watches in wonder as a shadow creature pulls itself out of the chaotic painting on the canvas. The canvas tears and clatters to the driveway, but Ina doesn't seem the slightest bit bothered by that. She watches it all with a look of wonder on her face.

"Jasmine, *look*!" Bea calls out.

She's pointing up the street toward Lyman Place, and Jasmine sees someone slowly jogging down the middle of the road, carrying something shiny in their right hand.

"No way," she mutters.

It's *Carl*, holding his saxophone. He slows as he approaches. "Jasmine?" he says, then gazes up at the sight above him. "What is this?"

"Carl?" says Mami. "You can see this, too?"

He looks down at his saxophone, then back up at the swirling mass. "Something . . . something came out of this," he says, his voice shaky. "I don't know. I followed it here."

His eyes find Jasmine's, and in the streetlight, she can see that they're red and glassy. "You," he says.

"Me?" She touches her charm.

"This is happening because of you."

But it isn't an accusation. Carl is *smiling*.

"I can feel your energy, young lady. You're special, aren't you?"

"I felt it, too," says Ina as she comes to Jasmine's side. "From the very first day I met you."

"¿Señorita Garza?"

From the west toward Vermont Avenue, two more people are approaching the whispering chaos. One is Diego, who looks so strange without his silver cart in front of him. He's clutching a beanie in his hands, kneading it over and over. Behind him is—

"Mr. Winters?" Jorge says. "What are you doing here?"

He merely points up. "It's him," he says.

"No lo entiendo," says Diego, looking to Mami. "Había una sombra . . ."

"Ya sabemos," she says. "You're in the right place."

The shadows.

All of them.

It suddenly comes together for Jasmine.

Everyone here lost someone.

She doesn't know Diego's story, but the expression on his face . . . she's seen it a million times. On herself. On Mami. On Tía. On Jorge and Bea and Mr. Winters. She looks up at the pulsating darkness, the whispering growing and growing, and another crack of thunder hits them. There's a terrible shattering down the street, and yet another shadow pours out of a house.

"Jasmine, you have to do something," says Bea. "How can you get them to talk to you?"

A bright flash sparks to the right, and the power in every direction goes out. Multiple horns blare at once from Vermont Avenue as darkness falls over everything.

This thing . . . it's destroying her neighborhood as it grows.

She tries one more time. "Please! What do you *want*?"

There's a bizarre tugging sensation, and Jasmine gasps as she feels her charm under her shirt moving. She goes to pull it out, but it slips out of her collar and . . . floats.

It's floating.

"This?" she says. "*This* is what you want?"

The unseen force tugs on the chain, and Jasmine rips it back.

It makes no sense. It's just a charm on a chain. It means nothing to these spirits.

It means everything to her.

But when the dogs start howling, when her neighbors come out of their homes, terror on their faces, when there's a frightening crash as a car hits a tree down the street . . .

Is it worth it to ignore what these spirits want?

But . . . this is her protection. That's what Papi said all those years ago. What if she takes this off and something terrible happens? What if she makes it all worse?

Standing there, though, watching the shadows spit and snarl, fear echoing throughout the neighborhood as the cats start yowling, she realizes two things.

This is her crossroads. This is the moment Tía told her about.

And this moment . . .

It can't get worse.

"Fine!" she says, defeated. "Is this what you want?"

She reaches behind and fiddles with the clasp.

"Jasmine, ¿estás segura?" Mami asks.

"I have to," she says. "I have to stop this."

It comes undone.

She takes hold of each end, then drops the chain and the charm into her right hand.

Jasmine holds it high.

"Here!" she cries. "Take it! Just please *stop*!"

The spirits freeze on command, and the whispers cut out.

And the darkness drops.

It hits the asphalt at Jasmine's feet and she flings herself back as the shadows split apart and spread over the ground. The breath is knocked out of her, and she gasps for air, watching as the shadow spirits twist and turn, and then there's a horrifying tearing sound, like someone is ripping the entire universe in two and—

"Ay, Dios mio!" Tía Selena cries out.

They begin to take forms. Not shapeless shadows, not syrupy balls of darkness.

One has legs. Another grows arms. Another . . . has a head.

There's one that's closest to Jasmine, and it rises up, sprouting legs as it does so, and it's *human*. There's a full head of hair and a face with eyes and a nose and ears and a smiling mouth and—

Her heart stops.

It's impossible.

"Jasmine," he says.

She pushes herself to her feet, hears her mami break out in sobs, and Jasmine lets his name fall from her mouth.

"Papi."

"I'm so sorry," he says. "It wasn't supposed to happen this way."

29

He's holding his arms out.

This isn't real.

This *can't* be real.

But she reaches out, expecting that much like what happened when Mami tried to attack a shadow, her hand will pass through her papi's arm.

But it doesn't.

She runs her fingers down his bare arm. He has on a black shirt with a pocket on the chest, and she recognizes it as the one he used to lounge around in at night. His arm . . . it's cold to the touch. But solid.

She gets to his hand. Puts her own in it, and then he's wrapping his fingers around hers, and she can't resist it anymore, and she is in her papi's arms, crying and sobbing and she can't breathe.

He shouldn't be here.

But he *is*.

The sensation is electric, and she can't pull away. She doesn't ever want to, because she's afraid that the moment she does, all of this will disappear like smoke in the wind.

Papi leans back, and he's still there. "Mi amor," he whispers. "We don't have much time."

Then he glances up, and his eyes fill with tears. She turns to see the others, gathered behind her in the small yard in front of her house, watching in shock. Mami steps closer.

"Jasmine, may I have a moment with your mami?" he asks.

She steps aside, even though every cell in her body is telling her not to let him go. Mami breaks down again as she slips into an embrace with Papi, and he rubs a hand down her back.

"Shh, Aida. Cálmate, cariño."

"Oh, I have missed you so much," she says. "How are you here?"

"We're all here," he says, and turns back to the shadows.

Which are no longer shadows anymore. All of them are people now: old and young, short and tall, all different shapes and sizes and—

"Abuelo?"

Jorge's voices cracks, and then he rushes forward, into the arms of an older Mexican man with a bushy mustache and a balding head. Mustache Papi follows, and the three embrace in a flurry of tears.

"I'm so sorry," Jorge cries. "Do you hate me? I was so mean in the end!"

"Never," says his abuelo. "Jorge, I don't even remember what you said! It doesn't matter in the end."

Bea cries out as she drops at the feet of a young man with tattoos down his right arm and a mohawk on his head. "Ramon, is that you?"

He lifts her up and swings her around in a hug. "Yes, Bea," he says. "It's me."

The Veracruzes rush to their son, and the entire family embraces.

There are more. Mr. Winters. Ina. Carl. Diego. Each of them comes forward, and each of them reunites with someone they lost: Keondre. Fatima. Carl's wife, who he introduces as Sheena. Diego's daughter, Mona.

Diego had a daughter!

"I have to be quick," says Papi. "You've had it all wrong. *All* of you."

But he focuses on Mami first.

"Your mami, Aida. She wasn't taken. She *left*. I've met her. She guides souls of the recently deceased to their resting place."

"Is she here?" Mami says, eyes wide.

"No, she's not," he says. "She's in the in-between, doing what she loves."

"Papi, I don't get it," says Jasmine. "Then how are you here?"

He places his hands on both sides of her face. "My beautiful daughter," he says. "You're special, you know that?"

"I told you!" yells out a tearful Carl.

"I gave you this," he says, and he reaches down to her clenched fist and opens it, then plucks the charm from her hand. "It was supposed to protect you."

"But it didn't," she says sadly. "It's been so hard without you."

"Mija, I didn't get to tell you what it protects you *from*," he says. "I died before I could. Your mami . . . she always worried about what might happen to you, and in that hospital room, I just wanted to make sure you had this so you'd be safe."

He gives it back, and she goes to put it on. Immediately, every spirit turns to Jasmine and yells, "NO!"

"Don't put it on yet!" Papi implores. "It protects you from *us*."

"What?" she says.

"My family . . . we come from magic, too. Oh, I'm so sorry I didn't get to tell you about all of this. I should have done it earlier. But magic has been in my family for hundreds of years. This prevents the dead from speaking to you."

And it all comes crashing down.

Her head spins. Her heart races.

No.

"Edgar, *what?*" Mami sucks in a breath. "Please tell me you're joking."

"You told me about your family," he says, "and I knew mine had something that could help her if she ever came into her magic. Mi familia, amor . . . they have their own magic. They imbue it in trinkets. Charms. Objects of protection. I reached out to my own papá and asked him if someone from our village could make you that charm."

He's shaking his head, his face full of despair. "I gave it to you to protect you. And then I didn't get to explain what it does."

"It was you," she says softly, and more tears pour from her eyes. "It was you all the time."

He nods. "It was me. And all of *them*."

He gestures to the spirits, now made whole, who gather on the street. She realizes there are so many more of them, wandering, looking for . . .

For someone to talk to.

"All of you?" Jasmine says, looking at the returned spirits.

"We all passed in tragedy," Papi explains. "We left abruptly, and it caused our friends and family so much pain. And we've been in this darkness ever since because the people who loved us couldn't let go."

"No," she says, choking on her tears. "No, Papi, don't say that. You've been stuck in the darkness for *years*?"

"Don't think of it like that," Sheena says, stepping forward. Her gray-and-white locs hang nearly to her waist. "For us, time passes in an instant. I feel I have been gone for maybe a day or two."

"Oh, Sheena," Carl says, pulling her close and kissing her cheek. "It's been ten years. I lost it all, my love. The house. My *life*."

Her eyes fill with tears. "Please don't be sad, Carl," she says. "Because we found this young woman, and she allowed us to come back."

"Think of it like a dark room," says Ramon, his hand in Bea's. "It was peaceful. Quiet."

"And then you showed up," says Fatima, a smile lighting up her dark eyes. "You walked into a dark room, and you turned on the light."

Papi examines her face, then finds the words he is looking for. "Like a firefly in the greatest darkness. We were drawn to you."

"Sabía que podía hablar contigo," Mona says.

When Bald Barrera looks to his husband, he translates. "She knew that she could talk to Jasmine."

"Your magic from Mami's side of the family meant you could talk to us and set us free," Papi explains. "But that charm I gave you . . . we got stuck, mija."

Keondre gives Jasmine a sad look. "We felt like we were supposed to come out of the darkness, but when we reached out . . . it was strange."

Mona leans in to Diego. "Me sentí . . . atrapada."

"Trapped," says Keondre. "Yes, that's the word. Trapped."

"So that means . . ." Jasmine begins, her horror mounting.

Papi nods. "Si, mija. We've all been here the entire time."

It's too much for her. She breaks into another round of sobs, but this time, her papi is there, holding her, and it doesn't feel as sad and impossible as it did before.

It feels relieving.

"You broke through," says Tía, her hand on her heart. "Every so often, you each broke through to this world."

Keondre walks over to Jasmine, and Mr. Winters trails behind him. "We weren't haunting you, Jasmine," he says. "We were trying to talk to you so we could move on."

"The spirit shadow things!" Jorge says. "Or whatever you called them, Jasmine. That's why they looked like that!"

"But how?" she asks. "How did you end up with *me*?"

"Glendale," says Keondre. "You lived underneath the apartment I died in three years ago."

"Clumsy, remember?" says Mr. Winters. "Always running into things."

"Oh!" Jasmine smiles at Keondre. "The glasses and mugs breaking all the time!"

He nods. "It was my way of breaking through for just a moment. That place . . . it's hard to muster energy. It's like a dark room, yes, but I thought it was kind of like being stuck in a giant pit of maple syrup."

"But not as tasty," Sheena jokes.

There's nervous laughter all around, and Keondre reaches out, strokes Jasmine's cheek.

"You brought me back to my love," he says.

Keondre pulls Mr. Winters close and kisses him deeply, then gazes at Jasmine. "You went to that library, and I felt him. I stuck around, and unfortunately, I think I haunted him as well."

"I knew it was you," Mr. Winters chokes out.

"Sorry about the camera," he says to Bea.

"So you could see things?" she says. Then her eyes go wide. "Could you watch me going to the bathroom?!"

"No, mija," Papi says between laughs. "It wasn't like that at all. Those moments that we broke through . . . they were so brief. Little glimpses of the world we came from. And so we did anything we could to get your attention."

"You keep saying 'we,'" says Mr. Veracruz, his arm looped around his son. "Could you all sense one another?"

Fatima nods. "Yeah. Absolutely. Jasmine, you ever heard that legend of the Pied Piper? Of the rat catcher who had a pipe that could lure rats?"

She frowns. "Sort of? I think we read a fairy tale about it in elementary school."

"That's what you were like. Once you started picking us up, we couldn't leave."

"So we worked together," says Sheena. "It's strange; we couldn't talk to one another, so to speak. It was more like . . . vibes. We just knew."

"Fascinating," says Mr. Veracruz, and he pulls a notebook

from his back pocket. But then his wife swats him on the arm, and he puts it away.

Bea laughs. "I can't believe this is happening."

They share their truths with her: Mona passed in the corner market next door to their Santa Monica apartment, which is where she worked when someone killed her. Every time she broke through to Jasmine, she opened doors and cupboards, thinking she was pushing her way out of the market itself. Fatima shares that her favorite thing to do when Ina spent the night in her Crenshaw apartment was to walk by and brush her fingers across the back of her neck. Sheena would spend hours dancing in her home with Carl, and the neighbor below them always used to complain about how they made the ceiling creak. Ramon was a bike courier, and he was hit by a truck in Westlake not long after Papi died.

"I was the one who was trying to whisper to you," he explains. "Me and your papi . . . we were together for the longest."

"You connected all of us," says Sheena, "and then somehow, you brought us all back to the people who lost us."

"You've been collecting souls for *years*," says Papi. "But we weren't supposed to linger. It's been building up and up."

"And we all tried to break through to get to you," says Sheena, and then she grimaces as she looks around her. "Didn't mean for all this to happen. With your papi's guidance, all we focused on in the end was getting you to remove that charm."

"So . . . I'm not haunted at all, am I?" she says to Papi.

"No, mi amor," he says, grinning from ear to ear. "You never were. You just didn't know what I'd accidentally done to you."

But then he kneels down in front of her, and her heart skips a beat. He looks . . . paler.

No, that isn't right. She can see the house across the street through him.

He's fading.

Mami grips Jasmine's shoulder hard, and Jasmine does her best to keep it together for Papi.

"Like I said earlier, we don't have much time," he says. He opens her clenched hand and pulls out the charm, then holds it up. "Tu abuela, Griselda, she made a choice to become what she is now. She was overwhelmed by all the spirits visiting her, and so she chose to transform into something else. I didn't know what you were when I gave you the charm, so I thought I was giving you something that would help you. I planned to get better. To recover. And then tell you about the world of the dead, and how some people can talk to them."

"But . . . did you think *I* could talk to the dead?"

He shrugs. "I had no idea. I had never seen evidence that you could."

He smiles wide. "You are allowed to make your own choices, Jasmine. You're becoming such an incredible person, so full of love and care. But you get to *choose* when to use your magic. You will never have to go through something like this again. You get to decide to use the power the Zamora family gave you whenever you want."

"We really are sorry," says Ramon. "We didn't know the impact this would have on your life."

"You heard me," she says. "When I yelled at you."

Papi grimaces. "Yes. And I knew then we were hurting you, so that's why things escalated . . . a lot. Magic should never be a burden. I am so sorry I hurt you while trying to protect you."

"Me too," Mami adds. "Clearly, both of us wanted the best, but we missed the mark. We kept too many secrets, and—"

She smiles. "The promise still stands. No more secrets, mija."

Jasmine's face flushes and she turns back to her papi.

And now, she can barely see him. See *all* of them.

"It's our time to go," Papi announces.

Her heart drops. "I don't want you to."

Each of the spirits, now fading gently, steps away from their loved ones. Bea protests, but Ramon gives her and their parents one last hug and moves back with the others. "I love you, Bea," he says.

"I wish I could watch you growing up," Papi says, tears streaming down his face. "But the time I did get with you? I wouldn't trade it for the world."

"Thank you," Jasmine says, holding up the charm and chain. "Now I know what this is supposed to be. And it's the best gift ever."

Papi doesn't get a chance to wave. Moments later, the spirits—all of them, including the ones she didn't get to meet—drift out of sight, and La Mirada is shrouded in darkness again.

Jasmine doesn't know what to do at first. She thinks she's going to start crying—like Diego does—but instead, she turns around and gazes back at the house. The living room window remains broken, and there's still a car alarm going off down the block. No sort of magic healed the damage done to their world after the spirits finally left.

It's like grief, she realizes. They can repair things, but there might always be evidence of what happened. They'll remember it. And sometimes, it's going to hurt.

But that's okay. Because it means that what happened was real.

Jasmine takes her mami's hand and stares at the empty spot on La Mirada Avenue. This time, though, she isn't waiting for Papi to reappear or talk to her.

She knows he's gone forever.

So she takes the chain and fastens it around her neck. For the moment, she needs to be with her family and friends.

The dead can wait.

30

"You're hogging the mirror," says Jorge, pushing in close to Jasmine as he tries to put on his face paint.

Jasmine scoffs at him. "This is *my* house."

"Still hogging the mirror," he adds, grinning.

"Does this count as a meeting of the Gay Supernatural Alliance?" Bea asks from the doorway. Their sugar-skull makeup is already done, and Jasmine appreciates how much detail there is in it. Bea had drawn tiny little flowers throughout their design, and Jasmine hadn't seen it done like that before.

"I'm the secretary, and I vote yes." Jorge draws the lines across his lips to give the illusion of teeth. "And where we're heading? That's definitely a meeting."

Jasmine instinctively touches the charm resting against her throat. Mami had finally gotten her a new chain, and she admires how it looks with the rest of her flowing outfit. But she knows she needs to wear it now as much as she can because there are a lot of spirits that want to talk to her.

She learned the hard way. Now that the spirits that had been "stuck" to her were free, Jasmine thought she could wear the charm less and practice speaking to the dead. Unfortunately, the first time a recently deceased person visited her, she was in the middle of a shower. They had poked their head out of a wall and both of them had screamed.

Since then, Jasmine had to enlist the help of her friends and the members of the Gay Supernatural Alliance to develop a routine. Using her knowledge of the supernatural, Bea helps track down wandering spirits for Jasmine, since they are often looking for someone to offload on before they move on. Jorge's secretary skills have taken on a new life because Jasmine finds that the dead have a lot that they want to say, so she needs someone to help her record them.

In the end, that's probably the thing she learned the quickest: the dead just want to talk to someone.

When Jasmine is done with her makeup, she heads to the living room, where Mami and Tía Selena are waiting for her next to the altar in the corner of the room. La ofrenda was Tía's suggestion, and she'd helped them set it up since she'd kept one herself for a long time. Mami's skepticism over all things supernatural had mostly faded, though she maintained that she didn't believe in any of the weird monsters that the Veracruz family did.

Like Mami, Jasmine appreciated having an altar devoted to Papi in the house. There was a photo of him as a teenager resting against a votive candle. They'd also placed a couple of his old notebooks on it as well, though Jasmine was always careful when a candle was lit so they wouldn't burn. And when Jasmine didn't need to use the charm, she left it on the ofrenda, another reminder of Papi and what he gave her.

She wouldn't need it that night. Mami helps her remove the charm, and she kisses it before placing it on the ofrenda. "Te amo, Papi," she says. "Hopefully, you and Abuela Griselda are helping the souls I'm sending on to you tonight."

There isn't an immediate presence in the house on La Mirada Avenue, but Jasmine suspects that their destination is the explanation for that. Bea and Jorge join them next, and then the five of them head out of the house into a night alive with possibility.

It is El Día de los Muertos, a celebration of the dead that the people of Tunapa practice. Jasmine is going to help those who need it. With the assistance of the Gay Supernatural Alliance, of course! There's a cemetery nearby where a ceremony will be held, and Jasmine wonders what her first holiday will be like with her powers unlocked.

The neighborhood is still alive post-Halloween. Jasmine sees Ina painting in her driveway. Her work seems livelier since she got to say goodbye to Fatima.

Carl's melodies hit Jasmine's heart differently when they pass him. She doesn't know if it's because of his reunion with Sheena or because he was able to get out of the shelter and into some assisted housing nearby. She's not sure it matters because Carl seems so much more alive.

Diego has expanded his business to sell helados during the warm Los Angeles nights. Mami doesn't want any of them to mess up their makeup, so she tells Diego they'll be getting lots on their way back home. He thanks them, but particularly focuses on Jasmine. "Gracias por ti," he says. "Now I know she's at peace."

She blushes, but he can't see it through her makeup.

After crossing The Intersection, they pass Kingsley, where Mr. Winters is standing with Mx. Chen and some other teachers, handing out sugar-skull snickerdoodles on the steps to those on their way to the celebrations. He looks . . . happy.

Happier than she's ever seen him.

Minutes later, they arrive. Tucked behind a looming apartment complex is a small cemetery that's unofficially been adopted by a lot of folks from Central America as their place to bury the dead and celebrate life beyond. Not everyone practices the same traditions involved with El Día de los Muertos, but this day is still special to many. She sees kids in sugar-skull makeup, sees others dressed up as dancing skeletons, while a mariachi group plays a lively song on a makeshift stage covered in candles.

But Jasmine is here for other reasons, and when the hair rises on the back of her neck, she knows it's time.

"Someone's here," she says to Jorge, who pulls out his own notebook, now a quarter full with messages from the recently deceased.

Bea swings their shoulder bag around and pulls out an EMF reader. After slowly waving it around them, they focus on an oak tree about twenty feet away. "There," they say, pointing. "Someone's over there."

Since that day a couple of weeks ago, the dead do not appear to Jasmine as dripping, shapeless shadow beings. In fact, they're no longer easy to spot at first when encountered out in the world. But as Jasmine slowly approaches the tree, her friends and family behind her, a form takes shape.

It isn't a shadow.

It's a person.

He's maybe in his twenties. Close-cropped hair. Wide nose. Color returns to his skin as he materializes, and it is a warm brown tone. He looks scared at first as he frantically gazes around him, until he finds Jasmine's eyes.

Then she watches recognition come over his face. He knows *exactly* what this is.

"You can see me," he says.

She nods.

"And hear me."

"All of it," she says.

Then she takes a deep breath. "Do you have something to tell me?"

He twists his face up. "I don't know. I don't know if he'll believe me."

"Leave that part up to me," she says. "Just tell me what you need to."

As he talks, Jasmine repeats what he says, and Jorge writes it down. Bea keeps track of the electromagnetic energy in case the spirit starts fading and they need to hurry things up. Mami and Tía stand back and watch.

Jasmine finishes.

Tells the spirit that she will get his message to the right person. Then she smiles.

"Go," she says. "You get to rest now."

Relief passes over him. "Thank you," he says, and then he fades away.

She's found the part that follows is hard. She hasn't always been able to find the people that the dead are seeking, and she isn't old enough that Mami is okay with her doing it on her own. So sometimes, she devotes an entire Saturday to passing on messages from the dead with Jorge and Bea. Some people appreciate it. Others break down. Some slam the door in their faces.

She still passes the messages on, though. And more important: the dead get to say what they've been holding on to.

Jasmine turns around after the spirit dissipates, and her mami is clutching her hands together over her chest. "What?"

"You know I'm proud of you, right?"

"I do."

"And I'm glad you have our family's magic."

"You are the perfect person for it to return to," adds Tía.

Jasmine wants to say more, but she can't. Bea's EMF reader is beeping, and Jorge has just finished writing down his notes.

There are more souls on this night of the dead. For years, she's desired someone to talk to about her life and what she was going through. Now, she gets to provide that to those who most need it. She has a purpose. And she isn't alone.

For the first time in Jasmine's life, she wants to be haunted.

ACKNOWLEDGMENTS

Thank you.

To my agent, DongWon Song, for your continued expert guidance and care.

To the team at Tor Teen / Starscape, who I am happy to call my new home for my middle grade stories! Most of you have worked with me on my young adult books, and I'm thrilled we get to do EVERYTHING together!

So, first of all: my respect and adoration to my editor, Ali Fisher, who saw the brilliance in Jasmine's story and helped guide it to where it is now. To our assistant editor, Dianna Vega, for keeping all this chaos deeply un-chaotic; my publicist boo, Saraciea Fennell, for being the best publicist I could ever ask for; to Anthony Parisi, for always finding creative ways to market my books beyond their publication date; to the production team of Dakota Griffin (production editor) and Steven Bucsok (production manager) for making my art a reality; to Genevieve D'Astous for the gorgeous cover and the very talented Lesley Worrell for the jacket design; and many thanks to William Hinton and Devi Pillai for continuing to publish me. All of you have changed my life.

Thanks to all my writer friends, educators, librarians, fellow chaos demons . . . I'm so blown away that I get to be making art at this exact time with all of you. Book eight! I wrote eight books!!!

Thank you to my readers. Thank you to the grievers. Thank you to the weirdos. I love us.

ABOUT THE AUTHOR

Darius Voncel

Mark Oshiro is the award-winning author of the young adult books *Anger Is a Gift* (2019 Schneider Family Book Award), *Each of Us a Desert*, and *Into the Light*, as well as the middle grade books *The Insiders* and *You Only Live Once, David Bravo*. They are also the #1 *New York Times* bestselling coauthor (with Rick Riordan) of *From the World of Percy Jackson: The Sun and the Star*. When not writing, they are trying to pet every dog in the world.

markoshiro.com
Instagram: @markdoesstuff
X: @MarkDoesStuff
Goodreads: Mark Oshiro